Helen H. Chambers
Xmas 73

PENGUIN BOOKS

THE FOOLISH IMMORTALS

Paul Gallico was born in New York City, of Italian and Austrian parentage, in 1897, and attended Columbia University. From 1922 to 1936 he worked on the New York *Daily News* as sports editor, columnist and assistant managing editor. In 1936 he bought a house on top of a hill at Salcombe in South Devon and settled down for a year with a Great Dane and twenty-three assorted cats. It was in 1941 that he made his name with *The Snow Goose,* a classic little story of Dunkirk which became a world-wide best seller and is now available in Penguins. Having served as a gunner's mate in the U.S. Navy in 1918, he was again active as a war correspondent with the American Expeditionary Force in 1944. Paul Gallico, who lives in Monaco, is a first-class fencer and a keen sea-fisherman. His books, which have achieved exceptionally high sales on both sides of the Atlantic, include *Jennie* (1950), *Flowers for Mrs Harris* (1958), *Mrs Harris Goes to New York* (1960), *Thomasina* (1957), *Love of Seven Dolls* (1954) and *Trial by Terror* (1952) – all of which are available in Penguins. His *Ludmila* and *The Lonely* have been published by Penguins in one volume. He has also written *The Steadfast Man,* a scholarly study of St Patrick, and *The Hurricane Story* (1959), a 'biography' of the famous fighter-plane. His latest books are *Love, Let Me Not Hunger* (1963) *The Hand of Mary Constable* (1964), *Mrs Harris, M.P.* (1965), and *The Man Who was Magic* (1966), *The Story of the Silent Night* (1967), *Manxmouse* (1968), *The Poseidon Adventure* (1969).

from

D1407276

PAUL GALLICO

The Foolish Immortals

PENGUIN BOOKS

Penguin Books Ltd, Harmondsworth, Middlesex, England
Penguin Books Australia Ltd, Ringwood, Victoria, Australia

—

First published by Michael Joseph 1953
Published in Penguin Books 1969
Copyright © Paul Gallico, 1953

—

Made and printed in Great Britain by
Cox and Wyman Ltd, London, Reading and Fakenham
Set in Intertype Plantin

This book is sold subject to the condition
that it shall not, by way of trade or otherwise,
be lent, re-sold, hired out, or otherwise circulated
without the publisher's prior consent in any form of
binding or cover other than that in which it is
published and without a similar condition
including this condition being imposed
on the subsequent purchaser

Chapters

Chapter 1

'For the living know that they will die' —
Ecclesiastes ix, 5

THE bartender behind the length of mahogany of Whaley's Café near the corner of Potrero and Clybourne in Burbank, not far from Megaphone Film Studios, jerked his head in the direction of the afternoon paper lying on the bar with its page-one photo of the fiercely ruffled, angry-eyed old woman with the hawk's beak and imperious mien and quoted the headline above it: 'To Live For Ever, says Multi-millionairess Hannah Bascombe', and then added, 'That's one she ain't gonna win, eh, brother?'

Joe Sears took a sip of his second rye and plain water and said 'Uhuh' mechanically and without concentration on the subject of the bartender's comment. His mind was still on the turn-down Ed Howland, who was heading up a new unit at Megaphone, had given him a few minutes earlier and his own immediate plight. Joseph Deuell Sears, aged thirty-six, smart, fast, experienced — and a failure. Three hundred dollars away from being rock-bottom, stony broke and no prospects.

He was remembering Howland's sudden burst of confidence: 'Dammit, Joe, you know how it is. I'd like to help you, but you're a corner-cutter. You could have written your own ticket at Supreme after the job you did on "Red Is For Danger". Then you get turned up taking kickbacks from agents for casting their talent.'

Sears had asked, 'Is there any law against biting an agent? They all do it in one way or another, don't they?'

'Well, of course it isn't like that dirty small-time racket of milking extras and bit-players,' Howland had admitted. 'I know you wouldn't get mixed up in anything like that. But when you get up near the top, Joe, they don't like to have someone around who *might* pull a fast one, if you get what I mean . . .'

Sears had said nothing further, left his address and departed.

There had seemed no point in suggesting that some of Ed's deals in buying, inflating and selling story properties had not been exactly ethical, though accepted studio practice. Sears' immediate concern was to reform neither Howland nor the world but to escape his own tarnished reputation somehow and find himself a job before he starved to death.

The bartender, moving through a momentary blaze of Technicolor when a shaft of late afternoon sun invading the bar splintered on a prism of the mirror and spilled a harlequin's colours over his bald head and white jacket, said, 'No sirree, brother. When her time comes she gotta go like everybody else. Ain't that right?'

'Yeah,' Sears said, 'that's right', but he was still worrying about himself and what he was going to do when his funds ran out. He was thinking, '*What I need is a Big Idea. I've got to cut out all this small-time stuff and come up with something that will pay off but good. I've got as much brains as any of these big operators.*'

It seemed as though, after weeks of walking the streets of Los Angeles, Hollywood, Beverly Hills, and the Districts, in search of what to do and where to win a living that was both quick and easy, he had reached the end of the line. There appeared to be no place left to go for a man with brains and energy.

As he saw it, you went along any street and passed the bakery and the drug store, the photography shop and the drygoods that sold nylon hosiery, the meat and vegetable market, the antique shop, the greasy-spoon restaurant, the hotel, the neighbourhood movie theatre, the dairy, the tailor, the cigar store – there they were, block after block, leaning up against one another, all making a living for their owners by means of some angle, whether it was merely buy cheap and sell dear, or the shady sideline.

They would let you in on the fringe for the least that they could pay you, to sweep, polish, serve, sell, or deliver, but they'd never let you near the jampots of their graft; and if they caught you being smart enough to figure one out for yourself, out you went.

And on The Strip, lined with the plushy agents' offices, cabarets and swank shops – as well as around the palatial homes in the hills and palm-lined avenues where the opulent lived and worked their pitches – they would really lower the boom on you if they caught you trying to outsmart them and move in on some of their angles.

Joe Sears had grown up with that sense of a self-devouring civilization, but it never had been so clear to him as it was now. He raised his glass and tasted the sour-mash tartness of the rye and set himself for the jolt and glow. His shoulder ached momentarily when he put it down, and he thought that his old football injury was advising him of a change in the weather.

And this reminded him of Joe Sears, star quarter-back of the Ventura High School football team – 'The Brain', as he was known in those days – with scouts from Palo Alto and Berkeley and Washington bidding for him. Then he had been caught speculating in the Big Game football tickets in a local scandal and fired from the squad, and with it went the college dream.

Whatever rancour remained at the memory was directed at himself for his stupidity in getting caught. Plenty of the kids had peddled worse things than football tickets.

Joe Sears was born and grew up in the little coast town of Ventura, opposite the Santa Barbara Islands. From the time he was old enough to go about with other kids he was determined not to be the fall guy. For there seemed to be two sets of rules for everything and everyone, and the world was divided into suckers and wise guys, the loose-lipped herd of patsies and the fellows who knew how to figure out an angle.

Everybody had an angle, and it didn't seem to matter what walk of life – whether it was the football coach who sent you in to cripple a kid on the opposing team in order to win a game that meant a new contract, or the penny-candy man who half killed a dozen kids with a batch of sweets he had bought cheap because it had been condemned, or the shoemaker who gave you paper soles, or the dentists who ruined good teeth to make you buy a bridge or a filling, or the doctors who never let you get really well, or all the politicians and angle-shooters in Washington or Sacramento.

Sears didn't go for the crooked stuff and he didn't like to see anybody get hurt. But only the yahoos worked for a living. The smart guy got himself a racket and then found out what the short cuts were and let the other guy sweat.

That this had not paid off for him he attributed partly to circumstances and partly to bad luck. He had tackled more jobs than he could remember – salesman, copy writer, police reporter, script writer, assistant director, clerk in a brokerage house, seller of mutuel tickets at the track, lawyer's runner, real estate, radio announcer – and between jobs had done all those things a young man will take on to keep clothes on his back and nourishment in his body: garage mechanic, dish-washer, short-order cook, stirrer in a candy factory, and of course, the long hitch in the army during the war.

Still, it hadn't helped him when he got out and settled on L.A. for the oyster he would open. In six years he had built up the reputation of a guy who was just too damned smart for his own good. 'Nice kid, Joe Sears. Clever, too. But you gotta watch him all the time . . .'

The bartender was looking down at the face of the old woman glaring up from the newsprint. He said, 'Yes, sir. We all gotta die, don't we? You – me – even the great Hannah Bascombe with all her money. The good Lord don't care how rich you are when He sends for you.'

The word 'money' snatched Sears from his reflections. He glanced down at the story under a San Francisco dateline. 'Hannah Bascombe, said to be the richest woman in the world, celebrated her seventy-first birthday at her Nob Hill mansion here today by granting one of her rare interviews.

'With her secretary-companion Clary Adams, the aged but dynamic heiress to the Bascombe mining and railroad interests met the press and blasted the government for its confiscatory tax programme and socialist policies. Breathing defiance against the Internal Revenue Department and other fiscal branches of the government with whom she has been conducting a running feud for the past twenty years, Miss Bascombe said, "They're waiting for me to die so that they can get their hands on my money. Well, they never will, because I'm going to outlive them all . . ." '

'It's a gag, ain't it?' said the bartender.

The story rang a bell in Sears's mind. Each year she gave out a similar interview, rasping, 'Well, I'm still here,' a kind of repetitive, bitter joke.

'Yeah,' Sears said finally. 'It's a gag. That's one thing you can't duck, and she's crazy if she thinks she can.'

But his mind was swimming at the thought of the fabulous, unlimited wealth of the woman and what life would be like if a man could latch on to some one as rich as that, work up an angle; set her up as a meal ticket.

He glanced back at the newspaper and re-read the name: 'Clary Adams, secretary-companion.' She had obviously got herself a good thing. She would be a tight-lipped, stony, forbidding spinster, possibly even a distant relative. When the time finally came for Hannah Bascombe to die, Miss Adams would inherit a tidy little fortune no doubt and be fixed for life, and in turn would hang on to her money like grim death. How they all clung to their money. Yet a lot of these financial wizards were supposed to be like children when it came to practical matters other than growing money out of money. A man with brains ought to be able . . .

Sears turned off the daydream with a shrug. A lot of people probably had had the same idea before him. A man would want to come up with something really new.

He nodded at the bartender. 'Yeah, brother, you're sure right about that one. Crazy as a coot.'

The two shots of rye had taken hold and the companionship of the talk had eased some of his depression so that he felt almost cheerful. He slid a dollar along the wet bar, said 'So long!' and went out.

But his shadow was not yet clear of the door when he came back in again. He indicated the newspaper on the bar. 'Mind if I take that along with me?'

The bartender said, 'No. Go ahead. Help yourself . . .'

Sears folded it and stuffed it into his coat. The woman must be worth a billion with all her enterprises and holdings, if not more. Somehow, just having that newspaper with him seemed to bring him a little closer to this fabulous and limitless wealth. It was almost like having money in one's pocket.

Chapter 2

'And all the days of Methuselah were nine hundred
sixty and nine years' – *Genesis* v, 27

SEARS stood for a moment beside the large canvas evangel tent
occupying the vacant lot at the corner of Potrero and Clybourne,
waiting for the light to change and halt the endless stream of
home-going cars moving in a bluish haze of gasolene fumes that
fouled the balmy air and clear twilight. The voice of the evangelist
emerged brassily from within:

'. . . And Adam lived an hundred and thirty years, and begat
a son in his own likeness, after his image; and called his name
Seth.'

The words hardly impinged on Sears's consciousness. The
drink had worn off. He was filled with the bitterness of failure.
Another day done, another day wasted into night, another turn-
down, another bar, another drink, another flop – and where
would it all end?

He heard him now, for the voice was beginning to rise with
fervour: '. . . And Enos lived after he begat Cainan eight hundred
and fifteen years, and begat sons and daughters. And all the days
of Enos were nine hundred and five years; and he died.'

Sears found himself trying to make a mental picture of the
evangelist and realized that he was typing him like a casting director, black frockcoat, lank hair, pale prophet's face. He moved into
the entrance of the tent to check and had to smile.

The speaker on the platform, surrounded by the usual crowd of
old women, seedy-looking chinless men with chicken necks and
assorted bums grateful for a chair, was a rotund, jolly-looking
fellow in a business suit, who looked like a stockbroker or a
chamber-of-commerce greeter.

He thwacked the Bible in front of him like an auctioneer knock-
ing it down and his expression was bland as he reeled off the
'begats': 'And Cainan lived after he begat Mahalaleel eight hun-

dred and forty years, and begat sons and daughters. And all the days of Cainan were nine hundred and ten years; and *he* died . . .'

Standing in the entrance to the tent, Sears suddenly felt grateful for the occupation of his mind, and listened as the preacher enumerated the list of patriarchs who had peopled the earth after Genesis:

'And all the days of Mahalaleel were eight hundred ninety and five years. . . . And all the days of Jared were nine hundred sixty and two years: and he died. . . . And Methuselah lived after he begat Lamech seven hundred eighty and two years. . . . And all the days of Methuselah were nine hundred sixty and nine years; and . . .'

'Hey!' shouted Joe Sears from where he stood by the tent flap, so that those sitting in front of him turned their heads and stared and the evangelist stopped abruptly and peered through his rimless glasses with a kind of friendly anxiety, to learn what this interruption boded. 'Hey! How come those guys managed to live so long in those days?'

Relief twinkled in the eyes of the preacher. 'It's in the Bible, brother!' he shouted and thumped the book three times with the palm of his hand. 'It's *all* in the Bible. Anything you ever need to know in this life, you'll find the answer right here in the Good Book. Bless you, brother. Go to the Bible.'

Joe Sears said 'thanks' and moved away.

The evangelist called after him, 'Stick around, brother. Come in and have a seat. Learn how it repented the Lord that He had made man on the earth and it grieved Him at His heart . . .'

'Thanks,' Joe said again. 'Some other time.'

He went out into the purple California dusk with his brain tingling and an arm crushing the newspaper in his pocket to his side, the newspaper that told of an avaricious old woman, rich as Croesus, who had passed her allotted span of three score years and ten but who was determined not to die. And once upon a time, this fat Bible-whacker had said, the sons of Adam had walked the newborn earth for eight and nine hundred years before turning up their toes. Somewhere, somehow there must be a connexion. 'Go to the Bible!' the man had said. Well, why not? Others had found an answer there.

Sears's budget didn't include the price of a Bible and the libraries would be closed. However, there were other means. He walked over to Cahuenga Boulevard and caught a bus for downtown Los Angeles. He was filled with excitement. He smelled money.

'In the beginning God created the heaven and the earth.'

Genesis! The earth without form took shape. Darkness gave way to light. Out of Adam, God fashioned Eve; Cain slew Abel; the patriarchs begat and lived nine hundred years; the earth was filled with wickedness so that it repented the Lord that He made man and He sent a flood to destroy him.

Noah built the ark and escaped; his sons, Shem, Ham and Japhet, lived to repeople the world. From their children sprang Abraham and Sarah and the new covenant with the Lord; Sodom and Gomorrah were destroyed; Isaac, Jacob, Esau and Joseph came into being. Names and figures danced before the glittering eyes of Joe Sears: '. . . so the whole age of Jacob was an hundred forty and seven years. . . . So Joseph died, being an hundred and ten years old.'

Sitting on the edge of his cot in the Brothers of Man Mission House, where bed, soap and towel cost twenty-five cents, but the Bible was free, Joe Sears came to the fulfilment of the promise made by the tent evangelist – 'It's all in the Good Book.' Here was the key to wealth.

For, in the worn, soiled mission copy of the Scriptures, Sears, avid and dazzled by the dream, discovered the germ of the plot that was to mulct the richest woman in the world and provide him with easy living. And later, when the boy came wandering into the drab dormitory, it set the seal on the design in Joe's mind.

To Sears, the youth, dark-eyed, black-haired, clad in worn sailor's pea-jacket and stocking cap, who dropped his sea-bag into a cot two removed from him, was like a figure come to life out of the Old Testament in which he had been immersed.

So must have young Jacob, or David, or even the Archangel looked; lean, compassionately saturnine, with dark luminous eyes at once filled both with fire and infinite sorrow and experience. Here was the thin, acquiline nose of high race, yet the thin lips and firm jaw were those of a fighter.

But over and beyond his Semitic beauty, pride of carriage and aura of self-confidence Sears was aware of still something else about the young sailor that at first baffled him and then, almost immediately when he understood and identified it, set up an exultation in his breast and a tingling in his nerves, as it always did when luck finally began to run his way. There was an ageless-ness about the boy.

He could be, Joe judged, twenty-one or twenty-two, or, if one looked at the corner of the mouth or the expression of the eyes, fifty, or seventy-two, or a hundred. There was a queer timeless-ness in the texture of his skin and the droop of his eyelids.

To Sears his coming was like being dealt the ace of spades needed to complete a royal flush, and the wheels of his mind revolved furiously to encompass acquiring him for his needs. But he was still riding the crest of his luck. Events took over.

The boy's presence created a stir in the dormitory inhabited by the flotsam of bums, drifters and down-and-outers, the scum washed up on the fringe of the Los Angeles tide. His youth, his self-possession, above all his clean and fantastic beauty, was an affront to them all. Animal antagonism made itself manifest al-most at once.

A big-armed, big-bellied beer bum on the next cot put down his comic book and said in a high-pitched unpleasant drawl of the male bent on nastiness, 'You're a Jew, ain't you?'

The boy replied, 'Yes, I am. What of it?' He said it right into Beer Belly's teeth and measured him as he said it. To Sears's sur-prise, he spoke with a British accent.

Beer Belly got up and said, 'I'll show you what of it. Git ahda here! I got no use for Limeys, and I don't like Jews around me.'

Sears' mind was lightning calculating: *'If the kid gets tough Beer Belly will half kill him. That means I'll have to get in it. I need him. It's as good an introduction as any. I hate fights. If I take his side it will bring in the others. The boy looks as if maybe he could go. This is going to be dirty. . .'*

Beer Belly said, 'Oh, you wanna git hoit!' A trucker came over and said, 'You hoid him. Beat it, kid, while you're all in one piece.' Two Oakies ranged themselves near Beer Belly, grinning and looking for trouble. Sears got up, went over and stood next the young sailor. 'I like this side,' he remarked succinctly.

The boy threw him a cold glance and said, 'I don't need you!' and then, 'Look out for yourself! They're coming!' Sears had an odd impression he was laughing inwardly at that moment.

Beer Belly aimed a kick straight for the sailor's groin, but the boy was out of range before it had even started, then he darted in low and hard. There was the sound of a bone snapping and a horrid choking cry. Sears aimed a punch at the head of the trucker, landed it, felt the return blow to his cheek and the scrabble of hands reaching for him, heard the scuffle of feet and whistle of breath and smelled all the whisky, sweat and unwashed body smell of the silent flophouse brawl.

Then the hands fell away from him and the trucker was down across the bed, retching and moaning with a ruptured eardrum where the sailor had clipped him a hatchet blow with the side of his palm. The boy was fighting swiftly, viciously and brutally with a horribly methodical and practised efficiency. Sears recognized it as advanced Commando stuff, but the spirit imbuing the scene was that of David and Goliath.

Beer Belly was out of it on the floor with a broken ankle. The boy was now working so fast the two Oakies never had a chance to get their hands on him simultaneously. The one he blinded, the other he kneed. A big drifter joined the fray, picking up an iron pitcher from the washstand, intending to bring it down on to the back of the boy's head and crush his skull. Sears stuck out his foot in time and the man went down, the pitcher making an iron clangour. Seemingly without a glance or a break in the smooth rhythm of his fighting, the sailor stamped on the fallen drifter's adam's apple with his heel, smashing it.

There was a moment's lull. The downed and crippled men were ringed by spectators staring with horror, but behind them there was a menacing movement. What frightened Sears was the look on the boy's face. If there was any more of it to come he would kill.

Sears caught his breath and said, 'Let's get out of here.'

The boy said, 'What for? I've paid!'

'Never mind. I'll stake us to a place. After this row they'll come up and put us out anyway. Be smart.'

The killer went out of the boy's eyes. 'Right-o!' he said. 'It wasn't a bad show.' He secured his sea-bag and jacket. Sears paused only to pick up the copy of the Bible. He would be needing that. Together they went to the door and down the stairs. Nobody made any move to stop them.

Chapter 3

'But every man is tempted when he is drawn away
of his own lust, and enticed' — *James* i, 14

LATER they sat in the coffee shop of the Union Hotel down by
the railroad station where Sears, now ready to invest some of the
last of his working capital, had taken rooms for them, the boy as
coolly indifferent and self-possessed as he had been at the height of
the brawl in the mission house, the older man studying him, probing for the weakness that might bend and expose him to his will.
The Bible, stamped in faded gold letters 'Brothers of Man
Mission', lay on the table between them. Sears smiled as he saw
the boy's glance stray to it.

'Souvenir,' he said, and then added, 'You familiar with
it?'

'Yes. When I was a child I learned most of the Old Testament
by heart.'

Sears nodded. 'Then tell me something. Right at the beginning
here, in Chapter V of Genesis. How come all those guys lived so
long — eight and nine hundred years?'

The young sailor replied, 'Because God willed it so.'

Sears looked at him sharply. 'Are you kidding?'

'No. I am not kidding. You asked me. I told you.'

'True enough. What is your name?'

'Ben-Isaac Levi.'

'Mine's Sears. Joe Sears. Shake. You can fight, kid.'

'Thanks. It was decent of you to want to help me even though
I didn't need it. What made you do it? You might have got hurt
defending a Jew.'

Sears shrugged. 'I have nothing against Jews. I didn't care for
the odds against . . .'

'We are used to them.' There was no bombast in the simple
statement of historic fact. The boy was cold, wary and no fool.
Sears felt he had been seen through by one who was almost as

18

cynical as himself. No one moves into a dirty fight for purely romantic reasons. He changed his tack:

'Where did you pick up that Commando stuff? And the British accent?'

'In Poland. A British major was dropped to us behind the lines to help organize the guerrillas. He taught me everything.' Ben-Isaac's eyes looked into the past for a moment. 'We had only one book – the English Bible. I learned that by heart too.'

Sears was astonished. 'Taught *you*! Were they taking babies in the Commandos in those days?'

Ben-Isaac said without emotion and as a plain statement of fact, 'I was a guerrilla between Lodz and Tomaszow and killed my first German when I was thirteen.'

'What happened to the major? He must have been an all-right chap.'

'He was caught and tortured to death. I killed the man who betrayed him.'

Sears thought, '*Tough – real hard. Lordy, and we thought we had a war.*' Aloud he asked, 'What about your family?'

'They were butchered by the Germans when I was eleven because they were Jews. I got away into the hills, where I joined the partisans. Then the Russians came. I have killed as many Russians as I have Germans.'

'Why? The Russians didn't hate the Jews . . .'

The young face went old and the timelessness had returned to the cold eyes that looked out at Sears. 'They always have and they always will.'

Sears had an inclination to shiver. He had never encountered anyone like this before. If this was the new Jew, he could understand how they had defeated three armies in Palestine.

'Have you nobody left?'

'There was an uncle – my father's brother . . .'

'Why do you say was? Isn't he living?'

'I don't know. He was always travelling. He was a great man.'

'In what way?'

Warmth came into Ben-Isaac's eyes, and pride. 'He was a rabbi who became a great scientist and teacher, an archaeologist and historian of my people. He has lived all over the world. His name is

Dr Nathaniel Levi. Perhaps you have heard of him.' The years fell away from Ben-Isaac's face. Here was someone he had loved.

Sears shook his head. 'Where is he now?'

'I don't know. I heard he had gone back to Palestine – ' He corrected himself with a sudden fierce pride, 'Israel.'

'Would *he* know why Methuselah lived almost a thousand years, and all the rest?'

'He knows *everything*!' This was the boy answering. But the man was never far removed, for Ben-Isaac added after a moment of reflection, 'He knows God.'

Sears made a mental note: '*Emotion. Could be paydirt. Maybe he's not so tough after all.*' He shifted his probe. 'Where were your people from?'

'We are Poles.'

'And before that?'

'Spaniards. And before that we were exiled in Babylonia. We are very old. My Uncle Nathaniel said we were of the tribe of Naphtali and came from the hills of Hazor.' He caressed the words like living things.

'Naphtali! I came across it in the Bible. Where is that?'

'In Israel. To the north, looking down on Galilee.' Then he quoted, "Naphtali is a hind let loose: he giveth goodly words." He added with simplicity, 'It is the most beautiful country in the world.'

'Have you ever been there?'

Ben-Isaac shook his head. 'No. But I have listened to my Uncle Nathaniel tell of it and of our forefathers there.'

The older man felt a thrill of satisfaction. It seemed as though, in crossing his life at this point with that of this strange boy, Fate had finally consented to smooth the devious path of Joseph Deuell Sears. He began to feel the confidence of the gambler when he knows his luck is on the upswing and holding. He said, 'Tell me, Ben-Isaac. What is it you want most out of life?'

The answer came with startling swiftness: 'To go and fight for Israel. To fight against everyone who hates our people . . .' He repeated the word 'fight!' with a terrible relish and then added, 'It is eighteen hundred years since we have taken up arms in our own defence. I could have killed those swine back there.'

Sears nodded. 'Yes, you could. It is just as well you didn't. And is that all?'

The boy reflected. His voice became softer. 'Perhaps I might find my uncle there if he were still alive . . .'

'Why don't you go?'

Ben-Isaac stared at him. 'I don't exist,' he replied. 'I have no papers. I can get aboard a ship where the master needs a hand and doesn't ask questions. I was on a tanker from Panama. She sailed a day earlier from San Diego, and I missed her. I'm ashore illegally. If I try to ship out on another now I'll be turned over to the immigration people. I have no right to be here.' After a moment's pause he added, 'I have no right to be anywhere . . .'

Sears said, 'That's a bad spot.' He looked at the boy calculatingly for a moment before he asked, 'Would you like to have a passport, Ben-Isaac – or valid travel papers, legitimizing and identifying you and enabling you to go to Palestine – or wherever you wanted?'

Ben-Isaac's laugh told Sears more than anything he could have replied.

Sears now drew the folded newspaper from his side pocket and opened it so that the startling, ruffled features of Hannah Bascombe glared up at them in the dim, smoky light of the coffee shop. He said, 'Tell me something, Ben-Isaac. What do you think of this woman?'

The boy took the newspaper and studied the harsh, rapacious face and then read the story connected with her and remained sunk in thought until the man at the table opposite him repeated the query. Then he replied, 'I think that she is very unhappy.'

'Would you be interested in making her happier?'

'Why should I?'

Sears discounted the blunt and almost inhuman reply. He guessed that, for all of Ben-Isaac's hardness and self-possession, he was bitterly hurt by what life had done to him and inwardly raw. He said now, 'Why, because if you were to succeed she could very well be instrumental in helping you to everything you most want – an identity, papers, a nationality, a home . . .'

The boy said with a sudden, tense fierceness, 'What makes you think I want a home?'

Sears laid a hand on his arm. 'Kid, everybody does.'

It was a hard, shrewd blow. But the boy, though visibly shaken, fought back immediately: 'How would she help? What could she do? What have I to do with this rich and blasphemous old woman? What's your game, mister? You're no almshouse Joe, with your good clothes and stolen Bible.'

'Right,' said Joe Sears. 'You've asked me. Now I'll tell you . . .'

When he had finished relating what he had learned by reading Genesis, the curious theory he had evolved and how it was to affect the old woman whose portrait stared up so fiercely and defiantly from the table top between them, and the narration consumed almost an hour, the boy sat reflecting silently. Then he said, 'You almost believe it yourself, don't you?'

'Why not? It could be, couldn't it?'

The boy shrugged. 'Uncle Nathaniel would know.'

Sears said, 'Ah yes. Uncle Nathaniel. The ex-rabbi turned archaeologist. You don't know where he is?'

'I have written to him, but I have had no reply. He is probably dead.' He thought a while again and then asked, 'How will all this get me my papers?'

Sears replied swiftly, 'If she believes my story she'll want to get them for you so that you can go with me to Palestine and search. This is the richest and most financially powerful woman in America. There is nothing she cannot buy.'

'Except her way into heaven . . .' said Ben-Isaac.

'Ah, but that is exactly where she does not want to go. If I can make her believe that with some of her fortune she can buy herself a little more time on earth . . .'

'Or a ticket to hell . . .'

'It isn't as though it were dishonest or crooked,' Sears argued. 'We're selling her an idea. Anyway, who is going to peg that first rock? Do you think that what the world has done to you is honest? Or that all of her manipulations would stand every test?'

Ben-Isaac said, 'Never mind what the world has done to me. I can look after myself.'

Sears replied, 'Uhuh. You've proved that up to now. You're

a tough kid, but you're in a bad spot. The Commando stuff won't go if the immigration boys pick you up, and they're getting very touchy about foreign-looking strangers in town these days. You'd find yourself on a ship headed for Poland, where the Russians would probably like to have a little talk with you. This is a way out.'

Ben-Isaac was uneasy. He countered with, 'She's wicked, but she's a woman . . .'

Sears replied, 'Right. But what does she lose? A couple of hundred grand backing my idea? She makes that over the telephone when she buys or sells a corporation. She earns that much in a couple of hours just by sitting still and doing nothing but let her money breed in the banks and on the books . . .'

The boy now sat silently and looked down at the face in the photograph. Sears wished he could guess what was going through his mind so that he would know better what stops to pull out to move him.

He said now, 'And, anyway, who said she won't be getting something for her money? And how does anybody know my theory isn't true until somebody tries to find out? We wouldn't be taking from her, but giving. Nothing prolongs life in the aged like hope and incentive. We give her an honest shake as long as we're on the payroll – organize an expedition and go to the Biblical lands . . . work, research, send back reports – we'd be guaranteeing her at least another five years of life just by providing her with something to cling to . . .'

Ben-Isaac interrupted suddenly, tapping the photograph on the table with long, graceful fingers that a few hours before had wrecked four men, 'She'll never believe you.'

Sears looked at the boy hard and penetratingly. 'Maybe not,' he replied succinctly, 'but she will believe *you*!'

They stared at one another now, the batteries unmasked. There was nothing more concealed between them. The issues were as clear as Sears had been able to make them. They were in that curious half-world of unrealized potentialities that men inhabit when they find that they have need of one another, when they have faced that whatever it is they want they can no longer achieve alone.

Sears let the silence last and the implications sink in. Then after a time he suggested, 'What do you say we have another cup of coffee? We can talk about it some more later if you feel like it.'

'All right,' Ben-Isaac said. 'What difference does it make?'

Chapter 4

'The heaven shall reveal his iniquity' —
Job xx, 27

Two weeks later, weeks devoted by Sears to voracious cramming of the Bible and Bible history, as well as research into back newspaper files on the life of Hannah Bascombe and her pioneer father, Iron Ike Bascombe, they presented themselves at the Bascombe mansion, that Victorian monstrosity of red brick and slate topped by towers and turrets, occupying half a block atop Nob Hill in San Francisco.

Sears was impeccable in dress, business suit, a conservative necktie, hat, gloves and stick — he knew the value of first impressions. The boy, still in his tight-fitting sailor's clothing, pea-jacket and stocking cap, was calm and self-possessed.

To assure entrance, Sears had spun an elaborate web of telephone calls to the Bascombe mansion, messages, telegrams and a fake transatlantic call purporting to be London trying to reach him, for which he paid one of the hotel operators twenty dollars to stage from their room. He knew that nothing created more of a sense of urgency and importance than an overseas telephone call.

The butler took the finely engraved card — 'Mr Joseph Deuell Sears' — and asked, 'Did you have an appointment with Miss Adams?'

Sears said, 'Certainly, else I should not be here. Please take her my card.'

The butler glanced at it and a gleam of recognition came into his face. 'I beg your pardon, would you be the gentleman expecting an urgent telephone call from London?'

Sears adjusted his cuffs. 'Yes. Has it come through? The Fairmount must have had it transferred here. I'm sorry about that.'

'There was a message for you to call Overseas Operator fifty-nine.'

Sears glanced at his watch. 'Thank you. It can wait until after I have seen Miss Adams.'

The butler placed the card on a salver and went out. Ben-Isaac said to Sears, 'You're slick. What if she refuses to see you?'

Sears said, 'She won't. I've spread confusion, created doubt as to whether there was an appointment, established an identity and I'm here. Are you nervous?'

'No. What have I to be nervous about?'

Sears nodded appreciatively. 'Good kid. Don't worry. We're as good as in. I've got a way with spinsters. They have a weakness for me. I'll handle Miss Adams.'

The butler returned to the ante-room. 'Miss Adams does not recall giving you an appointment, though she received a number of messages. However, now that you are here she will see you. Will you come this way.'

Sears arose. 'Of course. Ben-Isaac will wait here until I send for him.'

Sears followed the servant, the thick carpet deadening the sound of their steps and feeling good under his feet. How he loved luxury. Even hovering between nervousness and exultation he could enjoy this foretaste of it. The huge house was full of silence and darkness; there was a vast staircase, immense rooms opening off corridors, unlit, but stray beams of light fell upon heavy furniture. Sometimes a bell chimed, or there was the distinct ringing of the telephone.

They turned a corner and the butler opened a heavy oak door, preceding him into the room. Sears saw that it was a long, panelled study in warm reds and browns, with a massive fireplace in which a fire was burning. At the far end, in the centre of a small pool of light, stood a large desk at which a woman was seated, her head bent down, studying some papers. There were several telephones and a dictating machine on the desk. The only furniture in the room was a long, polished conference table and the accompanying chairs.

The butler said, 'Miss Adams, Mr Joseph Sears.'

Sears was conscious of a moment of exasperation. He would have to take the long walk up to this woman's desk like a boy marching up to teacher. Then he smiled to himself. There

26

were the props and psychological gambits in *their* game likewise.

He deposited his hat, stick and gloves on the conference table, adjusted his tie and walked the length of the room. When he was three-quarters of the way the woman at the desk removed a pair of horn-rimmed glasses, placed them on the desk before her, turned her head and looked at him, stopping Mr Joseph Deuell Sears as dead in his tracks as though he had come up against an invisible wall.

First blood, first damage, Big and Little Casino went to the enemy. He had geared his plans, his pitch, his mental approach to an elderly, tight-lipped spinster secretary. He was not prepared for a girl.

She was tall and her arms were strangely thin. Her skin had the pallor of one who spends little time out of doors but who lies soaking in soft baths and uses many creams and ointments. He saw that she had brown hair which was almost too soft and heavy, held back from the pointed oval of her face by a narrow velvet band. She wore a short-sleeved white blouse and a skirt of some dark, expensive material.

He felt at once that she was some kind of paradox – a staggering beauty under glass – a flower, half wilted in a tomb. Feminine and breath-taking and at the same time repellent. There was intelligence and appeal in the clear brow, the beautifully modelled jaw, yet there was a curiously unidentifiable weakness in the shape and expression of her mobile lips.

Her mouth was moulded in an expression of distaste. Her violet coloured eyes – large and disturbing – were levelled on him – penetrating, mocking – filled with a tolerant contempt for what they saw.

Standing there gaping, caught and stripped of all his pretences in one instant, Sears felt himself swept by a wave of violent resentment and anger against this person who had penetrated his disguise so quickly, smelling him out for what he was. This was not fair play to shock the carefully built-up personage that was Mr Joseph Deuell Sears – the big, International Something-or-other-Important – back into plain Joe Sears, Hollywood wise guy and would-be swindler.

Yet even while he was reeling under the impact of her presence and personality, Sears was gathering his forces and rallying himself. He thought, '*Oh, you've got me all right, my lass, but I'll be on to you, before long. I've been down for the count of nine, but I'm up again, and the battle's just starting.*'

She broke the spell she had cast over him by glancing down for an instant at his card on the desk before her. When she looked up again she moved at once to the attack from her position of advantage.

'What is it you want, Mr Joseph Sears?'

As always, she experienced a sense of satisfaction and justification from the confusion into which she had thrown her visitor and the ease with which she had penetrated his pretensions. She stood in need of these triumphs, for Clary Adams was a girl who had made a choice in life, and one that was less than courageous.

Rather than face the struggle in the highly competitive society into which she was born and in which her parents had made such a conspicuous failure, she had elected to bury herself as companion and aide to Hannah Bascombe in return for sheltered, luxurious living and the eventual security of a substantial inheritance.

Clary had been fourteen when her father died, his insurance barely covering the cost of the prescribed middle-class funeral. Three years later, when she lost her hard-working, ineffectual mother, Clary, still being a minor, came under the temporary guardianship of Hannah Bascombe, her nearest relative, though she was but a distant cousin on her mother's side.

The wealthy woman had been struck by qualities she observed in the girl over and above her breeding and good general education, such as her capacity for loyalty and her hatred and fear of dinginess and poverty.

Heretofore, Hannah Bascombe had been able to buy everything she ever wanted or needed with the exception of unswerving loyalty, coupled with constant attendance. In Clary, the poor relation, a beauty, whose temperament and weaknesses balanced out her strength, Hannah saw an opportunity to bind a creature to her side for life, someone who would fulfil her long-standing need for a female companion and buffer against the outside world.

Thereupon Hannah had offered Clary the life job, hedged about with certain protective clauses – protective, that is, to

Hannah. As an alternative the old woman had proposed to give the girl a business and secretarial education or send her away to school until she was of age and able to provide for herself.

Unhesitatingly, Clary had chosen the former with full recognition that it called for her to give up a normal existence, or the opportunities to fulfil herself as a woman – at least during Hannah Bascombe's lifetime. Her eyes had been wide open. She told herself that she did not regret her choice, for she lived a protected life of utmost luxury. Nevertheless, she took her revenge on any luckless caller whose business was illegitimate.

Chapter 5

'A sound of battle is in the land' – *Jeremiah* 1, 22

No better watchdog could have been secured by Hannah Bascombe to keep away the vultures, Sears thought to himself as he struggled to regain his poise and composure. Even men with legitimate business must find themselves weakened by an encounter with Miss Clary Adams, the inevitable prelude to an audience with her chief.

A glance was sufficient to reveal that she was possessed of intelligence sharpened and augmented by her woman's instincts. Added to this, she befuddled a man's senses, weakened his will, disturbed his self-confidence and moved him off balance with her appeal of repressed sexuality indicated in paradox by the challenging eyes and ripe mouth, guarded by the cold citadel of a body that in its rigidity and angularity proclaimed its inviolability. Sears was certain that he disliked her thoroughly.

Nevertheless, he was beginning to recover from the shock of feeling that with one look she had stripped him bare of all his carefully prepared pretence. To gain needed time until he could regroup and determine what line of attack might prove most effective, he said, 'How do you do, Miss Adams. Do you mind if I sit down?'

'No, do, please,' replied Miss Adams in a voice that was pleasant, polite and impersonal.

To Clary Adams, spinster, comfortably barricaded behind her imposing diplomat's glass-topped desk, secure in the authority of her position, the interview was already as good as over, and in her mind she was continuing with the work she had been doing when interrupted by this caller, of whose spuriousness she had not the slightest doubt.

He would stammer forth, or glibly produce, depending on what type of salesman he was, his 'proposition', his story of goldmines or oil-wells, his crackpot invention or world-saving play, or even some more bald-faced come-on, and in a few minutes she would have him on his way out.

Sears seated himself in the chair she had indicated next to her desk, asked her permission to smoke, and, when she gave it, lit a cigarette with careful and deliberate grace, thankful for the opportunity of collecting himself. 'I must confess,' he said to her, 'you took me completely by surprise. I was expecting someone quite different.'

It was an assay, as safe an opening gambit as one could make with a woman of such attractions. He had to find out where he was at. By her expression, subtle as it was, Sears saw at once that he had made a mistake. Most likely the majority of the callers at her desk made some reference to her beauty. She didn't like it. If she had any weaknesses, this was not one of them.

Clary said, 'Spare me, Mr Sears.' She found herself, as always, amused by the effect her personality had on men who saw her for the first time, but in this instance the amusement was laced with a rising anger at the arrogance of this male.

She resented also the smooth impertinence of his façade; the elegance of his clothes, their too rightness; the perfection of his recent haircut and shave; his almost aggressive cleanliness – all of which might well serve as a cloak and disguise for a scoundrel. In these first moments of their encounter her instincts told her that he was like an actor playing a gentleman who was in some part of his being enough of a gentleman to know how to impersonate, even though he might not be able to be one.

'It was a sincere compliment that was intended,' Sears said. 'I meant no impertinence. I must also apologize for what seems to be some confusion. I was under the impression that I had been given an appointment with you ...'

Miss Adams said evenly, 'No apology is necessary, Mr Sears,' adding, 'Now that you are here, may I ask you to state your business?'

Sears thought swiftly – what to call it: idea, plan, scheme, proposition? '*I would like to present a plan to Miss Bascombe*' – '*I have a little proposition that I believe would interest Miss Bascombe.*' He shuddered inwardly. The word 'proposition' placed before this girl who was appraising him so coolly was unthinkable. It was obvious that she was familiar with the methods he had used to reach her presence. Then why did she bother with him at all?

He had a sudden flash of insight into what life must be like for someone burdened with the responsibility of acting as sole channel to a woman like Hannah Bascombe. The rewards would be high, but errors would not be tolerated. In a far-flung financial empire such as Hannah's, mistakes could lead to disasters with world repercussions.

Thus, Miss Adams could not very well afford to take chances. Her business was to sift, analyze and evaluate every applicant. Hers was a job that must call for concentrated and unswerving loyalty. He wondered how such devotion would be rewarded and what was the secret of the relationship of these two women. He filed the thoughts away for future use.

'My business is with Hannah Bascombe. May I ask that you take a message to her for me?'

'And what is the nature of that message?' she asked.

Now it was she who studied him for any indication that she could have been wrong and that he might actually be on legitimate business after all. He had eyes which were spaced wide in his face. They were grey with yellow in them like those of a lynx. The brow indicated intelligence, the mouth recklessness, and the chin struck her as inclined to truculence and stubborness.

Her glance met his. His look, reflecting the change that had been building up slowly within him since he had come in, now conveyed a small shock to her, for she was made aware of an aggressive maleness about him, a confidence in his power as a man that was disconcerting.

His frank, appraising gaze turned full upon her left no doubt as to his estimate of his own ability to cope with that side of her which had heretofore proved her most formidable weapon. They had been exchanging polite sentences, the lead-up to business talk, but for the first time Clary began to realize that she was in a battle. She had shattered his initial campaign and put him on the defensive. Now she was aware that he no longer feared her, and in particular her damaging appeal to the senses. Most men were insecure and backed away from it. She determined to be rid of him even more quickly, for he had the good looks and sly promise of the predatory and uninhibited male. Clary Adams had long ago told herself that there could be no compromises. She was not interested in men, romance, sexual gratification, or love.

Sears felt the subtle shift in position and thought to himself, *'That's better. That's much better than compliments, or stalling. Now you know who would be boss in* THAT *department ...'*

Aloud he said, 'It is really very simple. Will you be so good as to take in my card to Miss Bascombe and tell her I am convinced that I can give her the one thing that she desires more than anything else in this world?'

'Are you joking, Mr Sears?'

'No, Miss Adams. I am quite serious.'

She was startled at his effrontery, for while she had been exposed to many strange approaches and impudent attempts to gain the ear of Hannah Bascombe she had never encountered anything to match this. But even more she was disturbed by the thoughts his statement had evoked in her. What did he mean by, 'The one thing she desires more than anything else in this world'? It was only she, Clary Adams, who, since seventeen, had lived intimately and closely with Hannah Bascombe for ten years, who knew the truth that beneath her apparently eccentric defiance of the government and her statements to the press lay a fearful and genuine obsession to defeat the Angel of Death.

Had this stranger, this man she immediately suspected of charlatanism, guessed it? If so, it made him a hundred times more dangerous. But it could not be, for then his proposal to gratify it was, on the face of it, ridiculous. She said, 'Surely, Mr Sears, you do not really expect me to take such an absurd message in to Miss Bascombe.'

'I rather hope you will, Miss Adams.'

She leaned back in her chair. 'Why on earth should I?'

'Because,' Sears said, 'it might just possibly be true.'

Now she said, 'I am sorry, Mr Sears. You will have to do better than that. We do not deal in riddles here. If you have something you think might be of interest to Miss Bascombe, I suggest you

tell it to me. I will then decide whether it is worth her consideration.'

'*Sure of yourself, Violet-eyes,*' Joe Sears thought. '*So sure of
yourself. And yet you're not. I saw your finger move towards the
bell and stop. You are not nearly as secure as you pretend. What
is it you are afraid of?*'

He replied evenly, 'If it concerned you, Miss Adams, I would
do so. But since it is a matter of urgent privacy and only for Miss
Bascombe to hear, I would be putting an affront upon her and
doing her a disservice by discussing it – if you will forgive me –
with you or anyone else.'

Honey was the better trap, but flies had been known to tumble
into the vinegar bottle. He wanted to see what would happen and
what she was like when angry. It showed in a hardening of the
curve of the luxurious mouth, and two red spots, the first colour
he had seen come to her pale cheeks. One of her long, thin fingers
moved towards the bell.

She said, 'Very well, Mr Sears. This interview is ended. Naturally I must refuse to convey your ridiculous message to . . .'

'Don't,' Sears warned, 'for you will regret it. If it ever reaches
the ears of Miss Bascombe what you have turned away from her
doors she will never forgive you.'

He saw a startled expression come over her features before she
could mask it. Her hand nearing the bell trembled. When she
looked at him again her eyes seemed to have undergone a curious
change. The challenge in them, the contempt for him, the mockery and the intelligent penetration were clouded. Even though
she said, 'I do not like to be threatened, Mr Sears,' he felt there
was no conviction behind it, and she made no further move to
press the ivory button.

Chapter 6

'For it is told me that he dealeth very subtilly' —
I Samuel xxiii, 22

AFTERWARDS, Joe Sears remembered that it seemed like a voice inside him crying in the manner of theatre ushers at intermission time, 'Curtain going up! Curtain going up on Miss Clary Adams!'

There she was, like a character walking across a stage. All the things he had suspected, wondered about, and guessed at came forth out of the files of his mind and he recognized her now; what kind of person she was, her position in the Bascombe menage, her weaknesses as well as her strength, and what she feared more than anything. It was just that simple. She was afraid of losing her job.

'Ah, no,' Sears said, and even felt a momentary surge of pity for her. 'I did not mean to threaten you. I only wanted you to understand the extent of what is involved. Supposing we start all over again. Will you let me show you how it looks from where I see it?'

The friendly reasonableness in his voice and attitude made it possible for her to acquiesce. It seemed as though he had opened a momentary line of retreat for her, an opportunity to rally her own forces and master herself, for the tide of battle had turned and she knew that somehow her early triumph had been snatched away and turned into defeat.

'Look here, Miss Adams,' he said quietly, 'what are the facts? Although you may suspect the worst, you do not really know who or what I am, or what it is I have to sell — or give away, or offer, or trade. And until you are certain it would not be the part of wisdom to turn me out. For if word reached Hannah Bascombe later as to why I came and that you had dismissed me . . .' He gestured with his hand across his throat to complete the sentence and then added shrewdly, 'For all I know, Miss Bascombe has been listening to some of what has been said here already.'

Clary's glance betrayed her. Her eyes strayed to the ceiling where there was probably an audio-box concealed, confirming Sears's suspicion that a woman like Hannah Bascombe would have means of eavesdropping on her secretary, or the entire house and staff for that matter, if she felt like it.

Sears's voice became soothing and impersonal. 'I am asking you to take her a message from me. What do you risk? You are at liberty to tell her your suspicions and urge her to have nothing to do with me. She has the choice of accepting your advice or of letting her curiosity get the better of her and seeing me. Either way, the final responsibility for her actions will then rest with her. Send me away from here and you stand to lose heavily, if not everything. Play the percentage, Miss Adams. It is really the sensible thing to do.'

She had replaced her horn-rimmed glasses and had somehow changed the attitude of her slender, too-thin body in the chair so that the woman had retreated and the secretary was now in the foreground. She sat at her desk again with head lowered over pad and pencil so that he could no longer see the expression on her face, and in a flat, unemotional voice asked, 'What is the message you wish me to take to Miss Bascombe?'

Sears repeated, 'Tell her I am certain that I can help her to attain what she most wants.'

He heard the soft sound of her pencil making the notation. Then she arose with the slip of paper in her fingers, leaving the room by a small door that opened in the panelled wall behind her desk. Sears felt tired and drained. He wished he had a drink. However, there was no decanter anywhere in sight and he coached himself, *'Never mind the drink. You're on the big time now, kid. Pull yourself together. You've beaten the girl. This isn't for peanuts any more.'*

Five minutes later the door opened and Clary Adams returned. She was able to look him in the face now, coolly and impersonally as if the taut struggle of a few minutes before had never taken place between them. She was again on dead-sure ground as Hannah Bascombe's machine, transmitting her orders and doing her bidding.

36

She said to Joe Sears, 'Miss Bascombe has advised me that she is greatly interested at the moment in acquiring the Seattle, Oregon and North Pacific Railways and the Alaskan and Orient Steamship Company, which is a subsidiary. If your business is concerned with either of these companies, or with her desire to purchase them, she would be willing to see you.'

Sears tried to keep the flush of triumph from his countenance at the words, '. . . she would be willing to see you.' He thought to himself, '*I'm in. Once I'm with her I can switch to what I am after.*'

Yet he did not reply. Something was warning him that it had been too easy; things didn't go like that, running for you without a hitch. Somewhere concealed in Hannah's message was a trap. You had to forget your small-time ideas when you went up to play with the big fellows.

In a flash of insight, coupled with an impulsive gambling instinct, he knew exactly what he must do and proceeded to put it into effect.

He arose, pushed back his chair, did those things about his clothes and person that a man will do when he is about to take his leave, and said, 'Thank you very much. I guess that will be all then. You have been more than kind.'

Clary Adams was plainly startled, and showed it by the widening of her eyes in the pale, luminous face. It was not at all what she had been expecting. 'You do not wish to reply to Miss Bascombe's inquiry?'

'Look,' Joe Sears replied, 'I don't like to be kidded. I came here on legitimate business and have acted in good faith. But now that I am here I don't care to go for the ride. The Seattle, Oregon and North Pacific business is not her greatest desire. I have no knowledge of or interest in this merger whatsoever and cannot assist her in any manner to achieve it. If that is her sole reply to the message I sent her, then that is the end to this affair. I am sorry.'

Thereupon he turned and took the walk that called for more nerve and courage than anything he had ever done in his life. He strode with just the right mixture of determination and injury down the long length of the room to the end of the table, where, with no perceptible hesitation, he picked up his hat, gloves and stick with three firm movements which had a touch of righteous indignation and walked to the door.

Only there, when he pulled it partly open, did he turn around as common politeness indicated, to say, 'Thank you, Miss Adams. Good-bye.'

She was standing beside her desk, the slip of paper still in her fingers. She did not reply. Well, there was no turning back now. There remained nothing for him to do but go. But before he could move he was halted by a voice that seemed to come from all about him.

'Wait a minute, young man! I want to talk to you.'

It was startling and eerie in its virility, its dry command. No one had joined them in the big conference room.

Then the voice boomed out again, seeming to come from above, beneath and all about him.

'Miss Adams!'

The girl involuntarily looked up towards the loud-speaker built into the ceiling as she replied, 'Yes, Miss Bascombe.'

'You may bring Mr Sears to me. I wish to speak to him.'

'Very well, Miss Bascombe.'

There was a click, and the room was again heavy with silence.

Clary Adams said, 'Will you accompany me, Mr Sears? I will take you to Miss Bascombe.'

Chapter 7

'If riches increase, set not your heart upon them' —
Psalms lxii, 10

HANNAH Bascombe was born in San Francisco in 1876, so Joe
Sears had read in the clipping files in Los Angeles newspaper
morgues. Before he and Ben-Isaac made the trip north he had
researched everything that had ever been said or written about
the eccentric heiress.

She was the only child of Isaac Gamaliel Bascombe, the leg-
endary Iron Ike of the Northwest. Her mother, Lavengro
Rydere, had been a school teacher from Virginia. She had died
when Hannah was three. Iron Ike himself was fifty years of age
and already twice over a millionaire at the time of their marriage.

Bascombe had come to California from Massachusetts as a
young man in 1850, in the wake of the great gold rush, and later
had thrown himself into the business of transportation, a game
that was made for him. He was a pioneer, a fighter, a gambler, a
full-fledged industrial pirate, and, according to his lights, a pious
man who never let a day go by without reading a chapter from
the Bible. When his wife died he could not bear to be parted from
the child even for a short time.

As she grew up there developed an extraordinary relationship
between father and daughter, proof of which yet existed in the
folders of old photographs Sears had examined in the newspaper
files.

In each one of them he was accompanied by Hannah at various
stages of her growth and development. In Nevada she was an
infant carried in his arms; aboard ship, en route to Nome, a
toddler, her tiny hand lost in his huge fist; in Oregon a little
girl dwarfed by the gigantic circle of the stump of a felled north-
western pine, or peering coyly out of the cab of a square-stacked
locomotive engaged in making the first run from San Francisco
to Oregon City.

The stories agreed that he adored this girl-child with the same fierce possessive love which he entertained for his grandiose and expensive money-making interests, and that she, in turn, worshipped her father beyond all else. Their lives, their wishes, desires and aims had blended as though they were really one. There was nothing that Hannah did not observe or learn of the rough-and-tumble of finance, politics, money and struggle for control and power in an expanding country and economy. She was no stranger to the panelled and plush conference rooms later where Iron Ike roared or wheedled, threatened or bluffed his way through the fabulous deals and combines that made and unmade men, bought or wrecked rival businesses and built the Bascombe empire.

It was apparent from the clippings that on the one hand Ike Bascombe could quote you the Bible from Genesis to Revelation, and on the other, without turning a hair, cut your financial life-line and starve you to death.

Hannah grew up in a country that was still wide open to the pioneer, a land of unlimited resources and opportunity for acquiring them and let the devil take the hindmost.

There had in all likelihood never been any idea that Hannah might some time marry and leave her father. No indication of any man in her life appeared in any of the newspaper stories. In 1910, when Ike Bascombe died at the age of eighty-six, Hannah was a spinster of thirty-four and by then wholly incapable of considering a man to supplant her father.

It was approximately twenty-five years after his death that it began to dawn upon those whose business it is to interest the public in stories of the doings of the wealthy that although the person of Iron Ike Bascombe had long since departed from the Bay area his freebooting spirit and powers of acquisition had not. It became evident that, far from diminishing or even remaining static, the transportation, mining and timber empire he had left his only daughter had been increasing steadily. Hannah Bascombe was labouring in her father's vineyards.

Single-handed all those years she had been competing against the greatest of America's new and rising generation of financiers. She was daring, aggressive, shrewd and ruthless; an expert at every facet of the game and particularly brilliant at concealing her connection with some purchase, merger or combine until the trap was sprung. By the end of the twenties she had more than quadrupled the fortune and holdings left by her father and stretched her tentacles into nearly every corner of the nation.

However, she did not become a semi-public figure, or newsworthy in the modern sense, until she encountered the one foe which up to that time no other single tycoon or large financial group had been able to defeat – the taxing power of the government of the people of the United States.

Almost at once, as news of her battles against the taxation she considered punitive and confiscatory leaked out, Hannah Bascombe began to take on the aspect of a legend.

Finally, in 1946, on her seventieth birthday, to put an end to the constant attempts on the part of reporters to invade her privacy, as well as to gain a voice for her determination not to surrender to the predatory tax-collector and the new philosophy of the reckless spending of other people's money, Hannah Bascombe consented to meet the press and the photographers.

A good deal of mystery and rumour were thus dispelled, for she turned out to be a woman who led a fairly normal life in consistently impeccable surroundings, conducting her business from the quiet of an office, a kind of miniature Exchange installed in her house, which included every kind and means of communication. She was known even, it developed, to spend an occasional evening at the opera or the theatre in the company of friends or her secretary-companion.

However, as she established the birthday interview as an annual custom and made it the occasion for reiterating her defiance against her enemies, and a restatement of her determination to outwit them by outliving them, a further aura and legend developed about her. With her challenging, 'I'm still here. I'm still alive. They're only waiting for me to die to rob me, but I'll outlive them all,' she grew to be something of a West Coast newspaper landmark. Assignment to 'Hannah Bascombe Day' was almost automatic. But every editor likewise had on tap an obit that began in effect, 'Hannah Bascombe, the heiress and financial genius who each year defied the government to dismember her vast financial empire via death duties, today at last surrendered to the one foe she could not vanquish, Death, which, as it must to all men, came to summon her at the age of . . . etc. etc.'

Hannah Bascombe, seated behind her huge, glass-topped diplomat's desk beneath the stern portrait of her father and flanked on one side by a large globe, on the other by a huge, brass-bound Bible on a stand, said, 'Sit down, Mr Sears,' and then added, 'Miss Adams, I wish you to remain.'

A sly smile at the corners of her mouth, Clary went to the secretarial table at the far side of the dark-panelled library that was Miss Bascombe's office and seated herself. Sears tried to drink in impressions in great gulps, anything and everything that would help him in his task now that the heiress had complicated it by ordering the presence of her secretary during the interview.

All of his preconceived notions and plans were already out the window. Hannah Bascombe might be a woman with an obsession, but she was neither an eccentric nor a fool. She was a powerful and dynamic personality.

He became aware at once of the startling paradox of a face of which only the upper half was alive in contrast to the cold, thin, bloodless line of a mouth that had never really lived. All of Hannah Bascombe was concentrated in and about her dark, intelligent, avid eyes that had remained untouched by time. The folds of the eyelids, gathered at the corners almost like drapery, contained cleverness, cunning, and a hint, too, of humour.

The fierce, dramatic youthfulness of her eyes denied the evidence of her three score and fifteen years; the blue veins at the temples, the shining wax-coloured flesh, the thin hawk's nose and the damage of the years to her throat. Her pepper-and-salt hair was piled on top of her head and laced with a bow; it had been done by a hairdresser. Sears noted the imperious and elegant pose of her head upon the slender neck, the finesse and delicacy of her wristbones, as well as the fact that her hands were perpetually balled into fists turned inwards – the gesture of one who cannot let go.

Her clothing was as up-to-date as today's newspaper. She wore a dark-blue jersey suit-dress with white collar and cuffs, the jacket trimmed with large ivory buttons. Three strands of pearls were wound about her throat. More were looped carelessly around her left wrist.

In the few seconds he had while he seated himself Sears' eyes roved avidly. He saw the portrait of Hannah's mother, Lavengro, with the unmistakable resemblance to Clary Adams, confirming her as a distant relation, and the framed photographs of rough-looking men in shapeless clothes and bowler hats, in various settings of the old west – railroad construction, timber, mining, ranching – and the theme that bound them all together; the girl-child-in-arms held lovingly by the biggest and burliest of them, Iron Ike. He noted the Bible was opened to the psalms.

Hannah Bascombe indicated a chair close to her desk and half facing Clary as well as herself. 'Sit down, young man.'

When Sears did so her temper at the moment and the kind of person she was became plain from her opening remark:

'I am seeing you, Mr Sears, in spite of the fact that Miss Adams here, who is charged with making my appointments, has not a very high opinion of you.'

Sears replied, 'I can understand that, since she caught me in a number of lies,' and he smiled openly and engagingly at Clary. He was certain that she had reported the frauds he had practised to gain admittance, and her angry look confirmed his guess. He thought he saw a hint of amusement emphasized by the folds of the delicately veined lids at the corners of Hannah's brilliant eyes. He concluded, 'They were justified by the fact that I very much wanted to see you and talk to you.'

She returned to the attack. 'That may be. You sent me a very clever and provocative message, and when I returned you one that was an untruth you had the wit to pretend you were going to leave. You may satisfy my curiosity. What is it you think I want more than anything else in the world?'

'Not to die!' Joe Sears replied, unlimbering his biggest gun and hauling away at the lanyard point-blank.

Chapter 8

'The days of our years are three score and ten' –
Psalms xc, 10

IF Sears expected a violent reaction from Hannah Bascombe, it did not come. The charge went off like a squib, but her darting eyes that searched him so directly seemed to be shadowed for an instant. Then she replied abruptly, 'Fiddlesticks! No one can live for ever.'

'That is true. But there is nothing to keep one from wishing to do so.'

'And you are under the impression that such is my desire?'

'No one really wants to die, Miss Bascombe.'

A light glowed on the button panel. Hannah Bascombe picked up the telephone and listened. Then she said, 'Thank you. No,' and replaced the instrument. Her mind was far off for a moment. She seemed to have forgotten Sears' presence. When she returned to him again, it was almost with a sense of impatience that he was quick to gauge.

'Is that all you wished to say to me, Mr Sears?'

He felt on the run. He could not reconcile the defiant-eyed person of the annual newspaper interview with this cold, self-possessed business woman. And yet he believed he was right, that somewhere, somehow the trigger of her obsession could be pulled. He felt that the interview was dangerously near an end.

He asked, 'Would you be interested in my real impression of you, Miss Bascombe?'

She did not reply to this, but neither did she by word or gesture deny him the opportunity of telling her.

'I believe you are implacably determined to resist dissolution.'

'Yes? Why, Mr Sears?'

There was interest with yet an undertone of grim come-on in her voice, as though she were prepared, for amusement's sake, to see just how much of a fool he was going to make of himself.

44

'Because when you die you will lose everything for which you have lived your lifetime, the empire your father built.'

Still she did not speak. He was launched and felt there was no turning back now. 'For twenty years they have been baying at your heels in Washington. Now they are simply waiting for the inevitable, when they will be able to get their hands on your fortune and empty it into the hopper of the new philosophy of tax and spend, spend and tax the earnings of men and women of vision, courage and enterprise.'

Hannah Bascombe said, with calmness and finality, 'You need not worry. They shall not have a penny.'

Sears wondered who was mad now, she or he. He plunged deeper. 'Oh yes. You will fight to live. You will not give up. When you can no longer walk you will crawl. Or you will take to your bed and fight on until only your eyes are alive, and when those are veiled you will struggle to keep a quiver in your breast or a flutter in your throat so that they cannot move in with their lawyers and assessors. But in the end . . .'

Clary half arose from her desk, her eyes burning with indignation. 'Miss Bascombe!' she cried. 'Stop him. Don't let him go on like that.'

But the older woman motioned for her to be still with a peremptory gesture and then concluded for Sears:

'I will die,' and now there was definitely amusement in her eyes. '. . . unless, as you indicated, you assist me to prevent it. Really, Mr Sears, you are the most astonishing man I have ever encountered. What are you selling? Is it a pill, a nostrum, something in a bottle, a diet, an electric belt perhaps? What will it cost me to learn your famous secret?'

'Nothing,' Joe Sears said. 'For you have it at your hand.'

He got up under her watchful eyes, went around her desk and laid his hand on the big Bible on the stand.

'It's in here, Miss Bascombe.'

She turned in her chair and looked up at him. 'What are you talking about? Don't you know what the Good Books says?' And then, without waiting for him to reply, quoted the tenth verse of the ninetieth Psalm: 'The days of our years are three-score years and ten.' Her voice rose, and it was astonishing how youthful and unaffected by years it was. '. . . and if by reason of strength they be fourscore years, yet is their strength labour and sorrow; for it is soon cut off, and we fly away.'

'Yet,' Sears said, 'it was not always like that.'

She looked at him with a kind of ruffled indignation. 'What nonsense are you talking now?'

'Turn back to Genesis,' and there crept into his voice something of the fervour of the evangelist in the tent in Burbank who had cried to him, 'It's in the Bible, brother. Hallelujah! Go to the Bible.' He flipped the heavy pages of the Book to the opening chapters. 'Look to Genesis and the lives of patriarchs, whose life-span was not threescore years and ten but eight and nine hundred years on earth: Adam and Seth and Enos Mahalaleel and Jared, Enoch and Methuselah . . .' And here he paused to read from the fifth chapter: ' ". . . And Methuselah lived after he begat Lamech seven hundred eighty and two years, and begat sons and daughters. And all the days of Methuselah were nine hundred sixty and nine years." And after that there was Noah and the generations of Noah, which began with Shem, Ham and Japhet.'

Sears had the impression that Hannah Bascombe now was genuinely diverted as one who feels herself in the presence of a harmless lunatic whose antics furnish a refreshing relief from the everyday and the prosaic.

'My dear man,' she said, 'when I was a little girl my father taught me the "begats" out of Genesis from memory. But what has all this to do with me?'

Sears *felt* like the evangelist now, standing there in the half-morning, half-lamplight of the library with his hand on the fat, polished Bible, the Good Book that had swayed the world.

'What if you were able to duplicate their years? Supposing you were able to outwit the Philistines waiting to trample your vineyards by outliving them, like Mahalaleel, Cainan, Jared and Enoch, generation after generation down through the centuries until no living man would remember when you were born and not even unborn generations of the future could hope to be alive when you died?'

46

Again a light flashed from her desk panel, but of a different colour. Automatically, her right fist unclenched and touched the surface of a mother-of-pearl button. Off to the left, behind her, a door set flush with the panelling opened, admitting a young man in striped trousers and short morning-jacket. He had a sheaf of papers in his hand. Paying no attention to Sears, he approached Hannah's desk, laid them before her and, leaning over, conversed with her in low tones.

Through the opening in the door that remained ajar Sears was afforded a glimpse of bright neon lighting and a room full of people, along with the chattering sound of printing machines, stock tickers and telegraph instruments. Close by, but cut off from the quiet and dignity of the library, the financial empire of Hannah Bascombe was running full blast.

The impeccable young man nodded his head several times in acquiescence, gathered up the papers and returned swiftly through the entrance by which he had come. When he had closed the door, silence absolute was restored. The teeming, heaving brokerage office briefly revealed was shut away, and Hannah Bascombe, her bright, avid eyes glittering, returned to the interview which now seemed to furnish her even with something like perverse pleasure.

'Now then, young man! What is all this nonsense you were talking? Clary, I believe you were right. This man is utterly mad.'

Her attitude had the odd effect of actually grieving Joe Sears. Hannah was the cold-blooded female calculating machine, the business brain steeped in facts and figures, while he was the creative artist. She was belittling and spoiling his brilliant, beautiful and imaginative story.

His anger crept into his voice and gave it just the tone of the quivering-with-righteousness evangel. 'You call it nonsense when I offer you triumph over time and victory over your enemies? Remember! No death duties. Put a dollar at compound interest, live a hundred years, and account your profits. Multiply this by the centuries enjoyed by Lamech, Cainan, Enoch and Methuselah, and the years alone must sweep every ounce of gold and silver above or below the ground into your lap. Add to this your financial genius, the world's resources and the speed of modern communications . . .'

He noticed that she was no longer listening to him but had pencil and paper before her, head bent over calculating earnestly, so that he could see the small black bow nestling in the carefully constructed tousle of her coiffeur. The thought struck him suddenly that, whoever and whatever she was, Hannah Bascombe was very human.

Chapter 9

'There were giants in the earth in those days' –
Genesis vi, 4

WHEN Hannah finished her calculations and looked up from
her figures her eyes burned with a new and more vivid light, as
though she had looked into some kind of paradise revealed. She
had been off into empyrean realms. But it died again when her
gaze fell upon the face and figure of Joe Sears.

This time Sears did not give her a chance to speak. It seemed
to him now that he was standing in a pulpit and that Hannah
Bascombe – yes, and Clary Adams too – were the congregation
to whom he would bring the reverberations of the thunder of the
ages.

'Do you believe in the Bible?' he cried.

'Certainly I do. It is God's word.'

'Then you believe that Adam, who ate of the fruit of the Tree
of Life, and Cain and Cainan and Seth and Enos and all his
progeny walked the earth as it is written here, each for almost
a thousand years, were potent and virile and begat sons and
daughters though they had passed the five-century mark?'

'Of course. It is written that God denied man life eternal when
he drove him from the Garden of Eden.' She began to quote
from memory: ' "And the Lord God said, Behold, the man is become as one of us, to know good and evil: and now, lest he put
forth his hand, and take also of the Tree of Life, and eat, and live
for ever: Therefore the Lord God sent him forth from the Garden of Eden to till the ground from whence he was taken." '

Sears retorted at once, 'Yet Adam must have eaten of the fruits
of the tree, for he lived for nine hundred and thirty years, and
his sons and his sons' sons after him also tasted it through the
generations of the patriarchs, and they were scattered far over
what was then known of the earth . . .'

Hannah Bascombe said, 'Nothing of the kind! The Tree of

Life was in the Garden of Eden. When man was expelled for his sin . . .'

'The Tree of Life was symbolic of the fruits of the earth. I am speaking to you of the Bible as history. These were people. They once lived and breathed. Legends have grown up about them. From father to son they handed down the memory of their struggle for survival, their wanderings, their encounters with God and their striving to lift themselves from the dust to His level. When it was finally written down it was a recording of remembered facts blended with myths, *but the myths had to be invented to fit the facts and not the other way around.*'

Hannah was sitting bolt upright now, listening to him, imperious head tilted slightly to one side, small hands balled into possessive fists. Even Clary's mocking smile had faded.

Sears, beginning to come under the influence of his own spellbinding, gained confidence.

' "There were giants in the earth in those days," says the Bible, the Niphilim. Moses cautioned the children of Israel against occupying the land of the children of Ammon, for it was accounted a land of giants and the Ammonites called them Zamzummims . . .'

Hannah protested, 'They were referring to spiritual giants . . .'

Sears cut her short, for he dared now. 'Nothing of the sort. They were referring to monsters that man remembered because they once stalked the earth. Two years ago I interviewed a scientist returning from a dig in the Far East. He had with him three human teeth, six times the size of ours, and a piece of jawbone large enough to accommodate them. He called the man that once owned them Gigantanthropus and estimated he stood nine or ten feet high. If you were a prehistoric Israelite measuring only five feet and saw one of them, you wouldn't forget it to your dying day. Man never did.'

Sears raised his voice a notch and threw a glance over to Clary, but could not interpret the expression on her face.

'Truth!' he cried. 'The Bible is a record of truth and facts. "God sent the deluge to punish man for his sins." The geological traces of the flood are there to be read. "The Lord rained fire and brimstone upon the heads of the wicked and destroyed their cities." Those charred towns buried for centuries beneath their own ashes have been found. Every new discovery of archaeology only serves to verify the stories and events set down herein.' And he touched the book again.

Lights again flashed on Hannah's panel and Sears was certain that the spell he had begun to weave was to be broken. But Hannah's eyes had turned to the Bible at his gesture, and her finger, touching a button, must have sent back a signal that she did not wish to be disturbed.

'Go on,' she said. 'What has all this to do with me?'

Chapter 10

'The sleight of men, and cunning craftiness,
whereby they lie in wait to deceive' — *Ephesians*
iv, 14

At once Sears picked up his thread smoothly and bending
his compelling eye on Hannah. 'Biblical man's life-span was
not reckoned in years but in centuries, up to a certain period
of this first recorded history of mankind.' He paused for
effect.

'*After* that period the length of his life was shortened. When
the generations of the patriarch Noah, through Shem, Ham and
Japhet, had repeopled the earth after the catastrophe of the
deluge had engulfed the population of that area, the life-span
was cut from nine hundred to five hundred, to four, then three,
then a mere two hundred years. Abraham was a hundred and
seventy-five when he died: Isaac, his son, a hundred and eighty;
and Jacob only a hundred and forty-seven. When Joseph passed
away in Egypt, far removed from the lands of his ancestors, he
was no more than a hundred and ten years old. And thereafter
there is no more record in the Bible of anyone surviving to an
unusual or patriarchal age. Why? What had happened to bring
about this change? What was the dividing line between long life
and threescore years and ten?'

Hannah asked impatiently, 'Well, what was it? Go on.'

He dropped his voice now, to give it import. 'The flood! The
rising of the waters that covered the earth.' When Hannah remained silent he continued, 'Noah, Shem, Ham and Japhet, who
represent the survivors of that recorded disaster, were of the
ancient stock who had lived on the fruits of the earth that existed
before the flood. Something there was in their daily fare that
postponed the processes of dissolution and decay, *something
that was no longer there, or was found only in diminishing
quantities after the land emerged from its forty-day inundation*

52

under water and killing slime — something that was eventually forgotten.'

Sears pinioned Hannah with his gaze as he drove home his arguments. 'I do not believe it has vanished completely. Matter is indestructible. Nothing has been actually diminished from this earth, nothing added, since the beginning of time. Somewhere this substance or element still exists, perhaps in altered form. I think I know where to look for it. If I find it for you I will make you the first woman to live, not for ever, but long enough to outlive every soul alive today and generations yet unborn.'

For a moment he thought he had won, for he saw her glance stray to her two fists on the desk before her, the symbol of her eternal acquisitiveness. But when she looked up there was no indication whatsoever that she had been carried away. From the line of the grim mouth emerged the single word 'Rubbish!' and his effect was utterly shattered by Clary's ringing laughter from the far corner of the room.

Hannah glared at him with something like triumph over the abyss created by the word before she continued, 'God prolonged the lives of the patriarchs to a more advanced age so that His world might sooner be filled. They lived longer simply because it pleased God, in whose will we abide.'

Sears struggled to control his disappointment and anger. Ben-Isaac had given him the same reasoning when he asked him why the patriarchs had lived so long. It was as though this Book cast a veil over the human mind.

'Besides,' Hannah Bascombe continued, and now her bright, calculating eyes were fixed on him, 'if there were any truth to what you say, why would not someone have looked for it already?'

'Because nobody else has thought of it!' Sears shouted at her. 'You read your Bible with your eyes and interpret it with your emotions instead of your intelligence. You accept its mysticism but neglect its history and the story it tells of human struggle. The secret of man's life-span then and now has been there all the time for anyone to read, but up to this moment no one has considered it. Had you?'

'Of course not. It is too utterly preposterous.'

53

'But possible!' Sears insisted.

A challenging look came into Hannah's face and a coldness into the vivacity of her eyes, as though blinds had been drawn. She turned abruptly towards the girl sitting at the other desk: 'Clary, what do you think of all this?'

For an instant Sears experienced a pang of pity for the girl because of the panic that sprang into her eyes. More than anything, it pointed up the extreme precariousness of her position and the difficulty of the decisions she was called upon to make.

He could picture the turmoil in her mind, the wariness needed to cope with a woman such as Hannah, the need to guess what answer Hannah wanted, the fear of crossing her . . .

A moment later he was admiring her cleverness, for with scarcely perceptible hesitation she replied:

'I feel that he has nothing to offer you, Miss Bascombe, that you cannot acquire by your own efforts should you desire to do so.'

And yet she gave something away. The obsession did exist. She was humouring the possibility that it would manifest itself. It was like the opening of a door to Sears.

'Exactly,' Hannah said with satisfaction and finality. 'You never had anything to offer me, Mr Sears. For should there be the slightest iota of truth in what you have told me, and your sole authority for your theory is the Bible, why do I have any need of you?'

Here was the true Hannah Bascombe of the legends, the hard, cold-blooded business woman who dealt only in terms of profit and loss, advantage and disadvantage, and in whose code there was nothing against the pirating of anything, an idea, a property, an industry, that was not fully protected. She could engage scientists and archaeologists by the hundred and start an army of agents combing the land of the Scriptures.

Sears said, 'How much time have you left?'

She made movements at her desk that indicated the interview was over. 'Thank you, I am not interested, Mr Sears.'

'And then,' said Sears, casting the last of the dice, 'you haven't got the boy. And without him you would never succeed. Really, Miss Bascombe, do you suppose I would come here to a woman of your reputation in the financial world and play every card on the table face up without leaving an ace in the hole for bargaining purposes?'

He had succeeded at least in distracting her again. She paused and looked up. 'What boy? What are you talking about now?'

He hesitated, with an inner regret that he would now be forced to use the bold lie he had worked out, coming up on the bus from Los Angeles, with Ben-Isaac's assistance and Biblical knowledge. He knew from past experience that lies were always a menace which rose up to haunt one later. He had practically succeeded in self-selling the merits and possibilities of his theory. He felt that the game would have been so much more artistic had Hannah accepted it as he had expounded it, and he would not have hesitated to cast Ben-Isaac adrift had he found he did not need him.

He seated himself again and leaned forward in the chair, fixing Hannah with his gaze, speaking slowly and forcefully. 'Ben-Isaac of Naphtali and Kedesh-Naphtali in the land of Galilee. He is a direct descendant of that Naphtali who was the son of Bilhah and Jacob, son of Isaac, whose father, Abraham, obeyed the voice of God and, with Sarah, departed from Ur of the Chaldees and journeyed into Canaan and the land of Ephraim, carrying with him the last remaining seeds of the fruit of the Tree of Life.'

Hannah seemed to be caught up in the sonorous roll of the ancient Biblical names.

'Ben-Isaac,' Sears continued, 'comes from the Hills of Hazor, overlooking the waters of Merom, where some of his ancient tribe have lived unchanged since the beginning of recorded time.'

'Who is he?' Hannah asked. 'What has he to do with what you were just telling me?'

Sears leaned forward. 'I said that the secret of the Tree of Life had been forgotten after the flood. But not by all. In the history of the family of Ben-Isaac is the record of that Barzillai who was still alive in the year AD 512, for the following year his death was recorded. No living man remembered when Barzillai was born or how long he had lived. But he spoke as one who had been an eye-witness to a certain turmoil in the temple of Jerusalem when the Man from Nazareth overturned the tables of the money-changers, sending the shekels rolling on to the stones while He whipped the unholy tradesmen from the forecourt. And this same Barzillai walked upon the hills of Golgotha one night of thunder, wind and quaking earth and saw there three corpses on three crosses, and one of them was crowned with thorns.'

A change had gradually taken place in Hannah as he talked, subtle but unmistakable. She was no longer a woman of ice, iron and whalebone. For an instant the grim line of her mouth unfroze and altered, down-drawn into a bow of pain.

It gave Joe Sears a queer pang. What cosmic irony it would be if this human, money-making machine, this unbendable will, this cold, mathematical brain, which had brushed aside a tenable theory that could contain more than a grain of truth, and cancelled it as rubbish and nonsense, were now to swallow the lie.

'What about this boy?' Hannah asked again.

'In his veins runs the blood of that Barzillai who died five hundred years after the Crucifixion.'

Now he saw the naked greed and possessive desire come into her eyes, the working of the scheming brain and the tighter clutching of the closed fists. He said quietly:

'You cannot buy him, Miss Bascombe. I found him in the south starving. He had run away from a ship from the east. He owes me his existence.'

'How old is he?'

'Who can tell. He is ageless.'

When she sat silent staring before her Sears wondered had he gone too far. He thought, *That may have torn it, kid. How preposterous can you get . . . ?*

But Hannah's lips moved and she repeated in a whisper, 'Three corpses on three crosses – and one of them was crowned with thorns . . .' Then she asked, 'Where is he now?'

'He is here with me – waiting below.'

Her voice was soft again. 'I want to see him. Will you let me see him?'

Sears nodded. 'Yes, Miss Bascombe. I hoped you would send

for him.' He turned to the desk at the far side of the room. 'Miss Adams: would you be so good and ask to have Ben-Isaac brought up here.'

Even he was shocked by the measure of scorn, contempt and hatred of him he caught in her expression as she picked up the telephone to do his bidding.

Chapter 11

'And mine age is as nothing before thee' –
Psalms xxxix, 5

ALONE in the ante-room below, Ben-Isaac Levi debated his best course: whether to remain and see this hoax through, always provided that Sears was successful in reaching the presence of the old woman, or walk out and take his chances on finding a ship that would sign him on without asking questions.

He felt no compunction at the thought of abandoning Sears. Life for Ben-Isaac was merely a continuation of the battle in which he had found himself since the coming of the Nazis. He was alone and a Jew. But he was permeated with the feeling that the days of passivity were done and that the time was at hand to fight back with every weapon at his disposal. News of the battles against odds in Palestine had thrilled him, and the new truculence and self-reliance filled him with pride and excitement. He felt momentarily trapped in an alien and hostile land where he might be either spit upon, as he was in the hostel, or used, as Sears was planning to do, for a shady purpose. He considered where he might gain advantage.

There was neither malice nor self-pity in his thinking. For all his youth, Ben-Isaac was a man schooled by what he had endured to regard people and events unemotionally and accept them realistically for what they were. He was certain that should Sears find him no longer necessary to his scheme he would be unceremoniously turned out. He did not find this unusual or disillusioning. Dispassionately, Ben-Isaac was able even to find something likeable about Sears and his frankly predatory attitude, but he remained an enemy. Friends were only to be found in that far-distant Israel where his people had become a nation and walked in dignity, armed themselves, fought and won battles against their hostile neighbours, and, forgiven their sins perhaps, were once more beloved of God as they had been many thousands of years ago when David was King and the lion of Judah ranged fearlessly from Lebanon to Egypt.

And yet Sears, that sly, slick man ruthlessly pursuing his own fortunes, had purported to show him, Ben-Isaac, a way out of this trap of being stateless and illegally in this foreign land, and one that might lead him directly to that Israel that was the goal of all his yearning. At the same time using the valid threat of what might happen if he were deported to Poland. It was quite true what Sears had guessed. The Russians did have a price on him. Ben-Isaac felt that Sears was quite capable of betraying him to the authorities, and did not think any the less of him for it.

He toyed with the idea of vanishing and letting Sears, that clever man, cope with an empty room. And, too, like a potent warrior, he calculated the risks of remaining.

His thoughts turned to the woman upstairs who was to be the key that would unlock the door to the paradise he sought. Was she indeed, as Sears had envisioned her, a monstrous spider lurking at the edge of her far-flung financial web waiting to pounce upon her victims and suck the life-dollars from their carcasses, an enemy of God and mankind whom it was no sin to mulct? Or was she only a victim of her own wealth, unable to face the day when she must put aside her gains and depart the world as poor and naked as when she entered it? What was going on upstairs? Were she and Sears already conspiring? The ante-room in which he sat was dark and gloomy, with heavy musty curtains, paintings veiled with gauze, slip covers over chairs; it inspired sinister thoughts and a yearning for the sunlight and blue sky without.

Ben-Isaac got up and went to the door. There was no one about, and a stillness, except for the eternally distant ringing telephones, filled the house and gave it a sinister aspect. Something rustled in his pocket, and he put his hand there and pulled forth the newspaper photograph of Hannah.

He went to the window and studied it again, though he already seemed to know every lineament by heart. And as always, behind the defiance, the anger and outrage expressed by the fierce eyes and the proud carriage of the head, he was aware of the unhappiness that had come through to him so strongly the first time he saw the picture.

Looking down upon her, it seemed to Ben-Isaac now as though he had known her for a long time, so long indeed that the harshness of the pose and expression had softened through familiarity.

He wondered to what extent he imagined this, yet he could not escape the feeling, or the appeal contained in her eyes. Some great misery was there, something she wanted from life and had missed. Ben-Isaac Levi had looked upon the face of tragedy many times in Poland where women sat weeping amidst the smoking ruins of their homes. He could not mistake it now or ever. He had an instant of feeling an infinite pity for Hannah Bascombe, and a strong desire to know her.

Outside on Sansome Street yellow taxis and trucks crawled up the hill; he could see a patch of blue sky. The momentary emotion left him frightened. What place had pity in battle? Whom dared he trust besides himself? Who in this world in which he was trapped had anything but hatred and contempt for a Jew?

The urge to leave was strongly upon him again. He heard a soft cough. The butler was standing in the doorway.

'Sir. Miss Bascombe has sent for you. Will you come with me, please . . .'

Ben-Isaac stuffed the paper in his pocket. In a sense, it was an answer to his indecision. And having chosen one of two roads, one could fight just as valiantly and cunningly down one as the other. He nodded and followed the man down the long muffled corridor and up the stairs.

Quietly Sears retreated to the shadows that lay about the entrance to the library so that he was half-concealed and inconspicuous, thus giving full effect to Ben-Isaac's entrance through the door, looking as male as Pan, as darkly proud as Lucifer.

The boy had removed the stocking cap from his head and carried the pea-jacket over his arm. The liquid, intelligent eyes shining from the bronzed face gave his aquiline features warmth and the breath-taking beauty of an archangel.

Sears saw Hannah's possessive fists, knotted on the desk before her, open once and then slowly close again. Speaking like a *regisseur* from the wings, he said, 'Miss Bascombe, Miss Adams – this is Ben-Isaac Levi of the family of Jehishai and Barzillai, of the tribe of Naphtali in Galilee, who were the sons of Jacob, Isaac and Abraham.'

Ben-Isaac stood without self-consciousness in the middle of the room opposite Hannah Bascombe's desk. He had seen the girl at the side of the room, his glance caught by the sudden movement with which she had removed her horn-rimmed glasses and placed them on the desk before her.

But for the moment he had eyes for no one but the small, dynamic woman who sat facing him, her face grim and expressionless. He felt a resurgence of the pity he had experienced at sight of her photograph, but to this emotion was added a strange warmth and yearning. He was aware of the urge to go to her, kneel at her side and place his arms about her. He had not yet discovered why she so touched his heart, but he was aware now that there were two reasons why he must conquer this woman. His passport to Palestine was still his prime motive, but the other was already pushing strongly against the doors of emotions rusty from long disuse.

He inclined his head with a kind of sweet courtesy and spoke the single word 'Shalom!'

Its use surprised even him, and he hardly knew whence it came or why he said it. He had spoken Hebrew once as a child, but the language had long since fallen into disuse. Was it the turmoil he suspected beneath the icy façade of the grey woman that made him dredge up the ancient Jewish word for peace?

His young yet maturely deep voice made it sound like not only a greeting but a blessing and a mystic word out of the far past; there was a singing in it. The room seemed to fall at once under the spell of his timelessness. He was but a momentary pause in the line of a thousand generations and at the same time ageless – youth, man and patriarch all in one.

Indeed, the first question Hannah Bascombe asked in a sharp, dry, schoolmistress voice was, 'How old are you, boy?'

Ben-Isaac replied, 'I am older than I look ma'am. Much much older . . .'

In the shadows by the door Sears smiled to himself. He had missed nothing. He had caught the swift glance to the side of the room where sat the handsome girl with the startled violet eyes, and had not failed to note the movement with which Clary had removed her glasses at first sight of the young sailor. So she was human after all! Armoured against sophistication, there was yet a femininity that reacted instinctively to the kind of beauty and inner innocence possessed by Ben-Isaac. He understood the boy's reply too. In the presence of these two women, Ben-Isaac did not wish to be taken for a child. But his manner of speaking, the way he had laid claim to greater age, had the odd effect of seeming to reveal a secret and confirming the impression made by his presence.

Hannah asked, 'What is the meaning of Shalom?'

'Peace. It is the greeting of my people.'

Hannah's eyes glittered, but her face remained bleak, and the severe line of her mouth harsh and repellent.

'Where are you from, young man?'

Ben-Isaac did not reply at once, for he was marvelling at how strongly he was affected by the severe woman sitting so uprightly and importantly behind the large desk, and the urge he felt to soften and win her to his purpose; to see the cold mouth melted by the warmth of a smile. The lie he spoke was almost unconscious, and eased by instincts that told him it was so much what she wished to hear.

'From the hills of Naphtali in Galilee, by the waters of Merom.'

The names falling from his lips were like music. The room rang with them. Hannah nodded her head slightly. Clary was unable to take her eyes from the boy.

The man who was pulling the wires to which the puppets were dancing so obediently chuckled inwardly to himself at his monumental cleverness. He thought, '*The kid's born to it. What a slicker. He's got the two women eating out of his hands already.*' He would have been less comfortable had he been able to look into Ben-Isaac's mind.

For in Hannah's iron rigidity, her self-possession, the regal poise of her body with its expression of indomitable will, and the stern, uncompromising eyes, Ben-Isaac had recognized the resemblance to the proud and able matriarchs of his own people, those women of force, honesty and single-mindedness that contributed so largely to the strength and happiness of the family. Only the warmth of the heart was missing in Hannah, and in his own mind he was already supplying it; prepared to find it beneath her hard core, or even breathe it into her if necessary to melt the icy crust that stood between him and what he sought. He was sensitively aware of many things about her and himself, though not yet the ultimate simplicity that he was a boy in search of a mother.

Hannah commanded, 'Come over here, Ben-Isaac, and sit beside me.'

He obeyed her instantly, unaffectedly slinging his pea-jacket under his arm as he crossed the room gracefully and sat down in a chair beside Hannah's desk. He took one of her cold, blue-veined hands in his with a tender, friendly smile and held it while he repeated 'Shalom!' and a moment later said, 'Shalom, Imma!'

Hannah withdrew her hands from his and said sharply, 'None of that!' She spoke gruffly, for she was out of countenance. She felt the reaching tendrils of affection and they frightened her, since she was not used to it. It made her rejection of him all the more severe.

Ben-Isaac was neither hurt nor abashed at her reaction. Partly he was like a lover who, suing for favour has received a temporary setback but knows he must conquer in the end, partly like an older son who regards his ageing parent with a kind of quizzical despair, tolerant humour, understanding and love.

Hannah said, 'Tell me about yourself. Where were you born?'

Ben-Isaac let his imagination reply. For he was now wooing her irresistibly, and invention in this instance was so much more beautiful than truth, particularly when he returned to his childhood dreams of the land of milk and honey, the fig and olive groves, the flowering green valleys, the rich hillsides covered with flocks, the rushing brooks and sparkling streams that emerged from the Scriptures, and the stories of the shepherd kings. Naphtali was as a hind let loose, and in his heart were the lines from the Song of Songs:

'For see, the winter has passed, the rain is over and gone; the flowers appear in the land; the time of singing is come, and the turtle-dove's murmur is heard in our land. The fig tree is reddening her figs, and blossoming vines give forth their scent.'

Thus he spoke to her of that Israel to which his soul was drawn, while Hannah sat bolt upright as though carved of stone, listening, and the girl at the far desk cupped her hand to her chin and leaned forward fascinated by both the sight and the sound of this stranger from another world.

When he finished, Sears was still unable to judge from Hannah's expression what was transpiring in her mind, whether she accepted or rejected.

Finally Hannah said, 'What was it you called me before? That strange word?'

Ben-Isaac's large eyes lighted up. 'Im-ma ... it is Hebrew for mother.'

Her look was stern and her voice forbiddingly harsh as she asked, 'Why did you call me mother?'

Ben-Isaac regarded her gravely and wondered about that himself. Was this what had always been between them since the first time he looked upon her features? He had the instinctive tact that knows when it is not yet time. Therefore he did not reply at all and let his silence and the clear, friendly look he bestowed upon her speak even more loudly and carry the message of his suit to her.

Hannah said, 'Never mind, then.' Her finger, which seemed to move independently of the rest of her person, pressed one of the buttons on the panel before her. The butler appeared and remained standing, just inside the doorway behind Sears.

Hannah said, 'Mr Sears, I will speak with you again later. I accept your proposition in principle. Both of you are to remain here with me in this house. Williams will show you to your quarters. In the meantime the boy must have some other clothes. It is necessary that he be properly dressed. Miss Adams will arrange at once for him to be supplied with a wardrobe.'

She turned to Ben-Isaac and said, 'Go with Miss Adams, Ben-

64

Isaac, and she will see to the purchase of what is needed.'

Ben-Isaac, as forward and shameless as any lover who knows that he has won, said, 'Thank you, Im-ma,' and reaching over, gently stroked her hand as he arose. This time she did not withdraw it but turned her bird-like face and peered up into his countenance long and searchingly.

Ben-Isaac tossed his pea-jacket over one shoulder and walked over to Clary Adams who was standing at her desk waiting for him, holding her horn-rimmed spectacles in her fingers. She was smiling, and Ben-Isaac smiled too.

He said, 'I saw how beautiful you were when I came into the room . . .' For a moment they exchanged the appreciative appraisal of two people who anticipate that their relationship is to be pleasurable. Then they went out together.

A moment later Sears followed the butler, feeling a queer pang of having been left out of something, of neither being wanted nor accepted by any of them even though he was to remain in the house. He was both surprised and shocked at its poignancy and the sudden feeling of loneliness that gripped him. But he quickly shook it off, substituting self-satisfaction, convincing himself that he cared little as to what the relationship of Ben-Isaac with the two women was to be. The point was that his scheme was on the way to success. The boy had put it over.

Chapter 12

'Let him kiss me with the kisses of his mouth' –
Song of Solomon i, 2

EVER since the arrival from Washington of Ben-Isaac's identification and travel papers, expedited by Hannah Bascombe's legal staff, Joe Sears had been contemplating their departure and escape from the strains and tensions that had been building up during the two months of their stay in the Bascombe Mansion, stresses that threatened at any moment to blow apart his elaborate hoax to win an easy living from Hannah Bascombe's obsession to protect her fortune by remaining alive beyond her time.

His accidental encounter one evening, at the turn of a corridor, with Clary Adams, lost in the arms of Ben-Isaac, sealed his determination. It was definitely time to take the show on the road.

When he came upon them the boy was in possession. In his arms Clary's body was limp with surrender, her mouth yielded, though when she took her lips from his she could still gasp, 'Oh no, Ben! No, Ben-Isaac, no, please . . .'

Sears experienced a momentary pang of sickening jealousy. Had this love affair been going on under his nose all of the time? The frigid Miss Clary Adams, self-appointed spinster, taking her nocturnal pleasure with this boy he had picked up off the streets . . . The force of the anger that overwhelmed him both surprised and alarmed Sears. What the devil was it to him whether this Polish stray and the frustrated, unhealthy fear-ridden girl were satisfying their appetites?

The next moment something about their attitudes convinced him that he had happened rather on a beginning than a climax, something that had just happened to a young and attractive pair, previously restrained, who had encountered one another in a passageway and had fallen sudden victims to their emotions and desires, something essentially human and comprehensible.

Sears wished now he had not intruded on their privacy, so exposing their moment of weakness and loss of self-control. For as he glimpsed the expression on the face of Clary, Sears had the impression that for the first time since he had known her she had become a woman.

The two had not heard his approach, but it was too late now for Sears to return without an undignified scramble. He heard the love-sick murmur of the boy:

"Look from the top of Amana, from the mountain-top of Shenir and Hermon, from the lion's den, from the mountains of the leopards: thou hast ravished my heart, my sister . . ."

Her head on his breast, denying him her mouth now, trembling from head to foot, Clary murmured, 'Ben-Isaac – let me go. Please let me go.' But she did not struggle.

Shortly thereafter they became aware of the presence of Sears. They did not spring apart conventionally. Instead, Ben-Isaac released Clary slowly, in a movement of gradual unfolding of their embrace, so that at the end his arm yet remained half about her shoulder. Then all three stood there looking at one another in tense and pregnant silence.

Sears refrained from speaking, for he had the quality that could recognize upon occasion the extreme indignity of words. He watched in silence for the change in Ben-Isaac's face, the darkening, the narrowing of the eyes, the perceptible recrudescence of the killer that from training and habit lay so close to the surface with him. It was a dangerous moment for all of them.

There was nothing left now of the melting womanly expression that had come to Clary's face and eyes. She was the first to speak after fixing Sears with a look of shame and hatred.

'Oh,' she cried with a bitterness and revulsion that was strange in its intensity even for her. 'Why did it have to be you?' Then she turned and fled down the hall, running hard and desperately until she disappeared around a turn.

Ben-Isaac said huskily, 'What are you doing here? Were you spying on me? I'm warning you, keep out of my way, Joe.'

Sears replied, 'Sorry, Ben-Isaac. It's just bad luck I happened to pass.'

The boy remained as sore as a bear. 'You picked a bad time to come by.'

Sears said coldly, 'A moment ago you were all man. Don't turn into a child. It's your life and your game, kid. Play it the way it seems right to you. Only remember that there is a lot more involved than just a girl. Getting mixed up with a woman on a deal like this can louse things up quicker than billy-o. We're in a tough enough spot as it is in this house. Think it over. Good night.'

Back in his room, Sears went over to the window, sat down in the dark, staring over the lights of the Bay, and assessed the situation.

There was no doubt it was high time to move on. Hannah Bascombe was difficult enough, but it was Clary who was most dangerous to his scheme. She feared him because he threatened her through his influence over Hannah; she hated him because he had beaten her in their first encounter. He was certain that she had had him checked by a private agency and held a dossier on his past, awaiting only a favourable opportunity to present it to Hannah. An alliance between Clary and Ben-Isaac might provide that opportunity.

It was another of the imponderables a man was called on to face when he involved himself in a big-time con, like the relationship that had developed between Hannah and Ben-Isaac. Everything that had been denied the childless, loveless woman who had spent her lifetime bound first to her father, then to his money – youth, poetry, imagination and a son's affection – had come to her since the advent of Ben-Isaac.

Sears had watched and allowed its progress, since it suited his designs, for Ben-Isaac was at one and the same time the bait and the catalyst of his hoax. Everything centred in Hannah's belief that the ageless germ of a patriarchal race ran in his bloodstream and that he could be instrumental in leading her to its source.

For Ben-Isaac the game had altered. He had long forgotten the original mood and circumstances that had led him to lend himself to the quasi-swindling of a rapacious old moneybag who would never miss the few dollars mulcted of her. He was no longer stateless or in imminent danger. His papers were secure in his pocket. Sears had been right. Through Hannah he had achieved his ambition and acquired his freedom. But something else had happened as well. In Hannah he had found a mother.

All the love in his youth's heart that for so long had had no outlet was now lavished on this grim matriarch who reminded him so much of the firm, capable women of his own kind, and during those days he thought only of making her happy; and one way he had learned was to keep her bemused.

He tried to repay her by bringing to life the poetry of the Scriptures, drawing upon chapter and verse of the Old Testament and the Talmud stored away in his memory, but animating them with his own inner fire, never realizing that with each word he ensnared Hannah more deeply and bound her more firmly to belief in the immortality that Sears had promised her.

For Ben-Isaac it was but a step to progress from saying 'In the old days my people came from the hills of Naphtali' to '. . . And we were of that ancient tribe of Naphtali who marched with Dan and Asher a hundred and fifty-seven thousand strong.'

Or he would lose himself, as he had done when he was a child and listened to the tale from his father or his uncle, in the song of Deborah and the Kings of Canaan who fought in Tanach by the waters of Megiddo, and he would declaim:

'They were *my* people that Deborah called down from Naphtali who jeopardized their lives unto the death. Out of Kedesh-Naphtali she called upon Barak, who was a great captain in those days. And he summoned his children to him, and we came storming down the slopes of Tabor, our spears and swords flashing, to descend like thunder upon the hosts of Sisera. Into Kishon we drove them, the river Kishon, where the dead in their armour were tumbled by the rushing water over the dark rocks.'

And Sears, noting the expression on Hannah's face, had felt the hackles of alarm go up at the nape of his neck.

First Hannah and now Clary. '*Watch yourself, Sears,*' he warned himself, '*or the next thing you know the kid will be taking over and moving you out.*'

Sitting there in the darkness, Sears let his mind return to Clary. Behind the languid pallor, the softness of her skin, the appealing loveliness of her eyes and features and the inescapable attraction of her beauty was something that repelled him.

It was some kind of inner failure, Sears told himself, with no suspicion of how closely, in a sense, it was allied to his own. Like most men who are themselves victim to a basic weakness, he was not prepared to tolerate it in a woman, and he was certain that he disliked her thoroughly. Denying herself everything called for by nature and her physical attributes, she seemed by deliberate choice committed to a life as ugly and barren as Hannah's had been. And yet in other ways she was exasperatingly feminine.

Who but a woman could be capable of the extreme sophistry whereby on the one hand she detested and feared Sears as a swindler who was bleeding her employer to whom she owed every loyalty, while on the other she accepted Ben-Isaac, believed in him, and even perhaps loved him? It was illogical, and illogicality tended to keep a man like Sears, in his precarious position, nervous and off-balance. Well, much would be solved when he took the boy away. He wondered what Ben-Isaac's reaction would be, and Hannah's as well, when he announced their departure for Israel.

He drew a cigarette from a pack and lit it, looking out from the darkened room, in which he had been sitting for what seemed a long time, on to the golden patches of the moving ferry-boats and the diamond bow of the great bridge span and not seeing any of them – not seeing anything but the memory of the face of Clary Adams during the moment of her surrender to the irresistible call of youth and beauty and the human urgency to love and be loved that cannot be denied. He wondered how long he would continue to see it, and what he would have to do in the end to escape from it . . .

Chapter 13

'Upon thy right hand did stand the queen in gold
of Ophir' – *Psalms* xlv, 9

Two mornings later, when Hannah Bascombe sent for him to
come to her in her office on the second floor, Mr Joseph Deuell
Sears, well-fed, well-dressed Director of Biblical Research for the
Hannah Bascombe Enterprises, found that his employer had a
question for him that was strangely unbusinesslike. It was:

'Supposing we are successful. What will it be like to live for
generations – for centuries?'

Sears was at once aware of a change of mood in her, and even
in appearance. Standing, a tiny, still arresting figure against the
tall red-velvet drapes of the high window that looked out over
the Bay and the austerity of the lighthouse atop Telegraph Hill
raised like an admonishing finger, it seemed as though certain ele-
ments of her bearing and that standstill in time that she seemed
to have achieved through sheer will-power had altered.

It was almost as though, waking that morning, she had found
herself perceptibly older than when she had retired the night before, a new line at the corner of her eyes, a tightening of the skin
over her cheekbones, and the shock had frightened her into some
semblance of humanity. She was like a queen out of the Dark
Ages who summons her magician to reassure her after a bad
dream.

Sears replied, 'For one thing, there would never be an end to
the show. Life is a cliff-hanger. Death comes to drag you away
from the theatre at the most exciting point in the story, just as
you think you are about to learn how it all turns out.'

He was temporizing, for he did not yet know her mood or
what she wanted, though he was rapidly becoming an adept at
his game of the donkey and the carrot. He had played upon her
obsession to the point where he was certain that, once he moved
out into the field and began sending back reports which would

always approach or indicate that they were on the verge of discovery, she could never let go. The excitement and hope engendered by the quest could well keep her alive another ten years. During that time he would have lived like a king and put sufficient by as well. But to bring her to this point he had had to feed her avidity and imagination constantly.

She said now, 'I have not that kind of curiosity, Mr Sears.' She sat down in a chair by the window with an expression of petulance at the corners of her thin mouth which made her even more human. Her veined hands were doubled up tightly into small fists in her lap. As so often, Sears took his cue from the horrible acquisitiveness they had come to symbolize for him.

'You,' he said, 'would become the queen of the world.'

Hannah stirred in her chair. The movement had in it the feeling of settling more comfortably, like a child preparing to listen to a favoured story.

Sears pointed through the window to the houses, docks, bridges, ships and factories of the Bay area. 'Whatever you looked at would be yours – *wherever!*'

It was as though he were administering a tonic. The straight line returned to her backbone and the youthful fire to her eyes. Those tell-tale indications of change that he had noted upon entering the room were no longer discernible. He thought to himself, *'That's the line she wants. I might as well lay it on thick.'*

'For in the end,' he said aloud, 'everything must belong to you. Even Jesus said, "For whosoever hath, to him shall be given." Money breeds money.'

The line of her mouth, the glitter of her eyes told him he was on the right track now. 'Your fortune must grow more quickly than it can be taxed away. As the sun sucks up moisture from the earth so must your possessions over the centuries draw themselves all the money there is in the world to pay the interest on your investments. And remember, there will be no death duties to break up your holdings.'

Hannah whispered softly. 'That's right. No death duties.'

'It will be like a gigantic snowball of gold, silver and greenbacks, growing, expanding, picking up everything it touches: currency, stocks, bonds, mortgages, debentures, notes and promises to pay, leases, deeds, titles, securities. Every man and woman alive will owe you their all; every child will be born already in debt to you . . .'

Sears himself was becoming hypnotized by the magnitude of the vista he was opening and his voice changed to the sonorous roll of the spellbinder:

'Every single thing on earth and all the ships that sail the sea or sky must belong to you. You will possess every kraal and thatched hut in Africa, stone or mud home in Asia, adobe lean-to in Peru or Mexico. Every house, mansion, villa, cabin, chalet, castle, hovel, palace, coop, hutch, byre or shack on the face of the globe where humans retire to lay their heads at night will be yours.

'Into your hands must fall every asset of this planet – its ore, cattle, grain, timber, coal, iron, copper, gold and silver, platinum and uranium – and with these will come to you the population of the earth, the peoples of every nation, for each of these is in thrall in one way or another, enslaved by these assets. Therefore you, and you alone, will own them all, body and soul. You will accomplish what men have tried and failed to do since the beginning of history – conquer all. You will be Hannah Bascombe, queen and *owner* of the world!'

Sears paused, breathless and excited by his own efforts, wondering whether he had carried it too far. But he saw that Hannah had straightened in her chair until she seemed inches taller, and the tip of her tongue showed at the straight line of her implacable mouth as though savouring an anticipatory flavour.

She said, 'Father would have liked that. Father would have made a great king – the greatest of all.'

For this was a part of her obsession too, that she and her father were as one and, though he had died forty years ago, he still lived within her. She had lost her mother when she was three and thereafter had never been separated from Iron Ike until the day of his death. He had left her not alone the vast fortune he had carved, stolen and battled out of the north-west, but likewise his truculence, free-wheeling individualism and the ability to come out on top in rough-and-tumble finance as well as the unquenchable expansionism of the pioneer. The modern encroachments of

73

government upon private ownership Hannah took as an affront to him as well as herself.

Sears said, 'You are closer to realizing it than you think. I have had possible confirmation for my theory. In a few days Ben-Isaac and I will be leaving for Israel.'

She could hardly contain herself. 'What have you found? Tell me.'

What did it matter now what he told her, Sears thought. For the first time since he had come into the house he felt well in control of the situation. The hook was truly set into his fish. He launched into his spellbinder's routine, and the weeks of study and research he had devoted to the subject since coming to San Francisco had made him glib and superficially knowledgeable. The Holy Land was giving up its secrets, he explained. Excavations at Megiddo, Hebron and ancient Beisan, in the shadow of Mount Gilboa, were furnishing daily corroboration of the Scriptures and the hand of God as revealed in the Testament. The secret of the fruit of the Tree of Life lay beneath the rubble of the centuries waiting to be rediscovered.

'We will go to Naphtali and the north, where that which Barzillai knew lies buried but not forgotten. We have come upon a clue in the writings of . . .'

'Must you take the boy?'

Sears was so startled by the question and its implications that he did not reply at once and she repeated it. He then answered with finality, 'Yes. Without him I should never be able to make contact with the ones for whom I shall be searching or recognize them when I find them. Ben-Isaac is the key. He must . . .'

Hannah cut him off with a gesture of her hand but nodded as though she understood and accepted his statement. She went over to the small desk microphone that connected with every room in the house, activated it and said, 'Miss Adams, Ben-Isaac. Will you both come to my office at once, please. I wish to speak to you.'

A few moments later they entered from opposite sides of the study: Ben-Isaac, in grey flannels and white shirt, looking like a young Oriental prince, Clary sedate with notebook and pencil.

74

Hannah said, 'Ben-Isaac, Mr Sears tells me you are to leave for Palestine shortly.'

The boy went to the desk, knelt and put his arm around her. 'It is true. But I will come back to you . . .'

Sears noted the gleam of tenderness in her eyes and the softness that came suddenly to the folds of the lids. Then she lightly touched her fingers to Ben-Isaac's cheek and said, 'Perhaps you would, and then, again, perhaps you would not when you found yourself home again in Naphtali. However, there will be no need. We will come with you.'

The impact of what she had said hit Sears like a blow to the pit of the stomach. He thought to himself, '*Oh brother! How successful can you get? You put it over all right. Queen of the world. She can't wait. . . . That's torn it!*'

Hannah was speaking again: 'Miss Adams and I will accompany you on your expedition, Mr Sears. You will therefore cancel any arrangements you may have made and wait to co-ordinate them with mine. You and Ben-Isaac may go now. Miss Adams, please remain and I will give you preliminary instructions. Thank you.'

Joe Sears had two impressions as he left the room, neither of which added to his peace of mind. One was the extraordinary pallor of Ben-Isaac and the expression in his eyes as he went through the door, and the other was the sly, knowing, satisfied smile at the mouth of Miss Clary Adams as she bent her lovely head over her notebook and waited to take down the instructions from her employer.

Chapter 14

'Rise up, let us go; lo, he that betrayeth me is at
hand' – *Mark* xiv, 42

THE Bascombe mansion had gone too quiet too early. Hannah
had retired, but Ben-Isaac was nowhere about, nor was Clary.
Sears's nerve-ends had moved right to the surface of his skin.
Standing momentarily outside his room, he could hear the distant murmur of voices rising from the floor below where Clary
had her office, but the sense of danger entered in through his
pores. Walking quietly and silently, he went there to see.

As he suspected, they were there together; he could see them
through the open door huddled at the far end of the room, their
intense faces dramatically illuminated by the sword of light from
Clary's fluorescent desk-lamp. It was at once clear from their attitudes that it was not love-making going on. Ben-Isaac was facing
Clary's desk at a quartering angle, talking earnestly and with a
fervour that shocked even Joe, since the boy was engaged in
selling him out.

Sears remained at the door listening for several minutes without shame, as the business concerned himself and now appeared
to be a matter of his survival or theirs. Then he coolly flipped on
several of the light switches, flooding the room with soft illumi-
nation, and walked in. He marched the length of the study asking,
'And what exactly are you going to tell Miss Bascombe tomorrow
morning?'

Startled, Ben-Isaac arose swiftly, facing him, but Clary was the
first to recover. With the supreme confidence of one holding all
the cards and knowing the game won, she replied, 'The truth.
I have known it for a long time, even before I had you checked
by an agency. But now Ben-Isaac has told me everything.'

Sears said dryly, 'I know, I was listening.'

Ben-Isaac asked, 'Did you like what you heard?'

Even though he had been half expecting something like this,

the bitterness of the pair arrayed in combination against him shook Sears. He had been prepared to cope with Clary as an openly declared enemy, but he had looked upon Ben-Isaac as an ally and a partner.

Sears replied curtly, 'Never mind. Let's get on with it. I missed the beginning part. What's the story for Hannah?'

Ben-Isaac replied, 'Why, since you want to know – that she's been had, of course; led up the garden path; swindled. That you're a crook and I'm a rotten cheat and liar who has never been anywhere near Palestine and . . .'

Clary cried, 'No, Ben-Isaac, no! He corrupted you. You didn't know what you were doing.'

Sears looked at her gravely and said, 'Could be . . .' He studied Ben-Isaac. 'I don't get it, kid. You seemed satisfied enough to go along with me. What's happened to change the picture? What are you afraid of?'

Clary said quickly, 'There's nothing he is afraid of.' Sears raised an eyebrow. Here was indeed an alliance.

Ben-Isaac said, 'We're finished, Joe. We wouldn't last three days in Israel with Hannah along, because when she gets there she's bound to find out our story is gammon. It didn't seem to matter about fooling her the way you put it first and the kind of person we thought she was, but it's different now.'

'Ah,' Sears remarked with no particular inflection. 'Different in what respect? Because you have your papers and can walk out?'

The boy stated plainly, without embarrassment or sentimentality, 'Because I love her. She has given me a home and treated me like a human being. For a while I thought I was helping her and keeping her happy with the things I told her and letting her believe. Well, it's gone too far. I won't lead her on a wild-goose chase. And, besides, now Clary knows, so it's all over anyway. We can't go on.'

Sears said, 'Yes, that's right. Now Clary knows . . .' He seemed defeated as he sat down saddlewise across a chair, resting his arms momentarily on the back. Then he began to speak, low and even, his voice in the beginning even containing a quality of deceiving warmth. He said, 'I love your conscience, Ben-Isaac.

Cherish it, kid, because it's one of the biggest luxuries in the world to be able to afford one.'

The boy said curtly, 'My conscience is my business.'

'Oh yes,' Sears agreed, 'and you've got to work at it too. It isn't easy to keep up one's sense of moral probity at the expense of somebody else. It takes real guts and a heart of flint to be that kind of a louse.'

Clary cried, 'Don't listen to him, Ben. He is wicked, corrupt and pitiless. He'll turn everything upside down.'

Sears laughed harshly. 'Wicked, am I? Corrupt? Oh yes, all of that. But not heartless.'

He lit a cigarette and pointed it at Ben-Isaac. 'Look at yourself, my noble paragon. All of a sudden your lily-white conscience means more to you than this woman who has been kind to you and whom you say you love.'

Ben-Isaac flushed and started to reply, but Sears was rolling and rode him down. 'Go in there, Galahad, and confess your sins to Hannah in the morning. Feel the thrill of righteousness when she falls to pieces before your eyes. Destroy her harmless beliefs and shatter her hopes of living beyond her time on earth. Watch the tears of disillusionment, loneliness and frustration fall from her eyes and then cuddle your dear conscience to your chest and hope its sweet perfume will drown out the stink of what you have done.'

Clary cried bitterly, 'How evil you are. And how useless what you are saying. Because if he doesn't go to Hannah with the truth I will. There is nothing on my conscience for you to twist and poison. I've been waiting a long time for this.'

'Yes, I know,' Joe Sears said. 'Too long.'

Clary looked at him sharply. 'What do you mean? Do you think you can keep me from ridding Hannah of a man like you now that I have Ben-Isaac for a witness?'

'No. I can't keep you. You will prevent yourself.'

'I will! What makes you think that?'

'Because,' Sears replied succinctly, 'you are a coward, Miss Clary Adams. You could have saved Hannah from me the very first day by having me shown the door. You didn't do it because you didn't have the guts. You were afraid for your job after I bluffed you. You're afraid for your job morning, noon and night.'

Clary cried 'It's not true!' before she realized that she was on the defensive.

Sears studied her for a moment. 'Oh, isn't it! I know all about you, sister. You're a coward and a quitter. You've never had the courage to face life. With all your looks, personality and brains, you haven't got the moxie of a twenty-dollar-a-week salesgirl in the Five-and-Ten. There is neither love nor charity in your soul, or even the normal emotions of a healthy bitch, because you've suppressed every natural instinct. All that's left is the colossal selfishness of a woman who has sold out body and soul for security and who is frightened silly because she cannot even count on that.'

Ben-Isaac moved angrily and menacingly. 'That's enough, Joe. One more word and . . .'

Sears stood his ground grimly. 'It won't help her to break my neck, Ben-Isaac. She knows it's the truth.'

But Clary had herself in hand now. She said coldly, 'Your opinion of me is about to become academic, Mr Sears. You and your miserable scheme to swindle an old woman are finished.'

'Oh, come off it, my girl,' Sears scoffed. 'You haven't really been worried about Hannah falling for my line and spending a few lousy bucks following it up. Ever since I've come into this house you've been scared that I might turn out to have something on the ball. I'm working to keep Hannah Bascombe alive, but *you* want to see her dead!'

She turned white and winced as though he had struck her. Sears whipped her now with horrible words and thoughts. 'Can you understand that? I said dead, *dead, Dead!* I can look into your miserable little soul. At night in your room, when you think nobody can see you, you lie there in the darkness wondering how much longer you will have to wait to pick up those bucks, the dead woman's handout for which you sold your youth. Okay! Finish her off, then, if you've got the guts. Murder her by telling her that because she's got a crack in her skull she was taken by a Hollywood phoney and his sailor pal. Truth isn't recognized as a lethal weapon. They can never pin her death on you. And then collect your lousy inheritance.'

79

Clary sat down, her face between her hands, and commenced to cry, her head turning slowly from side to side.

'I'm not saying that's how it is,' Sears concluded, 'I'm just saying that's what people might think.'

Support came from an unexpected source. Ben-Isaac knelt at Clary's side and put an arm about her. 'Don't believe what he says. But Joe is right in one thing. We can't tell Hannah now. It's too late . . .'

Sears said swiftly, 'Now you're showing some sense.' His voice turned gentle and persuasive again. 'Look here,' he said. 'We're all in the same boat now – you, Clary, Ben-Isaac, myself, even Hannah. Surely you must see how impossible it would be to turn back now. Even if she were tougher than I think and survived the blow, she would never trust you again. *You* wouldn't win. Much as any of us might wish to, we cannot undo what has been done. Events have moved away from us.'

Clary said, 'I don't know what to think any more.' She took out a handkerchief and dried her eyes.

Sears leaned forward. 'It isn't as though Hannah wanted to be made young, or beautiful, or find the fountain of eternal youth,' he went on, 'she just wants to stay alive to protect her money. How do you know we won't find some way of helping her in the land where so many great miracles once took place? How can you tell that just searching for it won't prolong her years? It's worth a try for her sake, isn't it?'

Clary said to Ben-Isaac, 'I wanted to save her from herself. She's sick . . .'

Ben-Isaac did not reply. Caught in the toils of what Sears had said, he was contemplating his own guilt in leading Hannah on and by his every word and gesture, in a sense, promising her eternity.

Sears continued swiftly, 'But since you cannot, isn't it better then to try to keep her happy? She's become wrapped up in Ben-Isaac as well as the desire to outlive her generation. He is like a son to her. As long as there is no retreat, why not go forward? Say nothing to Hannah, come to Israel with us, and I promise you when I get there I will do my best to deliver the goods. Is that a bargain?'

'Ben-Isaac,' Clary pleaded, 'what ought we to do?'

Out of his misery the boy replied, 'I don't see that we have any choice, Clary ...' He was bewildered by a mixture of emotions, desires, regrets, entangled in a web from which there seemed but the faintest and most unlikely possibility of extricating himself; and yet, because he was young and a born fighter, he could entertain that hope and even plan and build upon it. If somehow, as Sears had intimated, in that fabulous, misty land of the past to which he belonged by blood and race, a promise could be half realized, a cruel lie he had lived for Hannah made partly good. ... Once there, perhaps he could himself help to win her the added years she so desperately craved ...

Sears said, 'Well, Clary?'

Clary tried to think. The way he put it there seemed to be no other choice. And yet she felt sure that somewhere in his argument there must be a fault, some sophism or cynical twist to his reasoning, but she could not find it. To her horror and bewilderment, she realized that she was entertaining something almost akin to relief that somehow the breach between them all was to be closed, that this strange association was not to end, that on the morrow everything would be almost as it had been the day before. They would continue their preparations to leave for Israel. Was it, then, really true that she could be the coward he had pictured? Or was there something else that made her the victim of this man?

'I don't know what to say, Joe.'

'Then I gather that you agree,' Sears said. 'Good. We'd all better get some sleep now. We can talk about it further in the morning if you like. In the meantime, keep your chins up and leave everything to me. Good night.'

He got up and went out, leaving them both sitting there staring after him. He walked down the corridor and up the stairs, swelling with exultation. Had that pair of fools really thought that he was to be done out of this soft touch so easily? Well, they had found out. There would be no more trouble from that source.

But when he reached his room he was surprised to find a kind of enveloping sadness settled around his heart. The triumph

81

suddenly developed the taste of ashes. He sat down heavily in a chair, his legs stretched out before him, his chin sunk on his chest. His thought was, *'What a victory! What a smart, tough guy I am to destroy the only two people I ever cared anything about ...'*

Chapter 15

'Strengthen ye the weak hands, and confirm the
feeble knees' – *Isiah* xxxv, 3

JOE SEARS was in a mood to congratulate himself. He gazed
down upon the purple and crimson flower-beds and the floral
fireworks of palm and cactus from the terrace of his suite at the
Hotel Megiddo at Haifa the second day after their arrival; he took
in the blue Mediterranean, the golden scimitar of beach curving
northwards to Acre, the green coastal plain reaching to the
crumpled, dusty, brown hills guarding Galilee, and could not
suppress his sense of triumph.

He said to himself, '*Joe, you're not so dumb. You've finally
hit your stride. Look at you. You're living like a king.*' And only
a few months ago he had been on his uppers in Movietown, a bar-
fly and an object of contempt and pity to his friends.

They had sailed from San Francisco aboard the passenger-
freighter *Esdraelon*. In the hold were jeeps, cars, luxury trailers,
equipment and supplies to provide the transportation and background to the story released by Sears to cover the visit of so pro-
minent a woman as Hannah Bascombe to the new state – namely
that, interested in contributing to archaeological research and
excavation in the Holy Land, she was making a tour to examine
possible sites.

The voyage had been uneventful. Clary, for the moment, appeared to have buried the hatchet, though Sears did not permit
himself any illusions. She would never forgive him for having
trapped her into becoming a party to his conspiracy. But there
was a practical side to her nature. Having taken the step that
bound her to Sears, she appeared inclined to make the best of it.
Ben-Isaac, too, seemed reconciled to playing out the hoax, so that
a kind of *status quo* was established between them all.

Sears's plan was simple, if not yet fully formulated, and was
based on Miss Bascombe's reaction to Israel. Ashore but two days,

83

the mystery and attraction of the Holy Land, together with the stimulation of the teeming life and powerful growth impulses so akin to that same excitement she had known as a girl when men swarmed west to exploit the new lands and build their nation, affected Hannah powerfully. She was ready to believe almost anything.

It was Sears's intention to provide her with a good show of some kind, archaeologically speaking, calculated to arouse her cupidity further and cement her interest, and then send her home, since she could not remain away from her vast empire and business interests indefinitely.

Inordinately pleased with himself, Sears reviewed his situation once more: Clary his victim, Ben-Isaac silenced by love for Hannah – He made a mental note: Hannah would probably write Ben-Isaac into her will for a considerable sum; he must speak to the boy about shares, since, he, Sears, had dreamed up the whole idea and was therefore entitled to a cut. He could handle Ben-Isaac now. There appeared to be no flaw in his management. The situation was completely in his control.

The telephone rang in the room. It was probably Ben-Isaac, whom he had not seen since the night before. Sears went inside and picked up the receiver. It was Clary. Her voice sounded close to panic. She said, 'Joe! Can you come down here at once. I'm in the cocktail bar.'

He said 'Okay, sister!' and hurried below to the deserted red-and-silver lounge, where he found Clary seated in a corner looking frightened. It was ten o'clock in the morning. He asked, 'What's wrong, Clary? Trouble with Hannah?'

'No. It's Ben-Isaac. He's gone. I checked with the room clerk. He left last night some time with his bag and gave up his room. I found it out when I tried to reach him this morning. He left no word of any kind. Joe, I'm frightened. What will we do now?'

Sears did not reply immediately. So that was how it went, even on the big time. One moment you were sitting atop the world and the next somebody kicked the chair out from under you. It was small comfort to be aware of the new turn in his relationship to Clary, the fact that she was leaning on him and had said, 'What will *we* do now?' With the boy gone the whole show must collapse. They were finished.

He asked, 'Does Hannah know yet?'

Clary shook her head. 'But how long can we keep it from her? When he doesn't appear at lunch she will be wanting to know where he is.' Then she added, 'Oh, Joe. Why do you suppose he did it?'

Sears looked at her curiously. 'Are you kidding? He's done the smart thing. If I hadn't been so busy pinning medals on myself I'd have seen it coming. I thought I had him licked. Instead he had me fooled. After all, he got what *he* wanted, papers, and admission to Israel. Why should he stick around and take the rap for somebody else?'

Clary blinked back tears. 'But he loved Hannah . . .'

Sears added, 'And he loved you, Violet Eyes. But he wasn't getting anywhere. So he's checked out. As far as Hannah is concerned, he won't have to be the one to go in there and break it to her. He figured I'd doublecross him in the end, and so he beat me to it. You're looking at a wise guy holding a bag, Clary.'

She said, 'It's all over, isn't it?'

Sears pulled himself together. 'No. I'm damned if it is. Let me try to find the kid. Stall Hannah and tell her we're off checking a lead. As long as she thinks Ben-Isaac and I are together, she won't worry for a few days.'

Clary suddenly laughed bitterly. 'I suppose you're getting ready to run out yourself.' She shrugged, but her eyes were filled with despair.

Sears looked at her long and searchingly and wondered whether he was. Then he reached over and patted her hand lightly and said, 'Could be, but don't count on it.' He swore suddenly, 'Damn! I wish the kid at least had left me a note, even if it was only to say, "Go to hell".'

Clary said, 'You cared for him a little too . . .' When Sears did not reply she arose and held out her hand. 'Good-bye, Joe.'

He held it for a moment. 'Call it *au revoir*, sister, even though you believe I'm going to blow.'

'In your own words, it would be the smart thing to do. Oh, what's the use, Joe?'

'You don't chuck in your hand as long as there's still a chance.' He walked to the door. 'Keep your nerve, kid. You'll hear from me.'

For the first time since the beginning of the whole affair Sears felt pessimistic and close to defeat. The difficulties he had to face made his attempt to locate Ben-Isaac little more than half-hearted. He knew that his chances of finding him were slim and went through with it more for the sake of having tried, so that later he might not regret his failure at least to make an effort.

Language barriers harassed Sears. Israel was a babel of foreign tongues in addition to the official Hebrew, and English was more or less confined to the hotels and the business centres. It took him all the rest of the day to ascertain that a young man answering to Ben-Isaac's general description had boarded a bus for Tel Aviv the night before, and even then he was not certain. In America, Ben-Isaac was a standout. In Israel there were many more like him.

What little hope Sears had of locating Ben-Isaac vanished when he arrived in Tel Aviv himself and plunged into a huge, teeming, sun-drenched metropolis of more than three hundred and fifty thousand inhabitants, a feverish boom town of white stucco buildings with jutting balconies, rows of seaside hotels, banks, business houses, shops, cafés – much of which reminded him of Miami or Hollywood, and in other aspects defied comparison.

He could not find his way about. He had difficulty in acquiring a single room in a small hotel, and equal trouble to secure a vacant seat in a restaurant to get a meal.

Used as Sears was to the bustle and speed of Los Angeles, there was a breathlessness to the pace and push of this city that he found overwhelming. Never had he encountered so many people in one spot imbued with a sense of excitement. And it became obvious at once that he had no chance whatsoever of turning up the needle of Ben-Isaac in this maddening haystack unless he stumbled across him by a lucky accident.

Sears remained for another day, walking Allenby Street, looking into the principal hotels, strolling the seafront. Thinking the boy might have carried out his ambition to fight for Israel, he tried army headquarters, but without success. The conviction grew upon him that in all probability the boy had not come there at all.

The next morning Sears sat for an hour on the terrace of the Kaete Dan Hotel, overlooking the Mediterranean and some half-dozen tramp steamers anchored off the flat, sandy beach, and debated with himself.

He racked his brains to try and think of some way of continuing the scheme without Ben-Isaac, but there seemed to be none. The link between Hannah's belief in his theory and the boy had been forged too strongly to be broken. No, it was over, and the intelligent thing to do was throw in the hand that could no longer win anything and quit the game.

There remained then the question of the next move. Clary had read his mind correctly when she had accused him of harbouring thoughts of running out, and he considered the matter now carefully and from its practical side.

It had its attractions. He had plenty of money with him and was no more than an hour's drive away from Lydda Airport, one of the new crossroads of the world. In a day and a half he could be back in the United States and there would be an end to the affair. If Clary was smart enough to keep her mouth shut as to the extent of her knowledge of the plot against Hannah, she might even be able to ride out the storm. The best thing for everyone concerned would be for him to vanish as Ben-Isaac had.

Nevertheless, the thought of himself on an airplane whose every engine-beat would be taking him farther away from these people had a certain painful and unbearable quality that he did not understand. He finally set it down to pure sentimentality. He said to himself, 'Joe Sears, you are going soft. If they never saw you again, it would be too soon for both Hannah and Clary. Chuck it, kid.'

The picture arose in his mind of Clary sitting forlorn and frightened in the bar of the Megiddo and the pleading expression in her eyes when he had left her. And he remembered her unconscious appeal and the acknowledgement of her alliance with him when she had asked, 'What shall *we* do, Joe?'

It brought a quixotic thought to his mind. What was he being so tough about now that the party was over? With the game up and his beautiful racket ruined beyond repair he might afford to be sentimental for once. When you had nothing more to lose you could permit yourself a gesture. The idea amused and relaxed him, and, though he would not admit it, brought him a strange kind of relief as well, He got up, retrieved his bag, and shortly after boarded the bus back to Haifa.

Arrived there in the downtown business section, he went to the Savoy Hotel and telephoned Clary to take a taxi and join him there.

Shortly after she came into the lounge, and over small cups of thick Turkish coffee he broke the news to her.

'It's a washout, Clary. I thought he'd gone to Tel Aviv to enlist, maybe, but the army chaps never heard of him. It's a big city and crazy with people. He could hide out there for months. He doesn't want to be found. I'm sorry, kid. We're cooked.'

She was silent for a moment, inwardly contemplating the disaster. Then she bent a deep, searching look upon him and asked, 'What was it made you come back, Joe?'

Sears had a violent reaction. He thought to himself, *What is the babe trying to do, break me up?* Aloud he replied, 'What difference does it make?', an inner anger turning his voice cold and hard. 'If you must know, it was curiosity. It was too good a yarn to walk out on. If you read that private-eye report you had made up on me, you must have seen I used to be a newspaperman. I had to know how it was all going to come out. Satisfied?'

If Clary was disappointed she concealed it. Again her eyes seemed to try to pierce the façade of his outer being to fathom what lay beneath. She asked, 'What manner of man are you, Joe Sears?'

His anger left him. He went through the self-calming routine of lighting a cigarette, handling it like an actor. Then he replied, 'Just a guy who is out to get his'n, sister. Planned and patterned, cut and dried, to-hell-with-you, hooray-for-me, 1952 Homo Americanus. I didn't dream up this television civilization, the shiny car, white-enamel refrigerator, blonde in the checkered apron with the curly-haired tot, in the five-hundred-dollar-down bungalow, waving to the handsome young husband coming home with the news he's been promoted chairman of the board. It's a sales racket, but I ain't going to be its sucker. You've been around Hannah long enough to know all about the Big Divide in the U.S.A. – the Big Shots and the Little Shots. The little shot buys more insurance than he can carry, goes into debt trying to keep out of debt, wipes his nose on paper tissues and drops dead at fifty from overwork.'

He grinned at her. 'I could ask you the same question. What kind of a woman are you? When I elbowed my way to Hannah's trough I found you feeding there.'

Clary replied with a kind of lightness she did not feel, for she was miserably dismayed by Sears's estimate of himself. 'Oh, you know all about me. You guessed it back in San Francisco. I'm a coward and, I suppose, another product of the times. I'm the security girl. My mother preached it. She said there was nothing could take the place of money. We never had enough of it. Father was white-collar and died from the struggle to keep it clean. My childhood was spent wanting things I couldn't have. Now I have them.'

Thereafter they sat for a moment in silence and looked at one another across the unbridgeable gulf of their weaknesses. Then Clary asked, 'What's to be done now?'

'Go in and face Hannah and get it over with.'

'And then?'

Sears asked, 'Haven't you ever been out of a job before?'

Clary shook her head. 'No. But somehow, for the first time, I don't seem to be afraid. Is there no way she could be spared?'

'Spared?'

'I know Hannah is cruel and ruthless in business. I've seen some of the misery she has caused. I wouldn't care if she were legitimately beaten out of her money. But in this obsession she is as sick and defenceless as a child . . .'

Sears nodded. 'Okay. I'll box it around somehow. Keep your chin up and let me handle this.'

But when they returned to the Megiddo Hotel to face the music and went up to Hannah's suite after hearing that she had been inquiring for them, it turned out very quickly that here was something Joe Sears could not handle either . . .

Chapter 16

'Behold, the husbandman waiteth for the precious
fruit of the earth' — *James* v, 7

THERE were three people in the room Hannah was using as an
office. One was Hannah Bascombe herself, erect at her table,
imperiously triumphant and bursting with energy and excitement. The second was Ben-Isaac, clad now, like all young Israelis,
in khaki shirt and shorts and half-stockings, handsome, soldier-
like, standing close to Hannah. The third was a rather startling-
looking old gentleman, whose head was somewhat too large for
his body but contained the most friendly and affable blue eyes,
and who, in spite of country working-clothes, thick shoes and
brown calloused hands that gave evidence of recent hard contact
with the soil, did not appear at all out of place in the room.

Arising as they entered, he revealed a stocky but powerfully
knit body, the shoulders slightly rounded, but the carriage alert
and energetic. He had grizzled pepper-and-salt hair cropped
close to his skull and cut across his brow in old Roman fashion.
He could have been either a peasant or an emperor. He wore a
small, close-cropped moustache, but his chin was clean-shaven
and out-thrust, not so much in truculence as keenness of interest.
It was the kind of chin that wanted to be into everything, and yet
intruded itself with the utmost good humour.

Hannah cried, 'Come in, come in. Miss Adams, this is Dr
Nathaniel Levi, Ben-Isaac's uncle.'

Dr Levi smiled engagingly, looking like a friendly kobold.
'What a charming young woman,' he said. 'I welcome you to
Israel.' Then, more shyly, glancing at his fingers, 'I will not offer
you my hand. Not so many hours ago I was still digging up
winter potatoes and planting peas.'

Hannah continued, 'And this, Dr Levi, is Mr Joseph Sears,
the manager of my expedition.'

Dr Levi's smile was no less friendly as he turned to Joe. 'Ah yes, Mr Sears of course. You are the one who has hit upon that clever theory with regard to the longevity of the patriarchs. Ben-Isaac has told me all about you.' His voice was deep, cultured and pleasant, his English flawless except for the faintest trace of some unidentifiable touch of accent that added charm. He made no to-do about the condition of his hands here, and Sears felt himself strongly gripped.

Hannah Bascombe said, 'Dr Levi is a very kind as well as learned man. Ben-Isaac has told him the object of our visit here. Dr Levi has offered to guide us to the place we wish to find.'

The hackles were standing up at the back of Sears's neck. He was off-balance, off-base and unprepared. He said, 'You mean, of course, an archaeological site whose excavation you will finance, as we have announced to the press.'

Hannah looked at him sharply. 'Not at all,' she replied. 'Dr Levi knows the whereabouts of a people who still partake of the fruit of the Tree of Life Eternal. He is going to take us there.'

Sears exploded. 'He *what*?' He was genuinely shocked at the boldness of the manner in which Ben-Isaac and this bare-faced old fraud he had picked up somewhere were proposing to take over and operate *his* racket. 'Now just a minute. Let's get things straight here.'

He turned to the old gentleman and could not keep the scorn and mockery from his voice. 'You say you are Ben-Isaac's uncle?'

'Yes, that is so. I have been deeply thrilled to find my nephew alive.'

'And you know why we are here and what we are looking for?'

Dr Levi smiled gravely. 'Yes. It is nothing new. Man has searched for it a long time – ' He hesitated and smiled again, but this time winningly and with a kind of bland innocence. 'Ever since he was dismissed from the Garden of Eden, I think.'

'What is it called?'

Dr Levi said, 'It has been known by many names and has appeared from time to time in many forms. But here, where it is remembered, it is called very simply the fruit of the Tree of Life . . .'

Sears said, 'And when you swallow some you live to be five

91

hundred.' He was curious to see how far this shameless old faker was prepared to go.

Dr Levi's friendly blue eyes were turned full on Sears now. If he was aware of Sears's sarcasm he did not appear to resent it. 'If the legends connected with it are to be believed,' he replied, and then, suddenly looking as confiding and ingenious as a child, he explained: 'And here, you know, in this land legends mostly are believed, for they so often contain the germ of truth. People here *remember* so much. . . . Still, believing is always a matter of choice.'

Sears nodded. 'I see. And where is this stuff to be found?'

Dr Levi reflected. 'On the slopes of Mount Hermon there is hidden a little village called Beit Jebel. Not many are able to find it. I was there once many years ago. It is called the Village of the Patriarchs because of the great age of many of the inhabitants, who believe they are in possession of the secret of the fruit. If we are so fortunate as to reach it . . .'

Hannah interrupted sharply, 'We must reach it. You said you had been there once before . . .'

The friendly eyes were turned for a moment upon Hannah Bascombe and took on a kind of tenderness. 'That was more than a decade ago. Now it lies across the border of a country with whom we are technically at war. There will be difficulties, but . . .'

Hannah reacted characteristically. 'Difficulties were made to be overcome.'

Sears snorted. The plot was plain and incredibly naïve. Of course the 'lost' village would be somewhere that could not be reached. They had not even had the grace to come up with something new. He turned to Ben-Isaac. 'Where did you say you found this guy?'

Ben-Isaac replied curtly, 'I didn't.' He felt Sears's hostility and disbelief and it angered him, for he was still filled with the miracle of finding this relative he had not seen since he was a child, and enthralled by the man himself.

Sears said, 'Well, I'm asking.'

'In the north, at Metullah.'

When he had left Haifa on his quest Ben-Isaac had gone

directly to the Weizman Institute at Rehovoth, where he had learned that the famous Dr Nathaniel Solomon Bar Levi had given up his position and all his titles as well as his work and was now living somewhere near the Lebanese border under an assumed name.

'How did you find him?'

'I looked for him.'

Travelling by bus and on foot, Ben-Isaac had combed every *kibbutz* and hamlet in the area until, in the little garden paradise, Israel's most northerly outpost at Metullah, he had come upon an old gentleman in work clothes, labouring bareheaded in a field hoeing rows of sprouting carrots and beetroot. They had recognized one another at once.

The tiller of the soil had cried 'Ben-Isaac! You have been a long time in coming. You are welcome . . .' and taken him in his arms and kissed him, and Ben-Isaac had known that he was home.

Sears asked harshly, 'And you say this man is your uncle, the scientist fellow you told me about back in Los Angeles?'

'Yes.'

'What proof have you got?'

Ben-Isaac flushed angrily and the dangerous glitter came into his eyes, but Dr Levi said, 'I understand you. He was an infant when I left Lodz. How simple the proof would be could you look into our hearts.'

Ben-Isaac felt a wave of love for this man, the love and trust he had experienced ever since he had confessed to him his share in the hoax that was being perpetrated against Hannah, the story of Hannah's obsession, and his deep guilt at the part he had played.

Dr Levi had listened without condemning while Ben-Isaac told the whole story from beginning to end: his predicament, his meeting with Sears and later Hannah and Hannah's obsession, his growing love for her, and the circumstances that had forced him to aid Sears in bringing her to Palestine.

When he had finished the recital Dr Levi had asked, 'Does she still believe in God?'

'Yes. She reads the Bible every day.'

'You have been through hard times, Ben-Isaac. Do you still believe in God?'

'Yes, Uncle. I do. When I fought it was in His name. I called upon Him as our people always have. But He is *our* God!'

Dr Levi had smiled and said, 'You speak like a warrior of David. The Lord God of Israel has grown somewhat since then.' He had then fallen silent for a long time. They were in the sitting-room of the small house in which he lived on the outskirts of Metullah. At last he had arisen with a sigh, looking about him affectionately at things that were pleasing and familiar to him.

'Come then, Ben-Isaac. We will go to her. My life here is peaceful and my vegetables need me to look after them. But you have given her your word, and a promise is a promise. Perhaps we can make good the letter. To the north of here there is an ancient tribe such as you described. If we take her to them we will have fulfilled a part of your obligation . . .'

Then Ben-Isaac had cried, 'But, Uncle – what about the life eternal I promised her?'

The old man had reflected deeply, seemingly far lost in thought. 'Ah,' he had replied, 'that will be more difficult.'

Joe Sears's ironic remark brought Ben-Isaac sharply back. 'Never mind the heart. I'd like to look inside that head of yours, "Doctor" Nathaniel Levi . . .' It also brought a sharp reproof from Hannah.

'Mr Sears, I will ask you to show Dr Levi proper respect.'

For the first time Sears was rattled. He said, 'Miss Bascombe, as long as I am in charge of this expedition it is my duty to protect you. This man . . .'

'That will be all, Mr Sears. You will place yourself and our party, as well as all of our equipment, under the orders of and at the disposal of Dr Levi, who will be in charge from now on. If you can remain civil I am willing that the organization and responsibility for transport remain nominally in your hands while our original arrangement remains in force. Is that clear? Dr Levi will acquaint you with his plans later. And now, if you will excuse me, there are a number of matters I wish further to discuss with Dr Levi.'

An hour later, bewildered, angry, frustrated, Joe Sears was still pacing his terrace apartment trying to fit the pieces of the picture together and read them.

One thing was certain: at the last moment the game had been saved for him by the unexpected return of Ben-Isaac, only to have it snatched from his hands by the most palpable old swindler on whom he had ever laid eyes. Did Ben-Isaac really believe he was going to get away with stealing Joe Sears's con by digging up some amiable old farmer and passing him off to Hannah as a venerable rabbi, archaeologist and university professor?

There was not the slightest doubt in the mind of Sears but that Dr Nathaniel Levi was a crook, for he stood convicted *ipso facto* on the gall with which he calmly proposed to conduct Hannah to a mythical place that he, Joe Sears, had dreamed up, a kind of pseudo-biblical Never-never Land, to find a non-existent substance that was to prolong the life of Hannah Bascombe.

For the moment it was evident that he had convinced Hannah and, in the brief period since his arrival with Ben-Isaac, taken her over completely. For once Sears felt that he had encountered a faster, smoother talker than himself. The hoax was being carried on, except that he had been quietly and efficiently moved out of control of it. He had only been retained by Hannah because he had proved himself an able organizer. He had no doubt but that 'Doctor' Levi and Ben-Isaac would try to get rid of him at the first opportunity.

For a moment he wondered where and how Clary would fit into this new picture and whose side she would take in this fresh assault upon her employer's fortune. The answer seemed clear enough. She would be on the side where her bread was buttered. She would likewise be in the corner of Ben-Isaac. And if the humiliation of Joe Sears was thrown in with it, that would be all right with her too. Well, if they believed that Mr J. D. Sears was going to take it lying down they were all crazier than they seemed to be, from Dr Levi on up.

There was only one thought, however, that came to Sears that was more disturbing than the realization that he, the wise, hep, Hollywood angle-guy, had been taken over lock, stock and barrel by a refugee kid and a backwoods clodhopper and brazenly burgled of his own private prey, the richest woman in the world.

That was the remote, distant and wholly unlikely possibility that the man who said he was Ben-Isaac's uncle might be on the level!

But this Sears would not even let himself contemplate.

Chapter 17

'If a wise man contendeth with a foolish man,
whether he rage or laugh, there is no rest' —
Proverbs xxix, 9

JOE SEARS and Dr Nathaniel Levi sat together over a friendly
drink on the terrace of the King David Hotel in Jerusalem, facing
Mount Zion, the stone blocks and turrets of King David's fortress, and the walls, minarets and towers of the old city, but
friendship was not exactly what Sears had in mind. What he
was planning was a showdown.

Hannah was in her room sulking. She was angry at the delay
and impatient with the role of sightseer enforced on her by Dr
Levi, who, instead of proceeding immediately northward in
accordance with her wishes, had insisted they follow the usual
tourist route to allay suspicion and come first to Jerusalem while
he awaited the reply to letters he had sent off to his home in
Metullah. She was in one of her 'I want results' moods.

Sears was worried. The game, so narrowly and precariously
rescued by the sudden return of Ben-Isaac with this man he
claimed was his uncle, was threatening to fall apart again. At
any moment Hannah might suddenly turn on him, now that
actually she no longer needed him, and send him packing. It
was vital to him to get the reins back into his own hands again.
He remembered an old adage: 'If you can't lick 'em, join 'em.'

And so he had invited Dr Nathaniel Levi, farmer and truck-
gardener of Metullah, to join him for an *apéritif* on the terrace,
and there they sat now, Sears nursing a Scotch and soda and Dr
Levi appreciatively holding up a golden Martini to the light and
sipping it with evident pleasure as he remarked:

'Excellent. It has been many years since I have tasted one –
not since I have come to Israel, as a matter of fact. I rarely get
away from my vegetables. This is a treat, you know.' And he
took in the pleasant, civilized scene.

From within sounded the strains of a four-piece orchestra in familiar light European classics. The air was cool, clear, bracing, with a sundown nip. All about them from neighbouring tables sounded a polyglot babel. English, French, Hungarian, Spanish, German, Arabic, Russian and Polish were being spoken. . . . Dr Levi cocked his ears goodhumouredly and listened, smiling, for a few moments, then shook his striking head and made a kind of expansive gesture with his arms of pride and delight.

'Isn't it astonishing?' he said. 'All Jews!'

Joe Sears said 'Uhuh,' and then, without any change in tone or expression on his face, continued: 'You know, Dr Levi, I was wondering whether this might not be as good a time as any for you to let me in on your game.'

Dr Levi did not react as Sears had expected. He appeared to be neither indignant at the impudence of the remark nor did he fall back upon show of misunderstanding. He took another sip of his Martini, set it down before him, and said:

'Surely game is not the word you mean to use . . .'

'Game, racket, con – call it anything you like. I want to know what you're up to and what you're after. If it is reasonable, we might be able to work out a deal. I can help you and you can help me, but I want to know where I stand.'

Dr Levi nodded. He said, 'I can quite comprehend your anxiety. Where would you like to begin?'

Sears said directly, 'Well, with you, for instance. What is this farmer gag? Dr Nathaniel Levi, truck-gardener. Whom are you kidding, and what for? Ben-Isaac told me that his uncle was a former rabbi, an archaeologist and a university professor who holds degrees from universities all over Europe.'

Levi nodded a little sorrowfully and said, 'It is true I have many degrees – unfortunately in almost everything except agriculture, which I am most in need of at the moment.'

'Then what are you doing hiding away up north if you are actually the guy Ben-Isaac says you are? Why aren't you holding down a chair or teaching at the institute?'

Dr Levi regarded Sears evenly. 'Young man, when you have been here longer you will realize, as I have, that what Israel needs is not philosophy but food. Therefore I do what seems to me the most needful. Still, if it will ease your mind, when we reach Metullah I will show you my diplomas. Now then, what else is troubling you?'

Sears had the feeling he was being laughed at. Levi was no fool; he was a smoothie, and probably a bigger crook than he himself.

He replied, 'Plenty! Where are you taking Hannah – Miss Bascombe?'

'To Beit Jebel, the Village of the Patriarchs.'

'Where is that?'

'Across the border in Syria on the slopes of Mount Hermon.' He gave Sears a long, half-amused look over his Martini glass and said, 'The legend is, you know, that *two* mountains were not covered during the flood. Ararat was one. Mount Hermon is supposed to have been the other.'

'Is it dangerous to cross the border?'

'I told you that before. It may be.'

'Then why not approach it from inside Syria.'

Dr Levi nodded. 'Very sensible. But you forget we are still technically at war with the Syrians – and the Arabs *and* the Egyptians. I should not be permitted to enter their country.'

'Then why cannot we go on alone, without you? You could give us directions.'

'Less sensible,' Dr Levi said succinctly. Then he said, 'Do you mind if I have another Martini. It is such a rare treat for me. Let me order you another Scotch . . .' He summoned the waiter and talked to him cheerfully in Hebrew, a language he spoke with an odd kind of relish as though he were enjoying every syllable of it. 'Much less sensible,' he resumed. 'How would you find it, not knowing the country? How would you conceal your objective if you engaged guides? How would you keep the Arabs from cutting your throats if they felt like it, or holding you for ransom? And finally, should you stumble upon the village, in what language would you communicate with the villagers?'

Sears said acidly, 'You've got everything covered, haven't you?'

Dr Levi nodded agreement and said simply, 'Everything.'

'What is there in this village?'

'A few small huts and stone houses, some caves and a number of very old men and women, and several elders. They are members of a sect who believe they have preserved the secret of longevity of the original patriarchs.'

Sears thought to himself, '*Oh, you smooth, smooth, phoney. The gall of you, stealing my story*.' He asked, 'And have they?'

'I do not know.'

'What is this substance?'

'It is a fungus of some kind. I believe they grow it in the caves.'

'Have you ever been there?'

'Yes.'

'What did you go there for?'

The waiter arrived with the drinks. Dr Levi drew a leather purse from his pocket and paid. He said 'Ah' and 'To your health, Mr Sears,' and lifted his glass. Then he replied to the questions. 'You forget that I have been a scientist. I was curious.' He looked almost mischievous. Then he added, 'Also I wished to make the acquaintance of a man by the name of Barzillai.'

In spite of his determination to control, a cry was forced from Sears. 'Barzillai! ! ! You mean there really is a Barzillai?'

Dr Levi exhibited no surprise at Sears' astonishment and bestowed his bland look upon him. 'It is not an uncommon name,' he said, 'particularly not in our family. It is for this reason I take the trouble to look them up whenever I hear of one.'

For the first time Sears felt badly shaken. He had been not at all sure whether it was Ben-Isaac or himself who had made up the name. He asked, 'How old was this Barzillai?'

'I have no idea,' Dr Levi replied. 'He turned out to be one of the elders. He was very ignorant. Yet he had an astonishing memory for things that had happened long before yesterday.'

Sears felt his gorge rise again, choking him with anger. What did this colossal old humbug take him for? It was obvious that he and Ben-Isaac had cooked the whole thing up between them; but what a fool he must take him, Joe Sears, for, to think he would swallow such a naïve and time-worn concoction – the lost village on the mountain slope, the location known only to one man; the mysterious substance, the jealous priests, the carefully guarded secret. . . . The next thing, he would be producing the faded and time-worn map with a skull marking the location of the hidden entrance to the pass . . .

Dr Levi reached into his pocket. 'I have here a map, showing the general location and the entrance to the Wadi Beit Jebel, that I made when I came out ten years ago . . .'

There was no skull on it, but otherwise it filled the bill, and Sears' lip curled. He had called that one all right. It was clear now that Ben-Isaac had gone to the old man and told him the story, pointing out that, with his personal power over Hannah and Dr Levi's prestige, together they could take Hannah right out from Joe Sears' nose.

He drank from his glass, holding it so tightly that his knuckles were all white under his skin.

'Dr Levi,' he said, 'you're really a beaut – you and your nephew are a pair of beauts, as a matter of fact. Would you like to know what I really think of you?'

'Presently,' Dr Levi replied affably, 'I should be interested in hearing. But first there is a question I should like to ask you.'

Sears said, 'Fire away!'

'How did *you* come to hit upon your hypothesis with regard to longevity of the patriarchs? It is very clever, you know. It is really there for anyone who can read, yet you are only the second one I have ever known to formulate it. The other was Professor Liam O'Muir of the University of Dublin, fifteen years ago. He was about to leave for Palestine, Syria and Mesopotamia to test it out when he was taken sick and died. He would have been interested in the Wadi Beit Jebel on Hermon.'

Sears felt his head swim for a moment and then had the sudden urge to throw his head back and roar with laughter. What the hell was going on here? Who was kidding whom? On whom was this colossal joke being played? On Hannah Bascombe? On Joe Sears? Could it be true that, in framing his fraud devised to yank himself out of the rut of flophouses, cheap bars and sorry-but-we-have-nothing-for-you-today, he had actually hit upon a scientific truth? Had Joe Sears, Hollywood drifter, jack-of-all-jobs, wise guy and twister, dreamed up a secret known only to two other professors? And Hannah was going to find it and buy it with her gold, swallow the stuff and go on living and grabbing and acquiring for centuries just as Sears had made it up for her. . . . Why, he was a genius, a . . .

He checked his thoughts and cautioned himself: '*Steady, Joe. Don't be a sucker. Every con starts with a build-up. This guy is too smooth. It may be true, but he's got some scheme to move you out before the pay-off.*'

'But you were wrong in where you were going to look,' Dr Levi continued. 'It never could have been Naphtali. Geologically speaking, of course, Ben-Isaac, my nephew, led you astray there, I fear. He is long on romance like all young boys, but short on facts. However, he is truthful, for he told me everything.' And here he fastened his amazing blue eyes on Sears with a long, steady and completely inscrutable look while he relished another draught of his Martini. Then he smiled and said, 'You were going to give me your estimate of me?'

Sears' wits were rocking and he wished he had not had the second Scotch. The old man was apparently unaffected by liquor. '. . . Ben-Isaac has told me everything. . . .' What was everything? That he, Sears, was a liar, a cheat and a swindler of old women? If so, if this man's influence with Hannah was allowed to grow, then he, Sears, was finished. He racked his brains desperately for all his dealings with Ben-Isaac. He had never at any time admitted to the boy that he himself did not believe in the story he had cooked up for Hannah. He had always played it that it could be true and that he meant to prove it. Then what had he to fear?

Yet fear he did; he knew it, and did not understand why. There was something about this self-possessed, *knowledgeable* man that rattled Joe Sears.

Who was he? What was he? Ben-Isaac said he had been famous for his learning. Then why had he given up everything and returned to Israel to raise a few peas and carrots and beans? What was the secret of the penetration and the tranquillity that mantled him and which set Joe's nerves on a screaming edge? Sears had been afraid that Dr Nathaniel Levi was a fraud, a trickster and a crook, that he was not Ben-Isaac's uncle at all, but some local swindler the boy had latched on to out of revenge for what Sears had done to him in San Francisco. But now he was even more afraid that Dr Levi was everything he said he was.

He said harshly, 'Never mind. Skip it. That can wait. How long do we keep hanging around here? I know Hannah Bascombe. She's used to having her way. She is becoming difficult.'

A bellboy came up to the table, asked 'Dr Levi?' and handed over a telegram.

Dr Levi opened it and read it and a look of satisfaction spread over his features. He pocketed it, saying, 'We can start north now. The arrangements are under way. I think that that will solve your problem with Miss Bascombe, don't you? As long as she is going *towards* her objective. There must be no suspicion on the part of the government or anyone else where we are going, or why. You yourself very cleverly provided a cover for her presence in Israel. We should stick to that. Are you satisfied?'

Sears drew a deep breath. The battle between him and Dr Levi was far from over, but for the present his intelligence told him a truce was called for. He said, 'One more question. Why are you doing this? Why are you leaving your work to come down here and lead Miss Bascombe to – to this place?'

Dr Levi studied him for a moment before replying. He sighed finally. 'You are a strange person, Mr Sears. You have evolved a tenable theory. You have interested a wealthy woman in its development. You have come with her to Palestine to search for substantiation. Now that you are on the verge of finding it you strike me as being a nervous and unhappy man.'

Sears said, 'It's *your* angle I am interested in at the moment. What are you getting out of it?'

Dr Levi thought again. 'Ah well,' he said. 'Shall we say that my nephew made certain promises and commitments to Miss Bascombe, inspired, no doubt, by his youthful enthusiasm and imagination, and I, as his uncle and elder of the family, have accepted the obligations?'

Sears shrugged. 'If you say so.' But he was certain that there was something else and that he had not been told the whole truth.

The expression on Dr Levi's face as he contemplated the last of his Martini was bland and innocent. He said, 'This has been most enjoyable, Mr Sears, most enjoyable. I thank you.' And drank it off with enormous gusto.

Chapter 18

'And there went out a champion out of the camp
of the Philistines, named Goliath of Gath' –
I Samuel xvii, 4

THEY came down from Jerusalem by another road that led
them through the Vale of Heroes, passing by Zorah and Timnath, and, on the other side of the naked, sun-dried hills, the
long narrow Valley of Elah.

The procession consisted of two jeep-drawn trailers – one of
them for Hannah and Clary, the other devoted to the use of
the three men – a station-wagon that carried luggage and
supplies, and Hannah's big limousine, with chauffeurs to drive,
a cook, and the necessary staff to pitch camp, clean and serve.

They made an impressive but slow and leisurely caravan,
stopping often, for Dr Levi insisted it was of the utmost importance to maintain the fiction that Hannah was no more than a
wealthy American touring Israel inspecting possible sites for
excavation by a Foundation to be supported by her.

The many halts first tried Hannah's patience even though
they were at last northward bound on the expedition that Dr
Levi had promised her. Each time they paused at Dr Levi's be-
hest, however, the peculiar magic of the country through which
they were passing became more manifest, and in particular the
life with which the learned and friendly man seemed able to
endow it, for he was one who was equally at home in all worlds,
and loved the past, the present and the future of his country.

Zorah and Timnath were names that but faintly stirred the
memory. The former was a remnant of an Arab village clinging
to some hills, with a cement factory a-building in the valley
below; the latter, low conical mounds with traces of terracing on
their arid sides.

They were all riding in the limousine with Hannah. Dr Levi
pointed out the name of the factory-to-be – 'Shimshon Cement'

– and stirred Hannah's interest but faintly when he said, 'It is well named. For Shimshon was Samson. The place where he was born is buried somewhere on that hillside there, for that is Zorah.'

Hannah nodded absently, but when they were drawing away from the little vale she turned back to look and asked, 'Samson, did you say?'

Later, when they came to Timnath, Dr Levi pointed out the terraces on the rust-coloured mounds.

'Those were once green with vineyards and purple with grape. Do you remember Judges 14?'

Hannah shook her head. Her mind was in the north, where she had been promised a mountainside where men still retained the secret of the Tree of Life.

He quoted: ' "Then went Samson down, and his father and his mother, to Timnath, and came to the vineyards of Timnath: and, behold, a young lion roared against him. And the Spirit of the Lord came mightily upon him, and he rent him as he would have rent a kid, and he had nothing in his hand. . . ." It was here it took place in a green forest where now all is barren dust, yet these hills shall bloom again.'

Dr Levi leaned forward and said something in Hebrew to the driver, who thereupon left the main road that would have borne them north to Lydda, where they were due to lunch, and doubled back on a narrow, dusty track that carried them into the mountains again and along the top of a ridge until they came to a halt overlooking a narrow, fertile valley cut by two brooks.

Dr Levi said, 'Ben-Isaac, can you guess where you are?'

'No. Was there fighting here?'

His uncle continued, 'It is the Vale of Elah!'

Ben-Isaac gave a cry, 'Ah! I should have known.' He opened the door of the car eagerly. 'Imma! May we stop here for a moment? How often I have dreamed of this spot . . .'

Sears felt that he had gauged the temperature of Hannah's impatience and sneered, 'Well, so what happened here?'

There were hills on three sides, cut by a ravine, and below them the level plain a quarter of a mile broad, on which was growing wheat and barley and a yellow patch of golden sunflowers.

'Here,' replied Dr Levi, 'A little man of great faith destroyed a gigantic braggart who was very sure of himself.'

Sears looked at the old man sharply. Was there a double meaning in what he had just said, a double purpose in bringing them there? But Dr Levi's countenance was composed in innocence. He was standing on the edge of the road, the wind momentarily playing with the short fringe above his brow, his eyes peering beyond the valley below into its past.

'There, below,' he said, 'is where David killed Goliath in single combat.'

The simple sentence wove a spell about them, and even Sears experienced the little chill of drama even as he resented it. Hannah said sharply, 'Eh? What was that? Where are we?'

'At the top of Wady Es Sunt, which caps the ancient Vale of Elah where Saul and the men of Israel were fighting the Philistines.'

Clary asked, 'Is it really true?'

Dr Levi nodded and then pointed to the conformation of the land and said, 'You do not have to be a military expert to understand the reluctance of the two armies to fight one another here. Saul and Israel were drawn up on the mountain on this side, and the Philistines occupied the crest on the other. The valley is too narrow for anything but slaughter. Neither wanted or dared to give up the advantage of the heights, for to attack they would have to descend first. You can see from where we are standing that the Israelite position was the stronger, so that it was to the advantage of the Philistines to propose single combat, particularly with such a champion as Goliath. Yet Saul could not refuse.'

Clary murmured with a kind of amazement, 'Then they *were* real people.'

Ben-Isaac said, 'But of course they were. They were the greatest champions and fighters in the world – on our side.'

Dr Levi smiled at his vehemence and continued, 'Can you picture the sight? The days of stone weapons were past. They faced one another with spears of iron and shields and helmets of brass, thousands upon thousands of men, not daring to fight, not daring to let go.'

The two mountainsides became peopled with ancient armies. In the shimmering heat one could imagine the dust rising where they stirred and hear the brazen clangour of their equipment.

Dr Levi continued, 'And so the shepherd boy came armed with a slingshot, five smooth pebbles, and faith in the Lord. The pebbles, in all likelihood, he drew from the ancestor of that brook below. There they fought, probably near where the wall divides the grain field from those sunflowers, the stripling and the giant who was more than nine feet tall . . .'

Joe Sears said cynically, 'Do you believe that?'

Dr Levi turned his unruffled gaze on him and said, 'Don't you? It was you who pointed out to Ben-Isaac originally that the legend of the Nephilim, the giants of Genesis, had been confirmed by the discovery of the actual remains of gigantic humans. . . . We are near the Vale of Rephaim, the home of the aboriginal giants of Philistia. Goliath was undoubtedly a throwback.' His eyes twinkled. 'The Philistines must have used him like a tank. Nothing could have stopped him but a stone impelled with the force of unswerving faith.' He paused and looked at Hannah and asked, 'Shall we go on?'

For the first time the urgency was missing from her, and she did not answer him but stood looking down into the vale for a moment as though her eyes could see the brass armour of Goliath glinting in the sun and the flashing of David's arm as he twirled his sling above his head.

Then she asked, 'I want to hear the story again . . .'

Dr Levi said, 'Ben-Isaac, do you remember?'

The boy, dressed in khaki shorts and half-sleeved tunic, visored cap perched on the back of his head, was standing a short distance away on a rock, scanning the heights and the descent with the look of a soldier as in his own mind he went back to the days of Saul and David and weighed the military position of both sides and thought what *he* would have done had he been there.

He began to speak from the book of Samuel: "And there went out a champion out of the camp of the Philistines, named Goliath, of Gath, whose height was six cubits and a span . . ."

Verse after verse rolled from his lips as he retold the oldest battle-story known of the triumph of the weak over the strong.

And when he came to David's ringing words, ". . . Thou comest to me with a sword, and with a spear, and with a shield: but I come to thee in the name of the Lord of hosts, the God of the armies of Israel, whom thou hast defied . . .", he swept up Hannah with him so that for the first time since her advent to Israel she was no longer remembering the urgency of her pilgrimage.

Ben-Isaac cried, 'This day will the Lord deliver thee into mine hand; and I will smite thee, and take thine head from thee'; and for that moment he believed himself David. And so it was that Hannah saw him too, the young David reborn; his form, his voice, his faith, and his valour.

For a moment she had a vision of the brightness of the armour of the faith in God outshining the burnished plate of the Philistine. She was gripped by the mystery of the land, the boy, and the soaring spirit of the verse. For the first time, dimly, uneasily, she became aware of the aridity that in the past had surrounded her own approach to the God of her father, who was a word, a name, printed black on white paper and locked between the covers of a book, but here seemed to be thought of as a living force.

Joe Sears said, 'We want to get on to Lydda by lunchtime, don't we?'

The spell was broken. They returned to their vehicles and pushed on.

Later, they went to Bethshean through the vales of Esdraelon and Jezreel and the site of Megiddo, where Israel's battles of the Old Testament came alive again and Hannah looked upon soil that had once been soaked as red as umber with the blood of the Philistine, Canaanite, the Egyptian, and the children of Israel.

The old and the new blended here. In the village were the neat houses of the settlement, the flowered bungalows and garden patches, fresh-painted homes; to the west rose the great mound, and where the bones beneath it were laid bare by excavation they looked upon the remains of the walls from which the naked headless bodies of great Saul and his slaughtered sons were hung to glut the savagery of their triumphant enemies.

Here, too, in Bethshean the Old and the New Testament came

together for the first time in their hegira. As they were returning from the mound of the buried citadel, Dr Levi said suddenly, 'Jesus came here once. He healed two lepers.'

Hannah stared at him. 'Jesus here?'

'Yes. He surely knew this place, for not far off is Bethabara, where he was baptized of John. And Nazareth is less than fifteen miles away.'

'Nazareth?' Hannah repeated, and stood still, looking about her as though all the world had suddenly changed and she was seeing it anew – the fields, the hills, and the houses. 'Nazareth so near?' Her hands with their tightly closed fists were at her breast . . . She said, 'Should we not go to Nazareth?'

Sears spoke quickly. 'It is out of our way, Miss Bascombe. It will mean a detour and possibly another day if we stop. Our route north lies directly through Tiberias, and the sooner . . .'

She nodded, but appeared unable to make up her mind and asked, 'Is it far out of our way, Dr Levi?'

He stood there reflecting upon her question, an incongruous figure in khaki standing in a field of poppies and cornflowers, his face serious beneath a weird kind of floppy khaki hat, for he gave thought and attention to every question. He said finally, his gentle eyes on Hannah, 'Some people carry Nazareth in their hearts. For them it is but a step. Others may travel for thousands upon thousands of miles and never achieve it.'

Hannah repeated, 'A step – or many thousands of miles . . .'

They were all watching her. It was Clary who turned the scales. 'It is so near, Miss Bascombe. Could we not go?'

Hannah stared at her in surprise for a moment. Then she remarked curtly 'I wish to go Nazareth, Mr Sears' and walked on ahead of them by herself.

Sears shrugged and followed on, wondering about Clary.

Chapter 19

'Hannah, why weepest thou? And why is thy
heart grieved?' – *I Samuel* i, 18

ALL the time, as they proceeded towards their objective, the
unique quality of Palestine was chipping away at the hard shell
of the past that encased Hannah. For it attacked her where she
was weakest. In many places, with its rolling, brown-burned
hills, Israel seemed like the part of California she had known
during her girlhood when she had accompanied her father into
the American desert and seen his track-laying gangs wind northward to Oregon.

Everywhere that Hannah gazed there was ground-breaking
work and pioneering going on.

It was the finish that had been written to the horizontal building of America during Hannah's lifetime that was a part of her
sickness. When her father had died there were no new deserts
left to be conquered, forests to be hewn, or acres to be had for
the occupying. The vacuums had been filled. The knell of individualism had been sounded and limits placed upon the scope of
what a man might win for himself from the earth with courage
and ruthlessness.

But here, before her eyes, young men and old pioneered in the
production of a blade of wheat, the growing of trees on a bare
mountainside, the digging of a trench to lead a few drops of
water to a field, the raising of a factory wall, the setting up of a
house, the sinking of a well, the cultivation of a vineyard.

But there was yet another phase to the Israel efforts that engaged Hannah's sympathy and turned her thoughts back to the
days before the humanity in her had been calcified by the pursuit
of money and her father's dream of unlimited power. California,
Oregon and Washington had been virgin paradises of timber,
fruits and vegetation. But Palestine was a clinker. Nine-tenths of
the land was burned out, bare and arid.

And so the new pioneers of this land, the stocky youngsters with big, brown, piano legs and chests like wine casks, the husky girls and the old men with beards, all of them had first to restore what had been robbed from this country before they could reap so much as a blade of grass.

Nothing was so touching as the small rows of sapling trees, hardly more than a foot high, that they encountered along the roadside or planted to crest a rise, each plantation with its gang of workers bare to the waist, toiling in the burning sun carrying water in battered pots, empty tomato tins, or dippers from barrels mounted on lorries, water-ferried from distant well or spring to drench the roots of these gallant sprigs they hoped in a quarter century's time would again be the forests of Judea.

Their caravan was always halting on the way, for Dr Levi had an almost child-like love of gossip with these builders, the asking of a question, the exchange of a word or two. He was interested in everything that went on; like a juggler, he kept three worlds in the air at once: the past that pulsed beneath the mounds and tels hinting a buried city or fortress, the present before their eyes, and his extraordinary fascination with the future.

At one of these stops a huge bearded Russian, burned as brown as a cinnamon bear, his naked torso muscled like a wrestler's, was bent solicitously over a tiny, half-limp green shoot, patting the earth about it and leavening it with water poured from a rusty fruit tin.

He straightened up as they watched his efforts, and he looked into their car with enormous pride and cheerfulness, the sweat dripping from his broad face. He saw Hannah and called out something to her in Hebrew that sent Dr Levi into roars of laughter and brought a strange almost forlorn expression to the face of Ben-Isaac.

Dr Levi explained to Hannah. 'He is saying, "Shalom to you, little mother. It has been a hard fight, but I have won. It will live!" '

A workman near by said in English, 'He has been worrying over that little tree for days as though it was his child.'

The incongruity between the enormous man and the convalescing sapling made them all smile.

Hannah said, 'Tell him congratulations. It is a great victory he has won.'

Sears said, 'Tell him he'll be an old man before he gets any shade out of that tree.'

It was now the Russian's turn to throw back his head and roar before he replied.

Dr Levi interpreted. 'He says it is not for him, but his son . . .' He added, 'You see, there is no age in a country that works – only continuity.'

As they drove off, Ben-Isaac did a curious thing. He raised his right hand to the Russian in a half-salute. Their eyes met and for an instant gleamed with perfect understanding. The Russian saluted back and then waved until they were out of sight.

This was what Hannah could read in the faces of the men as they passed, and there was none who was not working. Whatever they did – whether they struck pick or mattock into the hard soil, or hammered stone, or piled up blocks of masonry to form a wall, or sawed a beam, or drove a nail – theirs was the gleam and the pride of those who are building a country as well as a home. At the same time they constructed their fields, their factories, their waterways or their houses, they raised their nation. This Hannah had seen before, and the memories it awakened brought alive something in her old, tough heart.

Leaving the fresh sun-soaked valley of Jezreel, they followed the winding road that climbed the parched hills of Galilee to Nazareth, where they arrived shortly after six, with the sun already low and close to the punch-bowl rim of the mountains that surrounded the old city.

They drew up at the Hattin Hotel, a run-down and bullet-flaked caravanserai, amidst crowds of curious Arab children and thronging Arab guides clamouring at once to lead them to Joseph's carpenter shop, the two churches of St Joseph and the Annunciation and the still flowing spring of the Virgin Mary's Fountain.

The streets were hot and dusty, the children dirty, the flies thick, and the babel irritating. For the first time they were conscious of the smell of an Arab town.

They went into the hotel for a wash and dinner. The lobby

was half a bazaar of tasteless souvenirs and cheaply made relig-
ious articles, the odour of frying fat pervaded everything, and
the dining-room was grim, empty and depressing, with soiled
table-cloths and flies everywhere.

Afterwards, Sears and Clary, with Ben-Isaac, went off sight-
seeing, Hannah remaining behind with Dr Levi, for she was
tired from the heat and dispirited by the disillusionment and
misery of the city whose name had always been able to bring
about a yearning within her.

Sears felt a curious kind of exultation as they set off up the
avenue that led to the supposed site of Joseph's carpenter shop,
over which the Church of St Joseph had been built by the Fran-
cisans. The way led through streets full of noise and squalor,
dirty old men in filthy robes and children with diseased eyes, and
he stole sly looks at Clary to see how she was reacting to the
surroundings.

For he was aware that there was a kind of struggle going on in
which he was involved, though he did not exactly know how, or
what it was he was fighting. He had almost sold Hannah on
pressing northwards swiftly towards whatever awaited them
there, when Dr Levi, aided by Clary, had diverted them to
Nazareth for some purpose of his own, he was almost certain,
for he was beginning to feel that Dr Levi never did anything
without purpose, even when he appeared to be merely sitting
in the sun or drifting through the countryside enjoying
himself.

Well, if this was the case, Nazareth must be accounted his first
failure. After a night in that shrieking redolent bazaar Hannah
would be only too glad to get on in the morning. Next time she
would probably listen to Sears when he made a suggestion.

The Arab guide, dressed in flashy modern clothes, was oily
and insolent until a warning from Ben-Isaac, whose teeth he set
on edge, frightened him into some semblance of politeness. The
interior of the church was modern, gaudy and in bad taste – it
was neither art nor spiritually stimulating, and the carpenter
shop of Joseph was nothing but a small rock dungeon with a dirt
floor some three stories below ground level in the crypt of the
church.

Sears snorted, 'What a sell. I'd like to know what Dr Levi would have to say to this.'

Ben-Isaac said, 'Perhaps that was why he didn't come. He does not like things that aren't genuine.'

Clary was standing in the middle of the dirt floor looking bleak and miserable while the guide rattled off his spiel.

Sears said to her, 'Well, this is Nazareth. Are you satisfied?'

She was too unhappy to resent the attack. She looked at him with eyes close to tears. 'But maybe it was a place *like* this in those days and looked different with a carpenter's bench and wood lying about . . .'

But it was no use. Somehow, without the presence of Dr Levi, the pictures would not re-create themselves. The guide droned on. Sears said, 'Let's get out of here. Maybe the other stuff is better . . .' He was hoping it wouldn't be.

When they returned to the Hattin Hotel, shortly before ten o'clock, they were surprised to find that the jeeps and trailers were no longer parked out in front. Sears had been looking forward to giving Dr Levi his opinion of Nazareth with considerable relish.

The desk clerk explained. 'The rich woman and the old gentleman have gone up into the hills. There is a car and driver waiting here to take you up to them if you wish to go, or they said you could remain here for the night and join them in the morning.'

Ben-Isaac said, 'I'm for turning in and sleeping in a real bed for a night.'

Sears said, 'No, we'll take the car.' He was feeling suddenly uneasy, his self-satisfaction drained away.

Clary said, 'Perhaps Hannah wants to be alone – she was very tired.'

Sears said, 'Wherever they've gone, you can bet it was Levi's idea; and if it was Levi's idea, I don't like it. I'm going on up.'

Ben-Isaac said, 'You make life interesting for yourself, don't you, Joe? It's probably cooler up there . . .'

They got into the car. Sears thought that Ben-Isaac might be right. Nevertheless the feeling of uneasiness did not leave him . . .

The road that mounted steeply through Nazareth twisted back

upon itself at the top around the western rim of the punch-bowl in which the city lay embedded and turned into a kind of flat shelf or plateau surrounded by a shallow semi-circle of cypress trees that in the darkness had the air of the smooth, stately pillars of a ruined temple area. The edge of the plateau was rimmed with spiny cactus and looked over the flat roofs of houses on the street below.

Hannah's trailer was parked at the rear end of the plateau, while the larger one, occupied by the men, lay in the shadows at the far end.

She had allowed Dr Levi to persuade her to leave the hotel and go up to the heights above the town. He had said, with that quiet confidence with which he always spoke, as though since he believed a thing everyone else must too, 'You will be cooler and happier outside the city. There is an old cypress grove just above the last terrace. If nothing else, from there you will see Nazareth by starlight.'

'And if else . . .'

'You will feel the heartbeat of Nazareth.'

Hannah went outside and sat on the steps of the trailer. There was no moon, but the stars were so intense, so close was the brilliant canopy, that faint shadows were cast and one could distinguish objects on the opposite hillside: white buildings, a slender tower, a grove of olive trees with a road winding through them.

The city fell away in terraces directly below at her feet almost; she could see a cobbled street, stone dwellings with barred windows, and flowers bursting from jars on the roof.

As her eyes became accustomed to the darkness and starlight she could see more and more of the soft contours of the hills that surrounded the city, the deep shadows of the clefts, the box-square shapes of the dwellings relieved here and there by the pure semi-circle of a dome, and the faint glow of lamplight behind window matting.

It was deeply still.

Hannah became aware that Dr Levi was standing there beside her in the darkness, his head lowered on his chest, looking out over the tranquil scene.

She waited for him to speak, but he did not do so for many minutes. Then at last he said, 'Now! This is Nazareth.'

And he said also, 'It was very like this when He looked upon it.... At night ... it was filled with this same tranquillity. He loved Nazareth.'

He did not say any more, and when she looked again he was gone.

The silence was broken by music that came from near by. Someone behind one of the barred windows was playing a reed pipe softly and with such sweetness as though the soul had to speak because it was so calm and beautiful an evening.

'He loved Nazareth. ...' The phrase came back to Hannah, and she breathed deeply of the night and smelled the perfume of oleander and rose, and knew that somewhere, too, there was dew glistening on honeysuckle and there were other odours rising from the sleeping city, unknown, oriental, pungent, like incense.

Where the sky touched the hills opposite and the stars burned like ornaments through straight cypress and gnarled olive there was movement, a stream of white objects flowing down the path, and she heard the distant bark of a shepherd's dog, and then saw the figure of the shepherd himself, late back from the hills with his flock, leading them home.

And Hannah's heart was touched.

For He had been evoked, though His name had not been mentioned. This had been the home of the boy Jesus. Here He had lived as a child.

The trees, the clefts, the unchanging rocks, the paths long trodden, the sky bending to dust His hills with stars had filled His eyes and gladdened His heart, and in the mystery of the firmament, the fragrance of the flowers and the innocence of the flock He had read the love and harmony of God.

He had once stood there, perhaps, where she had stood now, breathed the same air, heard the same sounds and looked upon the same sights. He who for so long had been but a name on a page and a mumbling of the lips came now so close, a large-eyed child, a tender man filled with the love of the Father whose gifts these were. Hannah was moved. Tears came to her eyes and she began to cry.

And the crying loosened something in her that had been a hard dry knot in her breast for so many years, and there she remained, an old and lonely woman who had never known gentle love or tenderness or understanding, looking down over Nazareth, weeping with love and compassion for a Jesus who for the first time had reached to her and laid His hand upon her heart.

She wept because of the Lord whom she had found, because of His peace that lay over the sleeping city and so filled it with His presence; she wept because she was a miserable sinner, because she had thrown her life away in pursuit of the vanity of power, and because it was good to let the tears soften the hard, brittle shell behind which she had concealed her lonely, unhappy heart for so long. She wished she could weep a river of tears to wash the feet of God . . .

She did not hear the car draw up, or the approach of Clary, Ben-Isaac and Sears.

Sears said, 'Is something the matter? Are you ill, Miss Bascombe? Where is Dr Levi? What has he done?'

Ben-Isaac ran to her side, knelt and put his arms about her. 'Im-ma – you are crying . . .'

Clary asked anxiously, 'Miss Bascombe . . . Hannah, what is it? Is something wrong?'

'Oh no,' said Hannah Bascombe. 'For the first time something is right.' Then she arose and went inside, closing the door behind her.

Dr Levi materialized out of the darkness. 'Ah, I am glad you decided to come.'

Sears said angrily, 'What have you done? Miss Bascombe is badly upset. What have you said to her?'

'I do not recall my exact words, but they had something to do with One who spent His childhood here.'

As always, Dr Levi's habit of making a considered and reserved reply to an aggressive question exasperated Sears. 'What kind of a game are you playing now? What did you bring her up here for?'

'To show her the true Nazareth. She has seen it. Perhaps, if you look, you will see it too ...' He moved off into the darkness again.

Clary cried, 'Oh, Joe! He is so right. It is here we should have come right from the beginning. Oh, look, and feel, and breathe – use your eyes and your senses. Doesn't this reach you?'

Sears looked from the starlit face of the girl to the star-bright city and the distant hills. She was a part of the all-pervading beauty that was invading him, crowding out anger, fears, soreness. . . . He had to summon all his resistance to hold out against it. . . . He felt that if he were to remain he would go soft, and if that happened he was lost.

He said, 'Not me, kid. It's been a long day. Good night.' He walked to the trailer, avoided the interested inquiring eyes of Dr Levi, and went to bed. It was not until much later that he realized he had been routed from a field.

Chapter 20

'I am the living bread which came down from heaven: if any man eat of this bread he shall live forever.' – *John* vi, 51

AFTER Nazareth the caravan adopted an even more leisurely pace. Though nothing had been said, it seemed as though some of the fever and urgency had been lifted. The change in the atmosphere disturbed Sears, for he did not understand it. He had still been unable to regain any measure of control over the expedition.

They followed the ancient road from Nazareth through the village of Kfar Kana that once had been the Cana of the Gospels and the scene of the first recorded miracle of Jesus, skirted the twin horns of Hattin, where legend held that Jesus had chosen his disciples, and broke from the hills of Galilee into the broad valley of the blue sea that lay shimmering there. They rolled on, past Majdal that once was Magdala, the low hill crowned with the cluster of eucalyptus trees said to be the site of Bethsaida, and thence along the shores of the lake towards vanished Capernaum.

At twilight the caravan rolled to a halt at a cool, green oasis fronting the north-west corner of Lake Tiberias, the modern name of the Sea of Galilee, where, in an exquisite grove of broad, leafy trees, pink and white oleander and many flowering shrubs, mimosa and palms, they came to a German Catholic hospice and a small chapel, where they were welcomed by Father Hofstetter, the resident priest and an old friend of Dr Levi.

This was Ain Tabigha and the Church of the Loaves and Fishes. There, permission was given for the trailers to be parked in the grove down by the lakeside and camp was pitched. But Ben-Isaac was sent on northwards by Dr Levi on a mission that he did not explain. The boy went by jeep. He was pleased and excited as he departed immediately after dinner.

Dr Levi said to Hannah, 'We may have to remain here for a few more days until I am certain it is safe to continue. You must wait again. Do you mind?'

Hannah replied, 'No. It is peaceful.'

But Sears was both alarmed and impatient at further delay and tried to call Dr Levi to account. He said, 'What's coming off now? Where has Ben-Isaac gone? Why wasn't I consulted?'

Dr Levi had been sitting on the steps of the trailer pulling on a pipe and gazing out over the vast expanse of the harp-shaped lake. He turned to Sears and said:

'Have patience. You need have no fears. In the end I will carry out my undertaking as I have promised.'

Exasperated, Sears said, 'I don't trust you, Dr Levi.'

'That is understandable. But you should be able to trust Ben-Isaac, for you know that he loves Miss Bascombe with all his heart.'

As usual, Sears felt frustrated, defeated and helpless. He thought of trying to find Clary and voice his fears, but put it aside as useless. Since the advent of Dr Levi she, too, had escaped him. He realized that he no longer had any hold over her.

Galilee held Hannah and, in the end, touched her even more deeply than had Nazareth, for nowhere were the Scriptures as precise and as vivid as when they dealt with what had transpired on the shores of this lovely and dramatic body of water more than two thousand years ago.

Here the fishermen still cast their nets by hand from their boats as had Peter and John until the eloquent and gentle Man had come down to them from the hills to enchant and capture their simple souls and make them fishers of men.

And though the surface conformation of the land had altered and the busy towns and villages that once throve along the lake had vanished beneath the topsoil of time, the shore-line, covered with millions of tiny, exquisite shells and edged with reeds, water grasses and marsh plants, was still the same, the shape of the lake was but little altered, and the masses of the surrounding hills had not at all changed from the days that Jesus had known them.

He had breathed the same sun-warmed air made fragrant by

the presence of the most beautiful plants and flowers. His eyes had rested lovingly and gratefully on the tranquil scene of blue waters and brown and dust-coloured hills and cliffs, His feet had trodden the fore-runners of the same shells strewn along the banks. It was impossible to follow those paths and not be aware of Him. Hannah would walk for hours, often without speaking, accompanied only by Dr Levi, seeking those sites and moments when she could feel herself closer to Him . . .

Along the barren shores they often came upon the blackened ruins of long-buried towns, thrusting a piece of wall, a pillar, or the top of a temple above the scrubby furze, or the pregnant mounds or tels that hinted at some village or trading post, perhaps, where Matthew had sat at his customs desk, and that had known the step of Jesus and the sound of His voice, or witnessed the multitudes that followed Him wherever he went.

Sometimes she wished only to stand and contemplate these sites in silence. At others she let Dr Levi resurrect them for her as they had been – busy centres of trade and life when the entire lake was surrounded by woodland instead of the dry and barren hills, and the plain of Gennesaret had been one flower garden perfuming the district with the scent of lemon and orange trees, mimosa and eucalyptus, nasturtium, hibiscus, ternaium and Persian lilac, oleander and honeysuckle.

There had been nine cities then surrounding the lake, and now there was none to be seen but Tiberias on the western shore, springing to new life as a resort. Outside of the grove of Ain Tabigha there was hardly a tree to be seen, and yet in the days of Jesus there was shade from oak and walnut, palm and fig, syca-more, plane, terebinth and caroobs, and wild flowers and flower-ing shrubs were everywhere along the shore. The now almost deserted body of the lake then was covered with the triangular white sails of small fishing craft.

What life had teemed here and was reflected through the voice of Dr Levi! Through him Hannah heard the rush of waters parted by wind-driven prows, the creaking of ropes and bang-ing of oars in oar-locks, cries across the water, the hammering of shipbuilders, coopers and caulkers, and saw the swarming wharves where the silver catches were dumped ashore wriggling in the sunshine, bought and sold and carried away in baskets to the pickling factories by ass and oxen.

Greek, Roman, Gentile and Jew had mingled here; roads were crowded with traffic, and the lakeside cities were a babel. And through these scenes, on these very sites, had wandered the Son of Man with His message.

They went one day by the lake to the supposed site of Capernaum and came to the ruins of the synagogue there, a rectangle of paving of square, stone blocks, with pieces of tumbled pillars, cornice stones and elaborately sculptured blocks lying about helter-skelter without apparent relationship to each other.

Hannah inquired then with a kind of swift anxiety, 'Was it here that Jesus preached?'

Instead of replying, Dr Levi asked a question.

'Does it say anything to you?'

Hannah looked about her for an instant with a kind of intent fierceness, as though she were both listening and with her mind attempting to reconstruct the edifice. Then she shook her head in negation.

Some stones have an inescapable eloquence; others are mute. Jesus did not seem to be there in spirit or memory.

Dr Levi said, 'Come with me, and I will show you something.'

He led her by a narrow path away from the lake, towards the north-east, along a fold of gently rising land for almost a thousand yards, until they came to a grove of cypress trees that stood by themselves in a shape that was no shape; yet form it had, or once had known, as though these were the dropped seedlings of other trees that had stood there long before these and in other places near by, planted by man to enhance and enclose something.

Yet now at first glance there seemed nothing to enclose but a flattish mound of springy turf carpeted with wild flowers, hummocked here and there in odd forms, long and low like a grave, or rounded like small tumuli but blending into the conformation of the ground, which was uneven and covered with young shrubs, saplings and the fresh greenery of spring.

But at the far end of the grove, almost vanishing against the background of a tall cypress, one single smooth pillar thrust from the ground topped by a broken piece of cornice, triangular in shape but of simple, sweet and harmonious design.

More than if there had been visible ruins, the single pillar multiplied itself in the mind, and the surmounting triangle swept inwards and upwards into the noble façade of a simple place of worship.

It filled the grove with its dignity and mystery. It was a forgotten site, yet here the past cried out with eloquence that was unmistakable; beneath the turf lay hallowed things.

Hannah cried, 'What is this *place*? Did He come here?'

Dr Levi nodded. 'Yes,' he replied simply. 'Beneath our feet lie the remains of the synagogue of Capernaum. I am certain of it' – he lifted his head and raised his arms in a gesture of embracing as he drew in a deep breath – 'by what I feel . . .' And then he smiled at her as though apologizing for becoming emotional. '. . . and also from what I know. It is my discovery, and some day we shall search here. There is evidence that in those times the water of the lake extended almost a kilometre farther north. Capernaum was not a Jewish but a Galilean town. The temple where the alien Jews met to discuss their God would have been a very simple one – such as, perhaps, this . . .'

The spell under which Hannah had been falling was upon her again. This was the perpetual enchantment of Palestine – that a swelling mound, a blue lake, a piece of broken stone could suddenly speak and say, 'Jesus knew me. His hand once rested on me, in me His eyes took delight, the ground beneath here once knew the tread of His feet. From these heights the prophets thundered, through these streets men preached the unity of God; from those mountain peaks the chosen saw their visions . . .'

She said, 'Yes, you are right. He must have been here.'

Dr Levi said gently, 'I have been sure of it since the first time I came upon this place.'

Something in his voice made Hannah tilt her head to one side in her characteristic pose of inquiry and ask, 'You love Him, do you not?'

'How is it possible not to love one so gentle and inspired?'

'And yet,' Hannah said directly and without embarrassment,

'you are a Jew. I thought that all Jews denied and hated Jesus.'

'A common error,' Dr Levi replied quietly, but then his voice took on warmth and animation and his eyes became singularly youthful as he continued: 'Here in Israel many of the old hatreds have died and are buried with the cities where they once flourished. There is no longer any time for them. Many of us have been liberated in more ways than one by our return. We may love whom we will. Jesus was a Jew, a teacher and a prophet. He took our ancient beliefs and through His exquisite spirit distilled them into such everlasting beauty that more than half the world has accepted them as the beacon for guidance in the darkness. It was man who created the gulf between Jew and Gentile, not Jesus. No one is forbidden to give love for love.'

Hannah said, 'I like to hear you speak of him. It is like no one has ever spoken of Him to me before. You make Him live.'

Dr Levi nodded gravely and studied Hannah for a moment. Then he asked, 'Do you remember what it was that Jesus said here?'

Hannah tried to think, but the words would not come. She said, 'I cannot remember.'

Dr Levi said, 'Here it was that He spoke the words that were to change the world.' Then he began to quote: "I am the bread of life: he that cometh to me shall never hunger; and he that believeth on me shall never thirst . . ."

The tenderness and force of the words, repeated on perhaps the very ground where once they had rung out before, brought the tears close to Hannah's eyes. Since Nazareth they always seemed to be not far from the surface.

She cried, 'Yes. . . . Now I remember.'

Dr Levi said, 'There was more. He said, "I am that bread of life. Your fathers did eat manna in the wilderness, and are dead. This is the bread of life that cometh down from heaven, that a man may eat thereof, and not die." '

Hannah looked at him sharply; but, oddly now, the old man did not seem to be aware of her. His gaze was fixed on the pillar of the ancient synagogue and his voice was sonorous and intense as he repeated the words John had attributed to Jesus:

"Whoso eateth my flesh, and drinketh my blood, hath eternal

life; and I will raise him up at the last day. . . . He that eateth my flesh, and drinketh my blood, dwelleth in me, and I in him. As the living Father hath sent me, and I live by the Father: so he that eateth me, even he shall live by me. This is that bread which came down from Heaven: not as your fathers and mothers did eat manna, and are dead: he that eateth of this bread shall live for ever." And thereafter Dr Levi said no more.

Hannah turned away. For a moment she could not bear to look at him. For now she was hearing within herself the last words that Christ had spoken on that occasion and that Dr Levi had omitted:

'It is the spirit that quickeneth; the flesh profiteth nothing: the words that I speak unto you, they are the spirit, and they are the life.'

And then, almost as an echo: 'He that eateth of this bread shall live for ever . . .'

'Dr Levi!' The cry seemed torn from depths that Hannah did not know she possessed.

'Yes . . .'

They faced one another, and between them the air was electric with the old man's humanity and pity and her need for help.

'Hello there! Miss Bascombe! Dr Levi!'

Sears' cry from the bottom of the cypress grove shattered the moment.

'Hello there! I've been looking for you.' He came walking towards them swiftly. There were a number of telegrams in his hand. He handed them to Miss Bascombe.

'These arrived for you an hour ago from San Francisco and mail as well. Miss Adams said it was urgent that they reach you at once. I offered to try to find you . . .'

She took the messages and glanced through them. Sears watched the grim lines of the business woman return to her face, the hardening of the eyes, the chilling of the thin mouth.

She asked, 'Is there a telephone line at Ain Tabigha?'

'Yes. Clary has already placed a call to your office in San Francisco. She is expecting the connexion within an hour.'

Hannah turned to Dr Levi, and it was as though she were speaking to a stranger. 'Business matters, Dr Levi. I have been out of touch with my office too long. I must return to Ain Tabigha at once and dispose of these.'

He nodded gravely. 'Yes, you must.'

They proceeded from the grove. Sears said to Dr Levi, 'An American boy arrived in a jeep. His name is Ed Avery. He brought a message for you from Ben-Isaac.'

Dr Levi nodded again. 'Ah yes. This means that they are ready. We can proceed north tomorrow ...' Then he walked on in silence, his massive head lowered.

Sears had a sudden, fierce moment of exultation. For the first time Dr Levi appeared to be depressed and defeated. He, Sears, had been right about his hunch to bring these messages, nerve ends of Hannah's financial empire, summonses from her past life, to her as swiftly as possible. He had arrived in time to spoil something for Dr Levi. As long as the cupidity could return to Hannah's eyes and the ice and iron to her mouth, the game was not lost to Joseph Deuell Sears.

Chapter 21

'And I will take the stony heart out of their
flesh, and will give them an heart of flesh' —
Ezekiel xi, 19

A WEEK later Sears found himself driving a jeep trailing another
piloted by the American boy, Ed Avery, with Clary Adams sitting
beside him, and containing Hannah Bascombe and Dr Nathaniel
Levi. It was early morning and still dark. Behind them at
Metullah, as cover and to maintain a show of activity, they
had left the cars and trailers and the staff of servants. They were
bound for Dan.

Avery, a strong, stocky boy in the inevitable khaki shorts and
shirt, with baseball cap added, came from a nearby *kibbutz,*
where a number of Americans were engaged in applying modern
methods and American machinery to farming and developing a
large tract covering several hills.

It was he who had appeared suddenly at Ain Tabigha, riding
a motor-cycle and bearing a message from Ben-Isaac that all was
in readiness for the expedition. He knew, of course, who Hannah
was and met her with frank and open interest; and when she
expressed surprise at finding an American there and questioned
him, he said, 'I was through here during the war, ma'am, and
decided when it was over I'd come back.' He waved an arm in-
dicating the horizon and the distant hills. 'Kinda gives you a
little room to stretch out here,' he said. It turned out he had
attended the agricultural school at Stanford University. He
added, 'Our family has always pioneered some . . .'

Hannah had asked, 'Are there many more like you in America?'

Avery replied cheerfully, 'Hell, yes, ma'am, only they're all
kinda spread out all over the world now. Most of 'em saw some
spot some place during the war where they figured a little enterprise would pay off and a feller could get ahead, and that's where
they are.'

Hannah had looked pleased and remarked, 'But you're not a Jew . . .'; to which Avery had replied with some surprise, 'What's that got to do with it? This is a fine country with a lot of fine people in it.'

Ben-Isaac had not been at Metullah when they arrived there, and Sears was as much in the dark concerning his whereabouts as anyone. Avery had said merely, 'My instructions were not to talk. I'll take you to him when we're ready to go.'

Apparently that moment had come, with Avery acting as temporary guide in the lead jeep.

Sears was glad to be alone with Clary. It was the first time they had been together since the day at Haifa following his trip to Tel Aviv. Yet the first words he spoke to her were aggressive.

They had backtracked southwards from Metullah down the valley of Lake Hulah and then turned eastwards toward Dan. As always, the rounded hills, the nearness of the sky, the evidence in trees and fields of the gallant struggle to cultivate moved Clary, and she gazed with sparkling eyes at the richness that unrolled before them as they entered country that was watered by nature. Sears leaned from the wheel and said, 'You're feeling pretty good these days, aren't you?'

Clary turned in her seat to stare for a moment at the man with whom it seemed she had been carrying on such a long and bitter feud. Sears was wearing khaki trousers, a khaki shirt open at the neck, and an old army khaki fatigue hat pulled down over his eyes. She thought that with the shedding of his city clothes he had left some of his slickness behind him and looked younger, but there was also now a quality of forlornness about him that succeeded in touching her heart in an odd way.

Even while she was considering her reply Clary wondered at this and decided that it was because he was a villain whose game had somehow gone wrong, and that there was genuine pathos in an evildoer whose carefully-built-up plot has come a cropper. All males, but particularly the more amoral ones, always looked helpless and pathetic when things didn't go as they had planned them.

She said gravely, 'It's true, Joe. I am happier and more peaceful than I have ever been before. It is so beautiful here.'

Sears said, 'Oh, come off it, Clary. I wasn't referring to the scenery. You figure I'm licked. Your precious Ben-Isaac and his uncle have taken over. You're out from under and sitting on top of the world. I'm just telling you before you move all the way over, watch yourself. Because I'm not finished yet.'

Clary nodded, but felt her heart sore for the weakness he was showing. She decided to ignore it, saying merely, 'I am happy, but not on that account.' Then she added, with a smile that was almost mischievous, for she wanted to cheer him up, 'Isn't it queer that I should owe it all to you . . .'

'To me?' It was his turn to stare at her now; and he was startled suddenly by her beauty, as though it were something he had not noticed recently. He was aware of how bronzing by the Mediterranean sun had improved her. She was no longer so thin and the sun had altered the colour of her hair and brought it to life and lustre. These, with the colouring of her eyes and the sensitive oval of her face, had suddenly created a loveliness that became almost unbearable. The bare, sun-drenched, unperfumed feminine fragrance of her reached him and filled him with a blinding longing. The sickliness, the unhealthy resignation that had so repelled him had all but vanished. It was a woman who was seated beside him.

Clary continued, 'It's true. But for you I should never have come here. And I would have gone through the entire rest of my life with Hannah living in fear. You did teach me not to be afraid if the worst happened, didn't you?'

Sears said nastily, 'I trust you are duly grateful.'

Clary asked, 'Why do you insist on being hateful, Joe? Doesn't it make you feel good to see green things growing and know that a country that has been sick almost to death is returning to life again? Doesn't any of where we have been and what we have seen touch you?'

Sears said briefly, 'I don't happen to be sentimental, sister.' Then he asked, 'What's happened to Hannah? When she came here she couldn't wait to start for the promised land. We practically had to pry her out of Ain Tabigha when that young fellow turned up. What has this guy Levi been talking her into? What do *you* think is his game?'

Clary said, 'What if he hasn't got a game?'

Sears moved sideways from the wheel to get a longer view of Clary. 'Are you innocent! A billion-dollar baby drops in on Israel, this smooth talker pops up out of nowhere and moves in and it isn't a racket? Even if it turns out he's only trying to get her to give her money to the State to buy some guns with, it's a ploy, isn't it? Come on, Clary, wake up. And pulling that line about the lost tribe, the jealous priesthood, and the carefully guarded secret of the thingummy . . .'

Clary gave him a half-amused, half-quizzical look. 'Jealous?' she asked.

Sears suddenly threw back his head and laughed with no trace of malice or cynicism. He was genuinely amused.

'Okay,' he said. 'It *is* funny, isn't it?'

Clary now asked, 'But what if somehow it *were* true?'

'That,' replied Sears, 'would be the biggest laugh yet. Levi might walk off with the lion's share of the loot, but your Uncle Sears would get paid.'

Clary asked curiously, 'Just what is your arrangement with Hannah, if you don't mind my asking?'

Sears replied with a kind of airiness, 'Oh no, no, not at all. Strictly play or no pay. Expenses for research and the rest on delivery. But I can live very nicely on the expenses, thank you.'

'But if you could deliver . . .'

The cynical expression returned to his mouth. 'If you like to talk dreams, baby. . . . She's protected, but so am I. Let's say we find it and she takes it. The doctors go over her. And I'm off the payroll for five years. That's to keep *me* honest. At the end of that time, if she is still alive, the medics look her over again. If the chart shows up the same as the first examination, I get a million dollars. And each succeeding year I get another million for so long as she lives – or I live . . .'

Clary sighed. 'How very wicked.'

'Uhuh! Ain't I!' Sears assented.

Clary said quietly, 'I wasn't thinking of you. I meant Hannah.'

Sears looked at her in surprise. 'Yeah? Do you think so? Well, money makes people wicked, and there's no two ways about that. It's the kind of wickedness I could enjoy if I had it.'

Strangely, Clary nodded and agreed. 'Yes, I know. Until you come across something that money can't buy. Joe, you asked me about Hannah. That night in Nazareth when I came back to the trailer and found her crying.'

'So what? Women cry.'

'Not Hannah. As long as I have known her she has never shed a tear.'

'What do you think happened to her?'

Clary replied with another question. 'Joe, haven't you experienced something since you have been here, anything at all?'

'Such as . . .'

She was serious and disturbed. 'I don't know how to express it . . . sometimes a sadness, or a catch at the throat, or a kind of longing, and above all a feeling of nearness . . .'

'Nearness to what?'

This time Clary did not reply.

'No,' said Sears.

Then they drove for a long while in silence, ascending from Lake Hulah into fertile hills covered with prosperous-looking farms and communities. The white tip of Hermon was just visible over the tops of the Syrian foothills in the distance.

Sears finally spoke, and he said the words as though he were repeating a litany.

'I don't care for this deal at all. I don't like where we're going, the way we're going, or who we're going with. I like no part of it.'

Clary asked, 'What is it you are worried about, Joe?'

Sears jerked his head towards two cases riding in the back of the jeep. Avery had put them there shortly before they had left Metullah. 'Do you know what's in those cases back there?' And when she was silent, he continued, 'Well, it ain't condensed milk or Wheaties. We've got a box of Czech grenades and the other is .303 ammo. There's enough for a small war. I didn't come here to take sides in this Israel-Arab thing.'

Clary asked without mockery, 'Are you afraid of war?'

Sears nodded. 'Uhuh. Especially private ones. You don't lug this much stuff around unless you expect somebody to get hurt. I wouldn't like it to be you. Or Hannah either, for that matter.'

Clary studied him. 'Could it be that you have a conscience, Joe?'

Sears shrugged. 'I doubt it. Call it a sense of tidiness. It just isn't Joe Sears to promise someone life eternal and then get them killed looking for it . . .'

Chapter 22

'Arise and be baptized, and wash away thy sins,
calling on the name of the Lord' — *Acts* xxii, 16

THE region of Dan proved to be open, sunny farmland that reminded Sears of the lush California valleys. Here they drove
their jeeps into the enclosure of a large community settlement
or *kibbutz* and remained for a lunch of black bread, sour cream
and salad. Then they pushed on afoot.

They were dressed for rough going, with heavy walking boots,
and all in khaki, which was protective as well as practical. Sears,
Avery and Dr Levi bore knapsacks with a day's food supplies,
and they could not be distinguished from the other groups of
walkers or wanderers afoot that one was always encountering
in Israel.

They had followed the road in a north-easterly direction for
several hours when they came to a narrow path leading due east.
Here, Dr Levi paused and addressed them, though his words
were directed at Hannah.

He said, 'Let us pause here for a moment. This is the beginning of the end of this affair. It is the point where the road
divides. The choice is still left us to go back after no more than a
pleasant walk in the country, or to take the turning and accept
the consequences of whatever lies ahead upon the path we
choose.'

Hannah cocked her head to one side in her characteristic gesture and asked, 'What are you trying to say, Dr Levi?'

'Only that you reflect at the cross-road. So frequently do we
become caught up in the pursuit of what we believe to be our
desires and happiness that we do not pause to listen to our own
heartbeats and question the strength of those desires when the
goal is in sight. I cannot promise you whether you will be happy
or unhappy once you have taken this path. I can only show
you the way. Do you wish to go on?'

Sears said, 'Certainly we want to go on. That's why we came here.'

But Hannah gestured curtly and said, 'Be still.' She studied the road, and the little trail branching off to the right, and then said to Dr Levi, 'Never, in all my life, have I paused at a cross-road. It is a new experience.'

She went a few steps forward along the path, then turned and came out again and looked along the road south. She said to Dr Levi:

'I think I understand what you are trying to say. If I turn back now, I shall be Hannah Bascombe still, and as I have been. And if I take that small path of my own will, there will be ines-capable consequences of my act. Isn't that it?'

Dr Levi nodded gravely and said, 'That is it.'

Hannah said to herself and to all of them, 'What shall I do?'

Clary, who had looked upon Hannah's tears and had heard her sobbing in the Nazarene darkness, said impulsively:

'Do what would make you happy . . .'

Hannah turned to Dr Levi, but he only smiled and shook his head. 'I cannot advise you,' he said.

Joe Sears rasped, 'Do what your father would have done!'

It was the deliberate pulling of the trigger that he had learned in those months in Hannah's house back in San Francisco, and he saw with satisfaction the change in her expression, the stiffening of her body and the convulsive movement of her hands.

In those days he had used it whenever she had seemed to waver. He had only to bring up a picture of her father, the kind of man he was and the lifetime he had devoted to amassing the Bascombe fortune, to set her once more on the path of her ob-session.

It was the first time in his duel with Dr Nathaniel Levi that Sears had counter-attacked, and he had well known what button to press to recapture her. He had again inflamed her mind with the memory of the man who had been her God and who had never hesitated in his quest for power, possession and more power to the day of his death.

Sears saw with satisfaction how the lower portion of Hannah's face froze again into the lines of grim immobility and watched the cold calculating light return to her eyes. Her expression reminded him of the first time he had seen Hannah when her face had appeared to him half living half dead.

She spoke sharply. 'Well why are we waiting? I wish to proceed.'

Dr Levi nodded, motioned to Avery to lead the way and fell in behind him, followed by Hannah and Clary, with Sears bringing up the rear. Joe was thinking, with the first relish he had experienced in many days, that he could still pull a string or two. It had been Hannah's cross-road, but *he* had made the decision. It wasn't until much later that he realized that it had been a cross-road for all of them, and for himself as well.

They began to mount almost immediately; a gentle, steady climb that was not yet taxing as the path led through small growth, occasionally emerging into high meadowland, where the air had great clarity and it was already cooler.

They heard the running of water and soon picked up a small mountain stream tumbling over a rocky bottom with force and verve. They pressed on through thickets of fragrant acacia, young oak and willow.

Here the path vanished altogether, and they soon found themselves laboriously picking their way through up the stream bed, stepping from rock to rock, as the way mounted steeply.

In some places human hands had jammed pieces of wood with crossbars to form a kind of improvised ladder barely raised above the rushing, green-black water, on which it was possible to gain a foothold for the more difficult parts of the climb. Sears was amazed at Hannah's agility and the speed with which she pressed forward aided by Dr Levi. He was satisfied that she was again under the spell of her obsession.

The angle of the climb eased suddenly as they came up over the edge of the brook's fall to a plateau of mossy turf carpeted with wild flowers that was a part of a narrow woodland glade like a green corridor. Here the stream ran still and deep with only a gentle murmur.

The corridor widened into a grove almost druidical in nature, so green and hushed and heavily still was it, and dominated at one end by a giant oak many hundreds of years old, spreading into branches over a radius of fifty yards. There were boulders and rocks piled up; some haphazardly, others, apparently, aided by the hand of man into something that might have passed for a throne. Close to one small pile of rocks there was a mound of fresh earth with a board at one end. The board was crowned with a steel helmet.

But the most astonishing phenomenon of this grove, and as dominating in its way as the giant oak, was the pools of fresh, dark water that welled up from the ground and poured forth from the crevices of rocks. It was here that the brook or small stream they had been following had its rise.

The thick carpet of green moss and dead oak leaves hushed their footfalls, but the strange quality of the place contributed likewise to their silence. Then there came a snapping of twigs, the sound of voices and the clinking of metal against wood and leather. From the brush at the southern end of the grove emerged Ben-Isaac at the head of ten boys approximating his own age, in shorts, knee-length stockings, khaki shirts and berets. They were armed with rifles, revolvers, Sten guns. Many of them had several hand-grenades fastened to their belts and carried back-packs of tents, supplies, entrenching tools and extra ammunition, topped by the British-type steel helmet. They all had the military bearing and alert, confident look of army veterans and first-class fighting men.

Ben-Isaac came over to them, accompanied by a tall, dark, loosely knit boy with a wide mouth, friendly face, prematurely grey hair, and the same air of absolute maturity and self-confidence that distinguished so many of the young men of Israel.

Ben-Isaac smiled at Hannah and said, 'Your army, ma'am,' and then introduced the other. 'This is Captain Schlomo Weinberg. He defended the Beit Hillel Kibbutz against more than four hundred Jordanites during the war. But of course the Palmach is all unofficial now. They're just coming along for the walk.'

Ben-Isaac himself had left much of his boyishness behind him and had become a fighting man from the top of his dark head, on which was set a Polish fatigue cap, relic of his guerrilla days, to the soles of his heavy army boots. He carried a rifle and crossed bandoliers of cartridges and a belt on which were hung a half-dozen Czech fragmentation grenades.

Hannah Bascombe looked them over like a general reviewing troops and nodded her head with a kind of grim satisfaction. She knew fighters when she saw them.

Sears noted the expression that came into Clary's face and eyes at the reappearance of Ben-Isaac, dramatized by the uniform and weapons, and said sardonically, 'So that's where you've been, Ben-Isaac. Where's the war?'

Ed Avery, who had slung his rifle and pack, brought by one of the others, jerked his head towards the bushes and said, 'Over there, about a hundred yards,' and then pointed to a mound topped by a tin hat on the edge of the grove.

The armed men had formed a semi-circle about it now, their heads bared, hands folded. Dr Levi and Ed Avery, too, bowed their heads. Schlomo Weinberg began to speak in Hebrew.

Hannah whispered, 'What is happening?'

Ben-Isaac replied, 'He was one of their friends, mother. He came from a neighbouring kibbutz, but they fought together in the siege during the war. He was ambushed here and killed three weeks ago.'

His words came as a profound shock to Sears. Were they, then, so close to enemy country, and the armistice actually meant nothing? He pictured the sudden rattle of small-arms fire from one of the thickets surrounding the glade and a boy like one of the ten stalwarts there falling to the turf, riddled with bullets, gasping and dying.

'Here?' Clary said, unbelieving. 'In this beautiful, peaceful spot . . . ?'

The little prayer for the repose of the dead had come to an end and the company fell back to the edge of the glade. Hannah asked, 'What is this place? Where are we?'

Dr Levi replied, 'We are at Tel-el-Quadi, one of the headwaters of the Jordan. The River Jordan is rising at your feet. The borders of Syria are fifty yards beyond.'

Hannah looked startled. She repeated, 'Jordan's rise. The River Jordan . . .'

Dr Levi indicated the boulders and throne-like rocks. 'It is more than likely that in ancient times the tribe of Dan met here for judgement. There is a legend that on Judgement Day the angel will appear here beneath this oak.' He then added, 'We had best be moving on. The men say it is not safe to remain here for too long.'

But Hannah only repeated 'The River Jordan . . .' for the third time. Then a curious expression came into her grim, cold face, a kind of hunger and yearning seemed to form beneath the hard crust of imperiousness. She said to Dr Levi, 'No. I will not go yet. First I wish to be baptized. I wish to be baptized in Jordan.' She stared at the dark waters welling from the ground like blood from a wound. 'Let my sins be washed away by Jordan!' she cried.

Sears suddenly felt a deep embarrassment mixed with anxiety. He stepped forward and said with some sharpness, 'Miss Bascombe, as I understand it, this is a bad spot. A boy was killed here only a few weeks ago. Dr Levi suggests we move on to where there is less danger, and if I . . .'

Hannah interrupted him peremptorily. 'Be quiet! I did not ask you. I gave an order. I wish baptism. Who will baptize me?'

No one replied. A look almost of panic crossed Hannah's countenance. She said, 'Anyone can baptize. . . . Dr Levi, will you not baptize me?' All of the imperiousness was gone out of her now as, with an odd break in her voice, she pleaded, 'Dr Levi – I beg of you . . .'

Everyone was watching them. There was no sound in the grove but the muttering of the emerging water and the occasional steel chink of rifle against belt. . . . Dr Levi gazed at Hannah keenly and asked sharply, 'Are you in a state of grace to receive baptism . . .?'

Hannah's hands, balled into tight fists, shook momentarily. She said, 'I don't know. . . . How can I tell? There is a memory of a psalm in me. I can hear it, but I cannot say it . . .'

Ben-Isaac quietly began to speak, his deep affectionate eyes on Hannah:

' ". . . from the land of Jordan,
And the Hermons, fom the hill Mizar,

Deep unto deep is calling at the noise of thy waterfalls;
All the breakers and billows are gone over me . . .
With a breaking in my bones, mine enemies reproach me;
While they say unto me all the day, Where is thy God?
Why art thou cast down, O my soul?
And why art thou disquieted upon me?
Hope thou in God: for I shall yet praise him,
Health of my countenance, and my God . . ." '

'Yes, oh yes,' Hannah cried. 'That is it.' Then she said to Dr
Levi, with almost child-like pleading in her voice, 'Can't you
understand . . . ?'

The old man glanced briefly at Sears, then went over to
Hannah, and with a movement of great tenderness he took her
hand in comfort and for a moment looked deeply into her disturbed eyes.

'Yes,' he said, 'I understand. I will do as you wish. I will baptize you. Prepare yourself . . .'

As Hannah knelt down to remove her shoes and stockings,
Sears whispered to Clary, 'For heaven's sakes, can't you stop
her?'

Clary said, 'Be still. Why should I? Look at her face. Can't
you see her need . . . ?'

Hannah went over to where the later afternoon sun slanted
through the dappled leaves and turned the flow of dark liquid
gushing from the rocks to gold and crystal and stood there so
that the icy waters washed her ankles. Dr Levi accompanied her
into the just-born stream.

He bent over and with his cupped hands he scooped up some
of the water and sprinkled it over the grey head so that some of
the drops ran down the cheeks of the proud countenance like
tears.

And he said only, 'In the name of the Lord God Almighty, I
baptize thee, Hannah Bascombe.'

Then they walked out of the pool together. A strangely incongruous yet touching note was sounded by the young American boy, Ed Avery, who came over to Hannah and shook her
hand. He said, 'Gee, Miss Bascombe, that was wonderful. I'm
awfully glad, for your sake . . .'

Joe Sears suddenly experienced a strange and inexplicable sense of defeat. It was as though a battle had been waged in and around and through him without his being able to take any real or active part in it or defend himself, a battle that in some manner concerned him deeply and that he had lost.

Chapter 23

'He saith unto him, Feed my lambs' – *John* **xxi**, 15

ROLLED up in a blanket and lying on the hard ground of their first encampment just inside the entrance to a deep gorge that penetrated the foothills which led to Mount Hermon, Sears could not sleep and badly wanted a smoke. Schlomo, however, had banned the showing of any kind of light, and Sears had savvy enough not to disobey.

They had managed to cross the border by the Queiteira road not far from Dan without incident after dark, the Palmach guard functioning smoothly in familiar country, and headed for the wilderness skirting the line between Lebanon and Syria.

This area had the advantage of comparative freedom from either Syrian or Lebanese military patrols, which both Dr Levi and Schlomo wished to avoid at all costs, but exposed them to the dangers of savage bands of roving Arabs who had been using the Arab-Israel war as an excuse for general raiding and looting expeditions. On the other hand, the going was sure to be easier for Hannah, the approach to Hermon lying through a series of shallow valleys at times no more than dry wadis or stony ravines that led through a series of gently rolling and ever-mounting hills.

The camp had been pitched shortly before midnight. With speed and efficiency, working in almost total darkness, the Palmach men raised tents for Hannah and Clary and inflated air mattresses for them. The men slept on the ground.

Sears' softened body was rebelling and he was unpleasantly reminded of his soldiering days. This was not exactly the way he had planned his sinecure.

Looking down the entrance to the gorge, he noted the outline of the figure of Ben-Isaac, silhouetted against the star-dusted horizon, standing his two-hour watch. Sears arose from beside Dr Levi, who appeared astonishingly inured to any kind of hardships and had fallen off to sleep without any difficulty, and, quietly picking his way, went down to where the boy was patrolling his area.

As Sears approached Ben-Isaac he saw his head come up, heard the jingle of his equipment being shifted and the metallic click of a weapon cocked. The older man said, 'It's okay. It's me, Sears . . .'

Ben-Isaac relaxed but said, 'You could get hurt wandering around in the dark. You ought not to be here. Orders were to bed down and stay there.'

Sears said 'Uhuh' but made no move to go. He felt about for a rock and squatted on it near Ben-Isaac's feet and remained silent for several minutes. Then he asked suddenly:

'Happy, kid?'

'Rather.'

'Like this sort of stuff, don't you?'

'Yes. Don't you?'

In the darkness Sears smiled to himself. 'Frankly, no. Remember me? I'm the original Peaceful Pete. I've had all the bang-bang I want.' Then he asked, 'What kind of trouble are we likely to raise?'

Scorn came into Ben-Isaac's low-pitched voice. 'If anything – Arabs.'

Sears said, 'An Arab with a gun can kill you just as dead as anybody else if he pulls the trigger when you happen to be in front of it. And don't forget, this is their country and we haven't been invited.'

Ben-Isaac snorted again. 'I wish they'd try it.'

'Uhuh. Sears's casting one wish they don't. What about Dr Levi?'

'What about him?'

'What kind of a guy is he?'

'Smashing!'

Sears smiled again. There were times when the young Pole was more British than the English. He said, 'I mean what is he really all about?'

Ben-Isaac said, 'You have seen nearly as much of him as I have. Cannot you tell that he is a great man?'

'He knows a lot,' Sears conceded. 'What is he doing here in Israel?'

'Raising vegetables.'

Sears snorted. 'A guy with all he has under his hat growing cucumbers and radishes? Don't give me that. What's it a cover for? Intelligence? Or black-market stuff of some sort?'

'Neither.'

Sears scoffed. 'Oh, brrrrother . . .'

Ben-Isaac said, 'You don't believe in anything, do you? But I thought you'd be clever enough to use your eyes. Where has five thousand years of culture brought Israel? Today, one Yemenite with strong arms and the will to work is worth a dozen doctors of theology – '

'Quoting Dr Levi?'

'Yes.'

'What made him come back here? From what I've picked up, he was doing all right on the Continent and even in the U.S. He's not an Israelite. He's a world Jew if I ever saw one.'

Ben-Isaac reflected for a moment, leaning on the muzzle of his rifle, then he replied. 'He was getting old. He returned here because he wished to find God. In his early days he was a rabbi, you know . . .'

'Is there no God over London, or New York, or San Francisco?'

Ben-Isaac said, 'Oh yes. There must be. But He is so much closer here. It is so much easier to communicate with Him. Hadn't you noticed?'

Sears did not reply.

Ben-Isaac continued, 'When my uncle first came here, a few years ago, he went up on top of a mountain and spoke with God and asked Him what he should do, and the Lord told him to remain and grow food, for that was what His children needed the most.'

Sears said, 'Are you kidding?'

Ben-Isaac said, 'No. I am not kidding. Why should I be? Men here used to talk with God all the time in the old days. Because my uncle is also a scientist he is a practical man, and therefore simple and direct in his approach to the source.'

'Did the Lord also tell him to lead Hannah to Mount Hermon?'

'Perhaps.'

Sears laughed. Then he said, 'What's his racket, Ben-Isaac? What's his game? What's he after? Why did he horn into this? Why has he taken Hannah over? Where is he leading us to?'

Ben-Isaac shifted in the darkness. Sears's eyes had become accustomed to the faint starlight, and he thought the boy's features had changed and that now he was grinning down at him. Eventually he replied:

'You're a funny chap, Joe. Back in Los Angeles you once filled me full of a yarn about a big theory of yours. There wasn't any reason why it should be true, but the way you put it there wasn't any reason why it shouldn't, either. When I told you about my uncle, who, if he were alive, would know all about such things, you were very much interested and said maybe we could find him and he could help us. Well, we did, and he is. What more do you want?'

'Plenty. For one thing, why is he doing it?'

'Why don't you ask him?'

'I may get around to it some day.' He fell silent for a moment and then switched his line of questioning. He asked, 'Look here, Ben-Isaac. Do you believe there is such a place as Beit Jebel, the Village of the Patriarchs?'

'Yes.'

'And that there are guys in it who claim to be three and four hundred years old who have found a mysterious something-or-other that they eat which keeps them going?'

'Certainly.'

'Why?'

'Because my uncle said so. He has been there.' Then he added, 'Is there anything else you would like to know?'

'Yes. What has happened to Hannah?'

'In what respect?'

'She's changed. Surely you must have noticed it. She isn't at all like she used to be. If she hadn't had religion before she came here, I'd say that she'd got it. That performance in the

Jordan. What was she up to in Galilee with Dr Levi? What goes on?'

Ben-Isaac said, 'We've all changed, haven't we, Joe? We're all a little different since coming here. Look back . . .'

Sears got up. 'Not me, I haven't.' He stretched. 'I'm still the luxury kid looking for a soft buck who doesn't like any one single part of this damn deal since we hooked up with Uncle. Well, good night, Ben-Isaac, and thanks for all the answers . . .'

But he was thoughtful as he picked his way back to his blanket and stretched out on the ground beneath the myriad eyes burning down on him from above.

It was shortly after three o'clock in the afternoon of the second day that Ben-Isaac got his wish.

They could travel by daylight now, for mostly the party was swallowed up by the folds of the foothills through which they were climbing. There was a blazing sun in a clear sky, but they themselves were in deep shadow, toiling laboriously along the bottom of a ravine with narrow sloping sides lined with rocks, scrub oak, pine and terebinth and picking their way across fallen trees and around huge boulders.

From ahead and far away there came a queer, pulsing cry, followed by a shot and a shout and then the sound of running feet, the jamming explosion of a grenade, and then, from both front and rear the crack of rifles and the ripping tear of machine-pistol fire.

Joe Sears, who had been walking with Clary behind Dr Levi and Hannah, said 'God damn!', reached for her and pulled her down flat behind a boulder with the instinctive reaction of the soldier who takes cover first and cases the situation afterwards.

Clary cried 'Hannah! Where is she?' and tried to get up.

Sears yelled 'God dammit, keep down!' and pulled her back. The sound of running feet came closer and, peering around the boulder, Sears saw that it was Ben-Isaac pushing hard, his face pale, eyes gleaming, mouth distorted . . .

Hannah was standing bewildered some ten feet behind Dr Levi. Ben-Isaac ran at her shouting, 'Imma! Mother! Take cover.

Lie down! Uncle – there behind that rock!' He seized Hannah and pulled her down between two logs of fallen trees, and pushed her half under one of them so that she had shelter from above as well. Then he stood up, looking left and right and all about him.

A bullet smashed from a rock near where he was and buzzed away angrily. Ben-Isaac raised his rifle, aimed it up towards the top of the ravine and fired, but there was no way of telling with what effect. Then he called to Sears, 'Stay down. Keep them all down. Ed wants me to go back and find out what Schlomo is up against. . . .' He went slipping and sliding along the rocks and tree trunks in the direction of the firing from the rear.

There was not a single thing to be seen, no attacking figures, no flashes or smoke. . . . There was only the noise of the firing. Clary again cried, 'Hannah . . .'

Sears said, 'Hannah's okay for the time being. Take it easy.'

'What is it? What is happening?'

For the third time Sears said, fervently, 'God damn!' and then added, 'We're boxed. They're ahead of us and behind us, and, from the sound of it, plenty. The boys are engaging 'em . . .'

Clary asked, 'Aren't you going to help them?'

Sears looked at her coldly. 'With what? Rocks? Let Ben-Isaac be the hero. He likes that sort of thing. I'll settle for a whole skin. This is going to be a stinker, sister. Just concentrate on staying alive.'

The firing increased in intensity up forward, and from their rear it sounded closer and more sporadic as though Schlomo, Ben-Isaac and their squad were falling back fighting as they retreated.

Chapter 24

'And deliver them who through fear of death were
all their lifetime subject to bondage' – *Hebrews*
ii, 15

THERE is a combination of innocence and deadliness in modern
battle action with small arms that only the old soldier knows and
understands how to evaluate. The combatants remain concealed,
the powder is smokeless. When there is no artillery, nature
remains undisturbed.

Sears, who had seen infantry action in France and Germany,
knew every tone of the deadly symphony that was being played
about them; but for the moment there was nothing to do but
keep cover and try to keep himself and the women from getting
hurt, for they were caught in the cross-fire from the action
against the front and rear guards of Palmach men, who were apparently putting up a good fight.

Ben-Isaac could take care of himself; he was a seasoned fighter.
What happened to Dr Levi, Sears did not particularly care. It
would serve him right for leading them into this trap. But it was
not his intention to get himself killed in a fight that was none of
his concern or to have Hannah's search for life eternal ended in
a ravine in Syria by a rifle or Sten-gun bullet.

Also Sears's already small stomach for this battle was still further reduced by the realization that whoever was attacking them
had a perfect right to do so, for he, Dr Levi, and his party had
provoked it by crossing a border with armed men, thus breaching
what was at best a delicate and uneasy armistice, aggravating the
situation between two countries that should be united in friendship.

The boulder behind which he and Clary crouched was ade-
quate cover from the north, though exposed to stray shots whining up from the south. He crawled about and moved some smaller
rocks closer, built them into a makeshift barricade and pressed

Clary's head down behind them, saying, 'Stay flat if you don't want to get hurt.'

He peered around the side of his shelter. A dozen or so yards up the ravine he saw Dr Levi lying behind several stones that were giving him fair cover. He appeared to be unharmed and unperturbed.

Between Levi and himself, at the bottom of the stream bed, well sheltered by the boles of the fallen trees, he could see Hannah, and he called out to her:

'Miss Bascombe! Are you all right?'

There was a rasp to her voice as she replied, 'Certainly! Where has Ben-Isaac gone? What is the meaning of this?' She sounded angry.

Sears said, 'Ben is fighting. We don't know yet exactly what it is. But whatever you do, keep down.'

She called back with asperity, 'You don't have to teach me how to take care of myself, young man. Where is Clary?'

'Here with me.'

'Look after her.' She called, 'Dr Levi?'

He replied, 'I am here, Miss Bascombe.'

'Can our men handle this?'

'I am certain they can.'

'Very well. See that you keep your head down.'

Sears wished he were as sure. He thought to himself, *'For the time being she doesn't know what a jam we're in.'*

From directly above there came an awful bubbling cry. A shower of small rocks and stones descended in advance of a figure with something white about its head.

Sears swore, and cursed himself for not having taken so much as a pistol, with which to defend himself or the women. This was it. While the two wings were engaged the rest would pour down the sides of the ravine and overrun them. With one hand he picked up a rock. With the other he reached into his pocket for his handkerchief. There might yet be a chance to save them by surrender.

But the expected attack did not develop. Instead a lone figure, barefoot, in a pair of ragged shapeless pants and a vest of some dark material, with a dirty white Arab *khabiyah* on its head, came twisting and tumbling down the side of the ravine, out of control; a grotesque figure that came to rest when a sapling oak some twenty yards up the side of the ravine halted its progress.

There it remained silently for a moment, a young Arab boy lying on his back staring up into the sky, his two hands clutched at his middle. Then he began to cry in range from the whimper of a child to the sobs of a man in mortal agony.

Clary cried, 'How horrible! What is it? What has happened?'

Sears said, 'It's one of theirs. Ben-Isaac must have winged him when he took that snap shot up the side of the ravine. He must have been in a tree or holding on to a rock. When he couldn't hang on any longer he came down.'

There was a moment of silence broken only by the awful crying of the wounded man.

Clary said, 'I can't bear it. It's too dreadful . . .' She raised her head. 'Why, he's hardly more than a boy.'

Sears said savagely 'Keep down!' and pulled her back. 'He asked for it. A boy can kill you as dead with a gun as a man. We're in cross-fire here.'

But he, too, could see how young the wounded boy was – hardly more than sixteen, with brown, oval face, exquisite dark eyes and white even teeth. Sears noted from the blood covering the hands where they clutched at his middle that he had been shot through the stomach and was probably bleeding to death.

The firing continued briskly from both ends of the ravine. A bullet struck the side of the boulder above Joe's head and flattened out. Another smacked into a near-by tree with a woody sound, and they could hear other ricochets buzzing and whining.

The boy's crying had settled into an awful monotone that became more unbearable each moment. One night in the Ardennes Sears had heard one of his own men cry his life away without being able to go to his aid because they were pinned down . . .

He heard Hannah's voice suddenly demanding loudly:

'Is anybody going to go and get that child, or must I?'

He heard the sound from behind him then, and turned around swiftly just in time to see Clary begin to climb and claw her way up the steep side of the ravine to where the wounded Arab lay.

He roared at her, 'Clary! Come back here, you goddam fool! This is a war. You're in the line of fire . . . Clary!'

He went stumbling up the hill after her, hating every step of the way, pulling in his stomach so that the bullet wouldn't hit him where it had the boy, shrinking his neck, enduring all the spasms of funk and anticipation that he had had during his months of combat, raging at the stupidity of the girl and afraid to look for fear that any instant he would see her jerk grotesquely, or stumble, or fall, or pitch, or sink to the ground and lie there with a stain spreading from her clothes or oozing from her head.

He kept saying 'No, no, no!' as he climbed. 'Clary, come back here!' But when he reached her at last and got his hands on her wrist and tried to drag her, she locked her other arm about the tree, crying, 'No, no, Joe. I can't stand it. I won't go back without him. Help me to carry him.'

Joe's training stood him in stead and he kept his wits. What was the difference whether they caught it carrying the kid down or scrambling back to safety without him? The chances were about the same either way now that they were both out in the open. He bent then and got his shoulder and arm under the boy, swivelled, applying the leverage of the dead-man's hoist, and picked him up.

He snarled at Clary, 'Get behind me on the way back and stay there, you nitwit. Come on.' At least she had that much more protection from one side. On the way down he felt the boy shudder and his leg twitch and thought that he must have been hit again, stopping one that might have been ticketed for the girl.

When they reached the protection of the boulder again, Hannah was there, and so was Dr Levi. Joe carefully laid the Arab down there, and was aware even as he did so that the fire seemed to be slackening off and falling away to isolated shots and bursts.

Dr Levi knelt by the Arab's side and loosened his clothes, shielding Hannah with his own body from the awful state of his wound in the belly and the second one that had shattered his knee.

But he could not conceal from her the stricken appealing eyes of the boy, or the dreadful contortions of his young features as spasm after spasm of pain convulsed him and robbed him of nearly every human aspect.

Sears said roughly to Clary, 'Don't look. The kid's cooked. He can't last much longer!'

Hannah said, 'What are you waiting for? Have you no band-ages?'

Dr Levi said, 'No. It's no use. There is no hope. He cannot live.'

The effect of his words on Hannah was even more horrible than Sears could have imagined. She started up, and for a moment the grim line of her mouth and chin had the awful quality of Death itself, while her eyes were lighted by a kind of fanatic fire.

She went up to Dr Levi and thrust her face almost into his and shouted, 'What's that you say – won't live?'

The old man said softly, 'Be quiet. He is dying.'

But Hannah screamed at him, 'No! No! I won't have it! Do you hear me? I didn't come here to find death! You are to stop it, do you hear?' Her tantrum gave the scene a horrible and grotes-que effect. Clary unconsciously moved to Sears's side, and he put his arm about her to quiet her trembling.

Dr Levi stood up and reached for Hannah's hand and held it in his own. He said, 'Look down. See what is happening. Do not be afraid.'

The boy had ceased to cry. His eyes had begun to glaze. He looked once more at them all, pleading. As he did so, Dr Levi spoke to him gently and soothingly, like a father to a child.

The agony went from the Arab's face and mouth. It became smooth and oval again, and even younger and filled with inno-cence. A little smile came to the corners of his lips, and thereafter there was peace.

'You see,' said Dr Levi. 'Death can also come as a friend . . .'

Hannah suddenly took her hand from his and covered her face. She sat down on a stone, turned away from them, but made no sound.

Clary cried softly, 'The poor boy . . .'; but Sears said gruffly, 'He's all right now . . .' and took his arm from about her.

Men were coming through the ravine. Sears saw that it was Ben-Isaac returning with Schlomo's squad, while at the same time Ed Avery's group appeared at the other end.

Sears asked, 'Is it over? Have you stopped them?'

Ben-Isaac said, 'For the moment. They've broken off. But we don't know what they're up to. It isn't finished yet.' He gave hardly a glance at the dead Arab.

Chapter 25

'For, lo, the wicked bend their bow, they make
ready their arrow upon the string' – *Psalms* xi, 2

A BATTLE finished brings a healing sense of relief, but a lull in
fighting contains all the cruelty of suspense and tension without
action to sustain it.

The two leaders, Ed Avery and Schlomo, were plainly worried,
and even the battle-lusting Ben-Isaac was uneasy.

Ed said, 'We gave them a bloody nose, but not enough for them
to withdraw. We don't know what's in the wind.'

Sears asked, 'Who are they? What are they after?'

Schlomo replied, 'Bandits. They want weapons and they don't
want any survivors. It's a mixed band of raiders.' He indicated the
corpse with his head. 'The boy is a town Arab.'

Sears's nerves were jumping badly. He asked:

'What's next? Do they come again?'

The Palmach men were engaged in carrying rocks and extend-
ing the wall of the shelter afforded by the large boulder so as to
yield more protection for the women. Ben-Isaac was looking the
ground over with the practised eye of the veteran and marking
out positions.

Ed Avery replied, 'Probably, yes.'

'The same way?'

The American shook his head. 'No. If something doesn't work
the first time they try something else. If we could hurt them badly
enough they'd get discouraged and quit.'

Joe Sears let out a yell. 'Look out!' He was too far from Clary
to reach her, but he was able to seize Hannah and throw himself
flat on the ground, half on top of her, just as a shattering roar
filled the ravine and a black geyser of dirt, smoke and flying rock
erupted from the near side, some thirty yards from their position.

Simultaneously two of the Palmach men cried out. One of them was down on one knee, the other had dropped his carbine and was clutching his neck with a dazed expression on his face.

Sears shouted, 'Mortar! They've got a mortar!' Out of the corner of his eye he had seen the black body of the low-velocity shell tumbling into the ravine, a moment before it exploded. He was too frightened to swear. He knew they were all only a few minutes away from being killed. Rifle and Sten-gun fire broke out again; this time from both sides of the rim of the ravine above them. Somewhere the raiding band had stolen a mortar and supply of shells. They had only to keep the trapped party herded together with machine-gun and rifle fire until the high explosive wiped them out.

Avery and Schlomo shouted 'Cover!' and deployed their men against the sides of the ravine. When Sears looked about for Clary he saw that she was outside the barricade by the two Palmach men who had been injured. One of them had been struck in the knee-cap by a fragment of rock, the other had a crease in his neck from a shell splinter.

It was pointless to shout at her or bring her back when the death of all of them was only a matter of moments.

The second shell exploded on the other side of the ravine and higher up, where it did no damage except to the nerves of the defenders. They had placed one short and one over. The next would be closer. When they found the exact range it would be all over.

He went out and helped Clary bring in the two men to the quasi-shelter of their makeshift fort.

He saw now that Clary was pale and dazed and her limbs were trembling even while she helped to support the limping boy. Realization of the deadly nature of the battle had come home to her for the first time. Sears had seen young and green troops grow sick under the same realization and funk it. But she was sticking it and looking after the wounded.

Sears thought to himself, 'Who would have thought it. Little Miss Hothouse Orchid!', and then felt a stab of pity that she was to be destroyed before he could ever tell her what he felt.

Hannah was sitting up, her back against the boulder, with a bewildered look on her face, and even Dr Levi was shaken by the shell fire. He staunched the bleeding from the boy's neck and bandaged him even as the third shell hit directly in the middle and at the bottom of the ravine, but up to the left. They were bracketed now.

Dr Levi said, 'This is bad, is it not?'

Sears nodded. What was the use of kidding anyone? 'We've got about three or four, at the most five minutes to live.'

The expression on Hannah's face was dazed. She said, 'I don't want to die. They will take all my money.'

Ben-Isaac suddenly appeared close to Sears on the outside of the barricade. He carried a Sten gun with two extra clips and had a dozen hand-grenades hung about his person. He said to Sears:

'Have you got any kind of fix on their position?'

Sears had made a calculation instinctively. He said, 'About in line with the two pines just to the left of that "V" in the top of the hill.'

Ben-Isaac nodded. 'That's about where I have it figured.'

'What are you going to do?'

'Get it!'

'You'll be killed.'

Ben-Isaac did not even reply. Sears heard Dr Levi say to Hannah, 'Give me your Bible . . .'

Ben-Isaac called to Ed Avery, 'Cover me!'

Schlomo yelled, 'Don't be a goddam fool, Ben. It's suicide. We'll go up with you.'

Ben-Isaac said, 'I know what I'm doing. Come up when I call for you.' With a swift gliding motion he went down on to his belly and began to crawl up the side of the hill.

Clary cried, 'Joe. Where is he going?'

Sears said, 'The damned fool is going up after that mortar.'

'He'll be killed.'

'Yes,' said Sears.

Behind him Dr Levi spoke:

"The Lord is my shepherd; I shall not want. He maketh me to lie down in green pastures: He leadeth me beside the still waters."

Sears turned to look. The old man was sitting next to Hannah, his back to the boulder, Hannah's pocket Bible opened to the Psalms, and he was reading.

His voice was drowned for an instant by the banging of small-arms fire as the attackers on the ravine's rim concentrated their fire on the figure of Ben-Isaac and as the Palmach men below pumped bullets to cover his approach and unsteady the enemy's aim.

Ben-Isaac was like a great cat as he stalked, climbing, oozing, insinuating himself, lifting himself higher and higher. Twigs fell, wood chips leaped, dust spurted all about him as the probing fire of the Arabs marked his course.

"He restoreth my soul: He leadeth me in the paths of righteousness for His name's sake."

A bullet smacked sharply into the boulder behind them and scattered chips and rock dust. Sears turned around to see Dr Levi calmly hold the book up to his face and with one breath blow the debris from the book.

By his side Clary screamed. Ben-Isaac's smooth, rhythmic, upward progress had been stopped halfway to the top. Then he began to slip and slide backwards.

Involuntarily Sears cried, 'Oh Christ! He's been hit!'

Clary leaped to her feet and would have run out had not Sears caught her and held her. She cried, 'Ben-Isaac, Ben-Isaac!'; and Sears was sick for her loss, and his as well. She commenced to sob hysterically.

Hannah cried sharply, 'Be still, Clary, and listen to what he is saying!' She was again in possession of herself.

Dr Levi had cleared his page. He read: "Yea, though I walk through the valley of the shadow of death, I will fear no evil; for thou art with me; Thy rod and Thy staff they comfort me."

High up on the side of the ravine, Ben-Isaac had begun to move again, forwards and upwards.

Sears shook Clary by the arm and shouted, 'Pull yourself together! He's all right. It was only a slip. He may make it yet.'

For now the boy was so close to the edge of the ravine that the men atop it could no longer see him, and Ed Avery and Schlomo had taken their boys over to the same side and poured such fire into the bandits on the opposite brow that Ben-Isaac had his chance.

They watched him stand up just below the 'V' notch atop the

ravine, take a hand-grenade from his breast hook, pull the pin with his teeth and lob it up over the top. Then with the flat explosion of the bomb he scrambled up on the rim of the gorge, his back to them, straddle-legged, and in rapid succession plucked, armed and flung five hand-grenades. They could see his right arm rising and falling, hear the crashing concussion of the fragmentation charges followed by the clatter of his Sten gun as he stood now slightly crouched and sprayed bullets. A moment later he turned and was waving. But Avery and Schlomo and the Palmach men were already charging up the opposite slope to finish the job. The firing from above ceased abruptly. It was all over.

The sudden silence that followed was almost more shocking than the awful detonation of the mortar shells and the riot of battle. Dr Levi finished the reading of the twenty-third Psalm:

"Surely goodness and mercy shall follow me all the days of my life: and I will dwell in the house of the Lord for ever."

Ben-Isaac came slipping and sliding down the side of the gorge looking like a young god of war, his accoutrement jingling and rattling.

Then he saw Clary's tear-stained face and cried, 'Clary! Are you all right? Is everybody all right?' He went to Clary and patted her shoulder. She clung to him, sobbing on his breast in relief from tension, and Sears saw how white her knuckles were from holding to him. Ben-Isaac soothed her gently for a moment, then said:

'Hush. There is nothing to be afraid of any more.' His eyes, however, were roving and still full of battle fever – he was looking for his comrades, for the possible dead and wounded . . .

Sears sat down and groped for a cigarette. A very pretty story-book ending, he thought to himself. The kid had got the girl, and why not? What woman could resist such a performance? She had probably always been in love with him. Her cry had betrayed her when she thought that Ben-Isaac was hit. Well, that was how things went. They belonged together. She had come a long way from the days in San Francisco, this girl who, when the chips were down, thought not of herself but only of others.

Ben-Isaac went to his uncle, put his arm around him and gently touched his cheek with his fingers, as though to make certain he was unhurt. He said, 'It was a good show. Did I not do well, Uncle Nathaniel? My British major taught me that.'

Dr Levi placed a hand fondly on his nephew's shoulder, but his voice was heavy with sadness as he replied, 'Yes, Ben-Isaac. You did well. You are a brave fighter. And I am a vain fool and a miserable sinner. I should have remained at home looking after my vegetables as I was bade. Because of me a boy is dead.'

Ben-Isaac said quickly, 'He was one of theirs.'

'No,' said Dr Levi, 'He was one of His.' After a moment he continued, 'That boy will be forever on my conscience. I am punished. I will atone . . .'

Ben-Isaac looked at his uncle sharply. 'It was I who shot him. What about *my* conscience?'

Dr Levi replied, 'I take your sin upon myself.'

Tears came into Ben-Isaac's eyes. An emptiness assailed him. The battle fever had abated and the glory had somehow vanished. He went some little distance away, sat down on a rock, his head bowed.

Sears went over to him. 'Come on, kid, get your chin up. That was the bravest thing I ever saw. You're a fighter. You've got all the guts in the world for my money. I take off my hat to you.'

Ben-Isaac looked up, his face bleak. 'Oh, leave me alone, Joe. My uncle is right. It is a sin to kill . . .'

Sears went back to the others. Clary came over to him. She said, 'Thank you, Joe, for trying to protect me.' She held out her hand.

Sears looked at her but did not take it. 'Don't thank me. I dogged it and let the others do the fighting. If it hadn't been for Ben-Isaac we'd all be dead. He's got all the courage in the world . . .'

She stared at him for a moment and said curtly, 'You have courage enough for me, Joe.' Then she turned away.

Sears gazed after her uncomprehending. He was brought back by the sound of the entrenching tools as the Palmach men prepared to bury the dead Arab. Hannah was looking to the injury of the boy who had been struck in the knee. She had recovered herself and was being grimly efficient, yet at the same time very gentle.

Sears suddenly remembered how she had looked listening to Dr Levi and the moment when she had calmed Clary. And it struck him that when things had appeared darkest and the end seemed at hand Hannah had no longer appeared to be afraid to die either. He suddenly felt himself very lonely, very old and tired, and utterly drained.

Chapter 26

'He that is greedy of gain, troubleth his own
house' – *Proverbs* xv, 27

THE third day after their arrival at Beit Jebel, the Village of the
Patriarchs clinging to the side of a rocky defile halfway up the
western slope of Mount Hermon, Clary sought out Sears in his
quarters at the edge of the village.

She said, 'Miss Bascombe is asking for you. She wishes to see
you at once.' Then she added, 'Where is Dr Levi?'

Sears replied, 'He and Ben-Isaac have gone to explore the
caves.'

Clary nodded reflectively and said, 'Hannah didn't seem to
want him to know that she had asked you to come to her.'

Curiosity mingled with elation in Sears. Dr Levi up to now had
apparently been unsuccessful in persuading the elders of the tribe
inhabiting the village to part with the mysterious substance to
which they attributed the longevity of those who were permitted
to partake of it. He said.

'I was wondering how long her patience would hold out.'

Clary was still introspective. She said, 'Things aren't going
well.'

'What's wrong?'

'She's tense and moody. She won't go out. She sits inside that
awful bare room all day, just staring ahead of her with the terrible expression about her mouth she used to get in San Francisco
when she wanted something that someone else had and meant to
have it. And her hands frighten me. They knot up so that sometimes she can barely get them open.'

Sears said, 'Hannah was never very relaxed. She lives on tension. That's what's been holding her together.'

Clary replied, 'Yet there was a time, a week ago, when she
seemed almost happy. She was like a different person.'

Sears said nothing. The 'different person' had been bad for

him. The avid Hannah that Clary had just described to him was the one that he could handle. If Hannah was sending for him it meant that she no longer fully trusted Dr Levi, and that was just fine for Mr Joseph Deuell Sears.

As he prepared to take the path to the cluster of white stone houses built into the cliffside where Hannah and Clary had their quarters, the girl said:

'Help her, Joe . . .'

Something in her tone and its unusual emotional content made him turn and regard her for a moment. She was looking at him with a kind of intense appeal that both mystified and surprised him.

He said, 'You bet. Leave it to me. I guess she realizes now that in the end it is going to have to be Sears who gets her what she wants.'

Clary watched him go with a kind of heavy sadness that verged on despair. He had not understood her at all. He was insensitive, self-centred, and apparently utterly unconscious of his hardness and amorality. Never once had she been able to penetrate his cynicism and self-satisfaction. She tried to comfort herself with the thought that Sears could not help but be as he was. Nevertheless, as always when she had to do with him, she felt let-down and unhappy.

Sears found Hannah standing in front of her dwelling gazing with impatient intensity at the white houses of the village proper, set off against their background of the dark mouths of the ancient caves behind them. She turned upon Sears almost savagely. 'Where is Dr Levi?'

Sears told her.

'Why is he not attending to my business? We have been forced to remain here three days now.'

Sears said, 'Dr Levi has explained that these people are primitive and cannot be rushed.'

'Are they aware of what I want?'

'I believe so.'

'Is it your opinion that Dr Levi has used his best efforts to secure it?'

Sears thought quickly. He did not know how far Hannah's sudden distrust of Dr Levi had progressed. He did not want to overplay this new hand that was being dealt him. He replied, 'I do not know. He has not confided in me.'

'Is this where you meant to bring me when you first came to see me in San Francisco? Is it here that the waters of the Flood failed to reach and the food of the original patriarchs was preserved?'

Sears replied smoothly, 'Theoretically. However, we have come here on Dr Levi's responsibility.'

She looked at him searchingly. 'There are some here who are very old. Very very old. Have you noticed?'

'Yes.'

'Tell me again. What is the substance called?'

'Dr Levi said the name, translated, means "Fruit of the Tree of Life".'

'What is it? Where does it grow? What is it like?'

Sears said, 'I do not know. I don't think anyone does but that tall fellow who seems to be sort of elder, or head of the tribe, and the other, the clever-looking one, the priest.'

'What did Dr Levi tell you about it?'

Sears thought to himself, '*She has got the wind up over old Levi.*' Aloud he said, 'He told us that, whatever it is, there is only a small quantity of it available. Due to climatic circumstances, or conditions that are not clear, the crop takes two or three years to mature. There is then only sufficient for one person. The elders of the village meet and decide who is the most worthy amongst them to have his span of years extended and to become a patriarch. And it is never revealed to whom it is given.'

Hannah said, 'Yes. That is what he told me,' and added fiercely, 'I believe it!' She came over to Sears, looked up into his face with hard and commanding shrewdness and said, 'There is some in the village now. I know it. Get it for me.'

He was startled. He had not expected this. He protested, 'Dr Levi . . .', but she brushed him aside.

'Dr Levi is studying prehistoric caves. I authorize you to act as my agent in this. Go and negotiate with them. I want it. I want it immediately and without further delay.'

Sears nodded. 'I will try. You understand, however, that it will be difficult. I do not speak their language. They may not even understand me . . .'

Hannah snorted in scorn. 'There is a language that is universal . . . money. They know what I want, and why I am here. Find out their price and buy it. Pay anything they ask for it. Is that clear?'

'Yes.' He turned to go.

'One thing more! Dr Levi does not need to know of this. If you succeed you will not regret it.'

The village of Beit Jebel was a small cluster of white stone houses that clung to a mound-like outcropping on the sheer face of a cleft in the mountain side. Behind it and on a higher level, entering the side of Hermon itself, were the dark openings of a number of caves.

The population of the village was no more than three hundred souls all told, men, women and children. Many of the men had the appearance of great age. The community appeared to be without contact with the outside world; neither telephone nor telegraph line entered it. Self-sufficient and self-supporting, it had none of the filth and squalor of the Arab villages Sears had encountered in Israel.

To reach there they had climbed steadily, emerging from the foothills on to the western slope of the mountain close to the snowline. Here they suddenly came upon an escarpment, at the base of which there was a narrow entrance that appeared to be no more than an opening made by erosion in the face of the cliff. But when Dr Levi took them through it they found that it was actually a corridor that turned into a narrow gorge, an old volcanic split in the solid granite of the cliff.

It led them then through a small green valley with evidences of agriculture and then climbed sharply to the hanging village and its dark, mysterious caves. There they had been received courteously and hospitably by the inhabitants, who proved to be a sweet and gentle people presided over by the tall, stately elder who went by the name of Barzillai and a kind of patriarchal priest called Amalkeh.

The villagers were not Mohammedans but a mixture of races: Arabs, Itureans, and descendants of the Nabateans. According to

Dr Levi, they were monotheistic and worshipped God almost after the simple and uncomplicated manner of the early Essenes. Their culture was primitive and recent. Indeed, as late as A.D. 41 Agrippa had visited that neighbourhood, then known as the Hauran, and had issued an edict to the inhabitants to cease living in caves like beasts and to emerge therefrom and build themselves houses.

It seemed still to be true that Nature had imprisoned Time in this cleft she had created by splitting the mountainside.

For the dominating feature of the village was the caves penetrating the lower west cone of the sacred mountain, the snow-cap of which could be seen looking along the split. They had been there since the dawn of man's birth, and exerted a powerful influence upon all of them, but in particular upon Sears. Who could say what secrets they concealed, what arts and rites had been practised there? It was unquestionably in caves that the first patriarchs, the ancestors of Abraham, Jacob and Isaac, dwelt. One tended to forget, reading the rolling verse of Genesis, that the characters one encountered were men of the Old Stone Age, and that when Cain slew Abel it was with a knife of flint. For the first time Sears had begun to wonder whether he had not, by colossal accident, blundered upon truth.

Freedom from all belief in the supernatural is the mark of the highly trained, cultured and educated mind, or one that is bolstered by a simple faith. Joe Sears had neither.

He was smart, brash and cynical, awake to the general facts of life, but he had no depth or solid foundation for his convictions. He was the type who denied marvels but inwardly did not wholly discount them. He knocked wood, refused walking under ladders, and avoided three on a match, as safety measures commonly recognized. He would not have been afraid to spend a night in a haunted house, but he was not prepared to swear that a house could not be haunted.

The Bible to him was a book of mysteries which modern science had made astonishing progress in substantiating and even in some cases explaining, like the miracles of Moses striking the rock and bringing forth water, which had been duplicated in modern times in that same country and proved to be a natural phenomenon of porous rock saturated with water retained behind a thin, hard surface of weathered limestone.

Sears's mind accepted the scientific explanations, but the possibility of marvels remained. Here in this ancient spot where Dr Levi had brought them they even acquired the aspect of the probable.

It was curious that up to the moment of starting off to carry out Hannah's orders Sears had actually never really considered the nature of the substance they had come to find, or its validity, even though he knew that Dr Levi had been closeted a number of times with Barzillai since their arrival on the same quest. He could not overcome his suspicions that Dr Levi was up to some game, and that in the end the whole affair would turn out to be nothing but an extension of his own hoax.

His summons by Hannah and her dispatching him to negotiate for the material had caused a sudden and violent shift in his beliefs and attitude towards the affair. Sears had been out purely to win the sinecure of continuing expenses. Now he suddenly saw himself reaching for the jackpot.

It was the fabulous wealth that might be his, indicated by Hannah's faith and belief in the fruit of the Tree of Life, that dizzied his brain and addled his mind, rattled and unsettled him and filled him with a kind of raging lust to succeed where Dr Levi had failed.

Chapter 27

'To another divers kinds of tongues: to another
the interpretation of tongues' – *I Corinthians*
xii, 10

CLIMBING the path that led to the house of the elders,
Sears passed the doorway of a tanner. He had almost gone by
when something that he had seen, or thought he had seen,
impressed itself on his brain and he paused and went back to
look.

The tanner was an old man. He was so old that there was no
possible way of judging his age, for he was bald and wrinkled and
shrunken, toothless and monkey-faced but for his eyes, which
were as clear and alive as those of a man of middle age.

Like all those in the East, his shop was open to the street; really
no more than a stone stall, in the middle of which he squatted and
scraped the inner surface of a goatskin hide to clear the shreds of
flesh still clinging to it. He was clad, like all others in the village,
in shapeless trousers and a woollen overgarment fastened at the
waist. His arms and legs were wasted, but his movements showed
no diminution of strength. He might have been ninety, or a hundred, or more.

What had caught Joe's eye, however, and startled him into
stopping was the implement he was using.

Sears squatted down beside him. The old man stopped work
and observed him with his keen and youthful eyes. Sears smiled,
pointed to the object in the tanner's hand and held out his own.
With complete trust and quick understanding, the tanner handed
him the object. It was a flint scraper of dark, polished stone, with
greyish surfaces where the chips had been pressured away to form
the cutting edge.

He remembered something then that Dr Levi had told him during the march as they had approached the village. He had said,
'You will see something very interesting there – a living people in

166

modern *times* making use of flint implements such as were employed in prehistoric ages.'

Sears reached into his pocket for his big two-bladed utility knife, opened the larger blade and showed it to the tanner. The little man nodded and smiled. But now he shook his head in a kind of bright and superior negation, and taking the knife from Sears's hand he applied it to the surface of the skin in the same manner that he had the scraper. Then he showed the result to Sears. Where the knife had been used there were a number of tiny cuts on the tender skin, minute openings, which, however, would spread with the drying. Then he handed the knife back and resumed with his flint tool, which left the surface clean and unharmed. A moment later he took up his stone awl, bored a perfect hole in the hide, ran a leather thong through it, hung it up, and took another.

Sears felt queerly shaken as he arose and stood there for a moment looking down on the man squatting on his heels, scraping away at his hide. His mind went back to the group he remembered having seen in the Museum of Anthropology in Los Angeles, the caveman squatting on his heels by the fire at the mouth of the cave, wielding his stone knife. Take the clothes off the old man, and by God . . .

How old could he be? Ninety? A hundred? A thousand? Ten thousand? Crazy, screwy, cock-eyed, but how could you tell whether he was not one of those selected to be given the fruit of the Tree of Life? They never revealed who had been given it to eat.

He shook himself back into something approaching sanity. The old fellow was probably between ninety and a hundred. In those countries and that climate men who lived to be over a hundred and worked up to the day they died were not exceptional. So a pocket-knife wasn't the proper implement for scraping. A properly shaped steel scraper would have done as well, only he didn't happen to have one.

Yet as he continued on up to the council-house in the midst of the cluster of houses farther up he knew that he hadn't talked himself out of what had come to the back of his mind.

These people were conversant with very ancient times, dating back to the dawn of man. If they still used implements from that period, preferring them to modern tools, might not other things have survived and come down to them as well? Things such as, for instance, the knowledge of how to live to the age of the first recorded dates and times of their ancestors who came out of Ur and Mesopotamia bearing with them the seeds of the Tree of Life Eternal . . .?

Sears arrived at the centre of the village, where the path broadened to the width of a narrow street, and walked to the square building he knew was used for the meeting of the elders. There were voices from within, but the door and single window were covered with a thick hanging.

Sears felt irritated at his own helplessness, for he did not know what he should do – shout, go in, remove his shoes – for he was afraid of jeopardizing what he had come for by breaking some local taboo or offending his hosts. At the time of their entry into the village Dr Levi had told him, 'Whatever you do, treat them with kindness. They are a proud and dignified people. At all times behave towards them with politeness.' But he had not told Sears how, or what might be considered a discourtesy.

Yet his appearance had been observed, for the hanging before the door was drawn aside and Barzillai appeared. He was taller than Sears, and the fact that he wore his hair long, swept back from his fine features and down to his shoulders, made him look even more imposing. The hair was still dark but streaked with grey, and there were lines about the splendid eyes, but the muscles and skin of the lean, handsome face were still firm and charged with tone and vitality. Sears judged him to be a man of perhaps sixty, but no more than sixty-five.

The American decided that manners were manners. He raised his hand in salute and then extended it. Barzillai shook it gravely and with a friendly expression. Encouraged, Sears pantomimed that he was asking permission to go inside. At once Barzillai inclined his head, drew the hanging aside, motioned Sears to enter, and then followed him across the threshold.

The council-chamber was hung with rugs and woven cloth, but was otherwise bare of furniture except for a small, low table.

Besides Amalkeh there were five others sitting cross-legged on the floor or squatting on their heels. Some of them were very old – older even than the tanner had seemed to be. But in every case there was a fabulous clarity and vitality in their dark eyes, as though, in spite of wrinkled flesh and wasted limbs, sunken cheeks, white hair, or mere wispy tufts – all the usual evidences of great age verging on senility – the inner fires burned on undimmed and with youthful vigour.

They all rose solemnly upon his entrance and bowed. Sears bowed and smiled in return and shook hands with each. They then motioned him to sit, Amalkeh clapped his hands, and a young boy appeared with a tray of bitter coffee served in small silver and enamelled cups of curious design in which a cross was woven. Sears had a feeling that they dated from Crusader times.

The coffee handed around, they sat and sipped it in a kind of friendly and affable silence that Sears found pleasant. It gave him time to collect his wits and reflect upon his idea, for he had thought of a means of overcoming the barrier of language and communicating his thoughts and wishes to these men.

He now drew a packet of American cigarettes from his pocket and offered them around. Each took one, lit it, and, holding it oddly between thumb and forefinger, smoked with obvious pleasure. Sears decided the time had come to experiment.

He had brought pencil and note-pad with him. These he now produced while seven pairs of burning, interested eyes watched him in silence. Sears was anxious to know whether they would be able to comprehend figures. He knew that the Western numeral system was Arabic and had been originally devised by them, but he could not be certain until he tried.

Therefore he pointed to himself, wrote the figure '36' on the pad and handed it to Barzillai, who showed it to Amalkeh. They both then nodded and smiled.

He then pointed directly at Barzillai with a questioning expression and handed him the pad and pencil. The tall native accepted it without hesitation, took the pencil and wrote in clearly interpretable figures the number '239' and handed it back.

At first all that Sears felt was a shock of disappointment. It was obvious they had not understood him, or figures had a different meaning to them than they had to him, for the number Barzillai had written made no sense.

The second shock rattled him to his core. He had remembered where he was. *What if it did make sense?* What if Barzillai had understood that Sears had given his own age and asked him his? *What if that was the answer?*

How test? He pointed quickly to the boy who had refilled the coffee-cups and was handing them around again. Barzillai nodded and smiled, took the pad again and wrote '14'.

Sears felt cold chills running down his spine.

But Barzillai was not yet through. He indicated Amalkeh, whose hair was snow-white and his skin drawn tightly over the bones of his face, and wrote '300'. Next he turned to the elder on the other side of him, the one who looked the oldest, and, with a twinkle in his eye, set down the shocking figure '410'. Then, with the gesture understood in any language in any part of the world, he reached over and gave the patriarch several affectionate pats on the back that said plainer than any words:

'This is Grandpop here. He's got it on all of us.'

Sears felt his head swimming, but it was the overwhelming calculations that crowded through his brain that were making it swim and no longer the shock of the revelation. He had not the slightest doubt but that Barzillai was speaking the truth. What was now bringing the sweat to his forehead and the blood to his eyes so that he could no longer clearly see, while his palms were clammily cold, was the lightning arithmetic he had been doing in his head on the basis of his agreement with Hannah. Whatever it was these ancients had discovered, or managed to retain out of the past, if he could get it for Hannah and she consumed it, when Hannah was ninety he would be hardly a year more than fifty, and already he would be a millionaire many times over . . .

He passed the cigarettes around again and lit another himself to quiet his nerves. Then he took the pad and pencil again, tore off the used sheet, which he stuffed into his pocket, and began to draw, having always had a knack of making swift, recognizable cartoon sketches.

So, in the manner of the strip artist with his panels, Sears tried to tell his story in a series of easily recognizable pictures.

There was a tree with a heart beating in its centre, fruit hanging from a branch surrounded by a halo, with Barzillai unmistakably standing nearby and Hannah with her hands outstretched towards it in supplication, which told of Hannah's desire for the fruit of the Tree of Life.

To show Hannah's wealth and importance he drew her seated on a cloud above the outline of the U.S., on which he sketched in ships, railways, factories, farms, mines, ranches, forests, all united by thin lines like reins leading to Hannah's hands, while from her head he sent the classic zig-zag radio waves to indicate that her brain ruled this vast empire of possessions.

The next panel revealed a drawing of himself with Hannah standing behind him, her right hand on his shoulder in the unmistakable age-old attitude of trust and representation. It could not have been said more plainly. 'This man is my agent and trusted friend.' Then he drew an anxious Hannah sitting in the stone hut by the window, waiting, tormented by doubt and desire. So that there should be no mistake about the torment part of it, he added several little imps and pitchforks stabbing at her head. He was fancying himself now.

He could tell he was hot and on the right track from the animation with which his drawings were passed from hand to hand and the discussion they aroused.

He felt now like a good pitchman who has his audience warmed, as though he ought to be pushing a hat back from his forehead, rolling up his sleeves and spieling, 'Now that we're all friends and understand one another, I'm gonna tell ya what I'm gonna do . . .'

He controlled himself, but nevertheless fixed Barzillai with a keen and calculating stare as he started on his last drawing. He caught the chief elder's attention immediately, for it was a flattering cartoon of Barzillai holding the fruit of the Tree of Life in his right hand. Opposite him he now materialized Hannah. In her right hand she had a large money-sack with a $ sign on it.

'Get it?' Joe Sears said, and suddenly realized that these were the first words spoken since he had come there, that everything else had been dumb show.

They were all watching him. He had the cartoon spread out on the ground before him now where they could all see it. With deliberate slow-motion he took the pencil and into the blank space on the side of the money-sack wrote '$50,000'.

Why be a sucker? Maybe that was a lot of jack to them. He knew his Hannah. The cheaper she got it, the more grateful she would be inclined to be to him. She might even give him a retainer through the five-year waiting period while she determined whether the stuff worked or not. When the sky was the limit, the smart thing was to start low.

Too low, he guessed, for there was no reaction. They stared down at the cartoon, and one or two of them exchanged looks, but no one said anything. But he still had his audience. With the same deliberation he erased the $50,000 and pencilled in $100,000.

'Double,' he said, just as though they could understand him. The stares became blanker now and the silence heavier.

'Tough, eh?' he said. 'Okay, then. Double again.'

He could not seem to break through and was conscious of the beginning of an irritation. He said, 'All right, all right. I was only asking. How about this?' He inserted '$500,000'. What kind of guys were these? If they'd only blink, or turn away, or shake their heads, or say, 'Go to hell! Quit kidding around and show us some real dough!'

Well, he knew it was going to come high, and Hannah probably did too. He had rubbed the paper in the centre of the money-bag raw, and, besides, he needed space for the big numbers. He looked into Barzillai's face and said, 'Okay, then, we cut out the clowning and get down to business. You tell me when to stop. This little lady's got all the coconuts in the world!', and he marked up the million underneath the sack.

This time it seemed to him that he saw the first faint glimmer of a smile return to the face of Barzillai, for he caught him exchanging a glance with Amalkeh. He let the million soak and then changed the 1 to a 2, and lectured with it. 'That's a fair trade, isn't it? She gets the stuff and you get two million boffos on the line.'

They had begun to talk to one another in their own language, but Sears could detect no signs of acquiescence.

The thought of what was at stake for him in this came up and hit him again and jangled his nerves. He was beginning to grow angry. What the hell! It wasn't his, it was Hannah's dough. He wrote in the five million.

Now a strange thing happened, for Barzillai gave Sears an extraordinarily sweet and understanding smile, placed his lean brown hand over the American's, the one that held the pencil as though he would keep him from writing more, and slowly shook his head in negation.

Sears pushed his hand away and snarled, 'Never mind that. I'm operating this bankroll. All I want out of you guys is to say "when".'

But at the ten-million mark his nerves broke. First the long silences of pantomime with all the words pent up inside him, then the speeches delivered into the void with no reply but the echo of his own words. He sprang to his feet and shouted at them, his mouth twisting all crooked, bitter and out of control:

'What's the matter with you jerks? Don't you understand money? Don't you know what ten million dollars is? What do you want, twenty? Twenty-five? Fifty? She's got it. She'll pay it. Cash on the line. What are you looking at me that way for? You know what money is! You're rich from then on, everyone in this crummy village. We'll buy Otto the tanner down there a brand-new platinum scraper mounted with diamonds so he can throw his flint away, and a fish-tailed Caddy to ride to work in. Don't you birds want enamelled refrigerators, vacuum cleaners and TV sets? Own your own homes, join the country club and get the missus a Paris wardrobe? Travel and see the world? Goddam you fatheaded saps, this is money I'm offering – fresh, red hot, off-the-press spendable money ... Can ya hear me?'

He was unaware that he was bawling at them at the top of his lungs or that the tears of frustration were running down his face.

He stopped suddenly and realized that the saliva was dripping from one corner of his mouth, and he fished out his handkerchief and wiped it. Then he saw that they were all standing and that Barzillai was taking him by the arm, and he knew that the game was up. Well, good old Joe Sears. Just so far and no farther. When the jackpot's within reach and ready to pluck, that's when he gums it up.

He managed a half-smile at Barzillai and said, 'Okay, boss, I know when I'm licked. You needn't get rough, I'll go quietly.'

He let Barzillai lead him outside the building. But when he looked into his face he was surprised to see that the elder did not appear to be angry. On the contrary, on his face had appeared an expression of extraordinary compassion and kindness.

He took Sears's hand and shook it, and then, even as he had done to the oldster on the council, he patted Sears several times on the shoulder, turned him in the direction of his quarters, and gave him a little friendly push in that direction.

Sears said to himself, 'Boy, Sears, you're something. Even that big monkey knows you're a flop and feels sorry for you. What do I tell Hannah now?'

He moved off down the path, stumbling occasionally, as befitted a man who knew that he has just cost himself some several tens of millions of dollars and a lifetime of security.

Chapter 28

'Thanks be unto God for his unspeakable gift' –
II Corinthians ix, 15

It was shortly after midnight that evening that the messenger from the council of elders came to the quarters of the three men. Ben-Isaac was asleep. Dr Levi was examining and classifying with the true collector's gusto a number of artifacts and flint implements he had picked up in the caves. Sears was reading, though his eyes only were on the page and he could not distract his mind from the failure of the afternoon. The scientist turned to Sears and said:

'Something has happened. There has been a council meeting and an important decision has been reached. The council of elders has asked that Miss Bascombe and all of us come at once to the council-house.'

Sears looked up startled and said, 'The hell you say!'

'Will you go and summon Miss Bascombe? There is a light still burning in her quarters.'

Sears asked, 'What is it? Are they going to come through? Have they decided?'

Dr Levi said, 'I do not know.' He gave Sears a long and searching look. 'I understand that you have interfered by visiting the council this afternoon. I do not know what transpired there or in what it may have resulted. That will be your responsibility. This summons may well be an invitation to leave the village. At any rate, we cannot ignore it.'

Sears put on a jacket and cap, for it was cold at that altitude, and went out. He climbed to the entrance of Hannah's quarters and called, 'Miss Bascombe!'

'Yes. Who is it?'

'Joe Sears. Are you still up and dressed?'

'Yes. Why?'

'Barzillai and the council of elders have sent for all of us. They wish us to come up to the council-house at once.'

Even through the thick hangings he could hear her gasp of eagerness. 'I will come immediately.'

For a moment Sears wondered whether he should tell her what Dr Levi feared, that they might well be about to be expelled from the village, and confess to her his share in the debacle to spare her the shock of disappointment. But he had a rule by which he was guided for good or for evil. It was simply, 'Play out the string.' What difference did it make really whether Hannah found out a few minutes sooner or later? And, anyway, how did anyone know what might yet happen? Things had looked bad for him before and he'd pulled through somehow . . .

Hannah appeared, accompanied by Clary. She had donned her mountain shoes and a heavy, woollen, parka-like garment with a hood, as protection against the chill air. Simultaneously, Dr Levi, Ben-Isaac and the messenger came up the path from below, the former carrying a small torch which was hardly needed for the brilliance of the stars and the crescent of the week-old moon. The narrow street and the white houses clinging to the cliffside were bathed in night-light, reflected from the snow-cone of Hermon, towering above them. Even in the dark, yawning mouths of the caves could be seen.

They came to the square stone council-house, where the messenger pulled back the hanging at the door and they entered.

Sears saw at once that it was the same gathering that he had attended with such barren results that afternoon; the seven arose at once upon their entrance. Barzillai then made a speech that was addressed to Hannah and which caused her to ask Dr Levi sharply:

'What is it? What is he saying? What is about to happen? Tell me at once.'

Sears asked Ben-Isaac, 'Can you understand anything of what they are saying?'

'No. But you may have spoiled everything.'

Only when Barzillai had finished did Dr Levi reply to Hannah's questions, saying, 'They extend you peace and greetings and say that they are honoured that you have come to their council.' Then he added, 'I will thank them. Whatever happens, Miss Bascombe, I beg of you to be patient . . .'

Clary placed her hand on Sears' arm. 'I'm frightened,' she said. 'What, that they won't give it to her?'

'No,' she replied with a little shudder – 'that they will.'

There followed the ceremonial handshaking and then the inevitable slow, silent sipping of coffee; a time that seemed interminable to Hannah and nerve-racking to Sears. He tried to make something of the greeting but found that it gave no clue. It was an oriental politeness and nothing more, and could quite well presage the news that their departure had been decreed.

To calm himself, Sears studied the faces of Amalkeh and Barzillai once more to try to solve the secret of their agelessness. Even in the dim, smoky light of the red-clay open dish-lamps with cotton wick floating in oil – lamps of a kind that were old when Joseph was yet young – he could see that it was not so much that they were not aged, but that the processes of ageing seemed to have been contained and somehow halted, as though something else had been overlaid. It was almost the effect, enhanced by the flickering yellow light, of looking through a thin covering of ice, or translucence, and seeing the contours of the skin and bones of faces just below the surface forever preserved.

Barzillai now arose and stood there silent for a moment, seeming to fill the entire chamber with the force and mystery of his presence and his noble height. In the quiet Sears could hear the banging of his heart against his ribs. With a gesture, almost like that of a magician, the tall elder reached within the folds of his long woollen cloak and produced a small, round, glazed bowl of bluish pottery, some four inches in diameter and closed by a lid.

Sears heard Hannah's long, indrawn draught of breath and felt rather than saw her start forward, and for a moment entertained the awful feeling that she might lose all control, dart up, snatch the bowl from the brown hands that held it, and commence cramming the contents into her mouth. He put out his hand and laid it gently on her arms to restrain her and was surprised to note that, on the other side of her, Dr Levi had done the same.

Clary's eyes were wide with anxiety and her hand had gone to her mouth in a gesture of despair. Ben-Isaac leaned over and whispered something to her.

Barzillai now motioned for Dr Levi to arise likewise, and when he did so, facing him, he commenced to speak in his own language, slowly and carefully, with measured cadence and deep emphasis. It was a long speech, and during its rolling, sonorous course Sears watched with his eyes and with his eager and all newly re-sharpened wits, and with the pores of his skin and his tactile senses, for any clue as to what might be forthcoming.

He saw and felt many things. He noted that Hannah could not tear her eyes away from the blue-glazed bowl; that when it moved in Barzillai's hands, as he swayed or gestured in emphasis to what he was saying, her gaze followed it like that of a cat watching a bird or tracing a moving object.

Several times Barzillai looked down at Hannah as he spoke, and there was something very moving in the expression of his eyes; also his gaze from time to time rested on Sears.

But strangest was the look on the face of Dr Nathaniel Levi as he listened to what the chief was saying, and one that Sears felt contained considerable bewilderment and surprise, but also, he would have sworn, harboured a glint of amusement. Several times the doctor glanced away from Barzillai to Sears as though something were beyond belief.

At last Barzillai ceased speaking and inclined his head to Dr Levi in a bow that was full of charm and dignity. It was several seconds before Hannah seemed to realize that he had finished. Then she turned on Dr Levi:

'Quick! What has he said? Tell me at once!'

Dr Levi stood looking down at both her and Sears as though he did not know how to begin. Then he returned the salute of Barzillai and commenced to speak:

'Barzillai has said that in his hands he holds the substance that, since times even beyond the memory of man, has served to defeat the ends of the Angel of Death. It is the fruit of the Tree of Life ...'

Hannah sucked in her breath again.

'The fruit of the Tree of Life is the gift of the Lord to the descendants of the children he drove from paradise. It is meant for the innocent, who are forgiven the sins of their fathers provided they do not sin anew ...

'Each third year the small and precious crop of the fruit of the Tree of Life is harvested and prepared. On the seventh night of the new moon the elders meet in council to decide who amongst them in the village has been worthy of God's gift of years. They have met tonight. They have decided.'

Sears thought to himself, *'One more word and I'll know. Millionaire or a bum!'*

In the silence he heard Hannah's hoarse, penetrating whisper, 'Who?'

And now it was that Dr Levi seemed to stumble and from time to time appear at a loss for words or how to express himself. He glanced first at Barzillai, then at the seated elders, at Hannah and at Sears, before he spoke again. Then he said carefully:

'They have made their decision. They have said, Miss Bascombe, that you have conferred great honour upon their humble village by visiting them, and that you have journeyed a great distance. Further, that you are a person of great importance in your country, old and venerable and greatly respected, and that their poor hospitality has nothing to offer you but perhaps the trifling gift of years contained in the blue jar. Therefore they are giving you all that they have garnered this year as a present. If you wish it, it is yours.'

Sears somehow managed to suppress the shout of exultation that rose within him – *'Bingo!! Millionaire!'* Then he had a queer thought, *'She's got it. But the Doc wasn't telling the whole truth!'*

Ben-Isaac said with a kind of fierce relief, as though what had just happened had purged him of the guilt he had been carrying, 'She's got it. We've kept our promise.'

Hannah struggled to her feet. As she did so, Barzillai, with a dramatic gesture, removed the lid momentarily from the bowl. It was covered with a few leaves. Beneath the leaves was a smooth, grey-green substance. A pungent, bitter-sweet aroma, reminiscent of night-flowers, hyssop and wormwood, filled the air in the enclosure. He spoke again.

Dr Levi interpreted. 'He hopes that you will accept their humble offering, and that the Lord will bless every added year of life that is contained therein.'

Hannah spoke hoarsely. 'What shall I do? What shall I say? Is this true? Is there nothing they demand in return?'

'Nothing! Thank them. This has entailed sacrifice on their part. Do not hurt them by attempting payment. Say to them that you accept their generosity in the spirit in which it is offered, and that it is your hope that their gift will add to your wisdom and that you can devote it to the praise and glory of God and all His works. But you must say these words to them yourself and then I will interpret for you.'

Sears could see the effort with which Hannah pulled herself together and spoke the words dictated, one after the other, like someone who is hypnotized and does not know what she is saying, and he was aware of the almost ecstatic shudders of triumph that were shaking her frail body.

When she had finished and Dr Levi interpreted, Barzillai bowed and, with a gesture that contained both sweetness and a kind of eternal understanding and compassion, handed the bowl to Hannah.

Her fingers made a dry and scaly sound as they closed around the smooth, glazed surface, for her fingernails, too, became involved in the convulsive grip with which she clutched the bowl and held it to her breast.

She looked up into Barzillai's face and said:

'Thank you. Yes, yes, thank you.' Then she turned to Dr Levi and repeated, 'Thank you. Thank you. Is that enough? Can I go now?'

He nodded assent and made as if to speak, but she said quickly, 'I can find my way back. You need not accompany me.' The blue-glazed bowl held firmly to her, she hurried from the room.

A minute or two later, when Sears, Dr Levi, Clary and Ben-Isaac emerged into the cold, clear night, the street was deserted and there was no sign of Hannah visible on the path between them and their quarters, several hundred yards below. But far above them, on the rocky path that led northwards from the village, they heard the sound of shod feet beating out a note of panic, and in the distance, as she breasted a rise and for a moment was outlined against the snow-covered slope of Hermon, they saw it was Hannah.

Dr Levi said softly to himself, 'Poor soul. Poor, poor soul.'

Clary cried, 'What has happened to her? Where is she going?'

Ben-Isaac said, 'She doesn't know what she's doing. She'll get lost. I'm going to get her and bring her back.'

He started off as Sears snarled, 'Leave her alone'; but it was Dr Levi who restrained him. 'No, Ben-Isaac. . . . Let her go, we have interfered enough. She would only run from you until she died. She is afraid we want to share her immortality.'

Exultation returned to Sears. 'I pulled it off. She's got the stuff. She's got it. But you were lying back in there, Doc. What was it the guy really said?'

Dr Levi said, 'Yes, you are right. I could not tell the truth in front of her. You are a very clever man, my friend. You convinced them somehow that Hannah believes she is the queen of the world, holding in her hand the reins of power over all and sending forth the lightnings and the winds from her head. They think you are her son and have brought her here to seek help from them in her quest for life eternal to rule the earth. Because she is mad – and, to the oriental, the mad are touched by God and people deserving of the deepest and most special consideration – they have given her what she desires. That is what he was saying . . .'

For a moment Sears stared at him, unbelieving. Then his mind went back to the scene of that afternoon, the series of drawings he had made, and he wanted suddenly to yell with laughter. They had misinterpreted them into seeing them as Sears' plea for help for his insane mother. Oh, but that was rich, and Levi was right. He *was* clever. Everlastingly, dingbustedly, monumentally clever. Maybe that wasn't exactly what he had intended, but, after all, he had gone there, had braced them, *had* thought of communicating with drawings and cartoons.

And only then the real impact hit him. He had pulled it off. He was rich. Five years from now he would be a millionaire.

He stopped there in his tracks and shouted. 'Hey, Doc! Clary! Ben-Isaac! I'm in!' He seized Ben-Isaac by the hand and began to pump it. 'Kid, shake the hand of Millionaire Joe Sears! We're in. I've done it.' All the let-down and disappointment of that afternoon now turned into a kind of hysterical outburst of uncontrolled exultation. He shouted, 'What's the dif how it happened? We made it, didn't we? You brought us here, Doc, but I put it over. Who cares? There'll be enough for everybody. I'll take care of you, Doc, and Clary and the kid too. Goddam it, you sourpussed old coot, cheer up. You wanted her to have it or you wouldn't have brought us here. I'll see you don't lose by it. Millionaire Joe Sears knows how to look after his friends.'

The hysteria of joy affected his limbs. He seized Dr Levi in his arms and whirled him around and around in a dance. The old man neither protested nor seemed to take offence at the indignity.

He let him go, but his exuberance and triumph still filled him. He looked back up at the shimmering white breast of the mountain where Hannah had vanished and crowed:

'Money in the bank. She's taken the stuff up on the mountain where she can be alone. She's going to have it all by herself and make Joe Sears a millionaire.'

'Perhaps.'

The word fell heavily upon Joe Sears. He stared at Dr Levi. 'What do you mean, "perhaps"?'

Dr Levi regarded him not unkindly. 'It was just a thought I had. I will tell it to you. It is that no one is ever wholly alone up on that mountain. . . . Good night.' He walked off down the path.

Joe Sears stood there with Clary and Ben-Isaac and watched him go. He felt like shouting 'Sourpuss!' after him, but he did not do so. Why pick on the old guy? After all, this was one Joe Sears couldn't lose now.

Chapter 29

'Verily, verily, I say unto you, He that believeth
on me hath everlasting life' – *John* vi, 47

EMERGED from the council-house, the jar clutched convulsively
to her breast, Hannah had given way to the panic that gripped her
ever since the fruit of the Tree of Life had come into her possession, and commenced to run.

She ran northwards, away from the village, in feverish escape
until her breath began to come in sobs and her throat burned. Yet
she could not stop. She was like an animal that has acquired a
prize and is fearful of having it snatched away.

She kept to the path that led upwards past the caverns and
higher, her pace slowing as she climbed where it narrowed to little
more than a goat track, but clearly discernible in the moonlight.
She fled from those she had left behind as though they were her
enemies.

Sears, Dr Levi, Clary – and even Ben-Isaac. Now that she
clutched to herself the key to an eternity of living and power,
she could trust none of them.

Below her she could yet see a few lights in the village, and they
seemed to her like covetous eyes looking after her.

Close to exhaustion, nevertheless she continued to press on-
wards. Not until she was certain that they would never find her
would she dare to open her jar and partake of immortality. At last
she emerged from the cleft to which the path clung and stood for
a moment poised on the skyline on the snow-crust of the mountain slope.

Hannah's strength was at an end. There was insufficient oxygen
at that altitude and she could not catch her breath; her legs, un-
used to such exertion, would no longer carry her forward. There
was a long, low, flat rock nearby, worn smooth by many generations of shepherds that had used it as a rest. Nearly blind with
fatigue, Hannah staggered to it and half fell, half sat upon it, but
with the instinct left to protect the precious jar.

Gradually, as her eyes began to clear again, the action of her heart quieted and her burning lungs were relieved by the clear, cold, sweetness of the air, passion and panic commenced to subside and she looked about her to see where she was.

Behind her, upwards to the stars, swept the twin snow-peaks of Hermon. The third crest of the mountain she could not see, for it lay to the east. Below her the snow-covered slopes fell away to meet the hills, crumpled like bed-clothes through which they had toiled.

Hannah Bascombe was alone and on top of the world.

The air was sharp, yet not unbearable. Never had the stars seemed so many or so close. Hanging low on the western horizon, just over the dark line of the hills rolling like billows to the stormy seas of stone that were the mountains of Galilee whence they had come, was pinned one great star, brighter than all the rest.

She was fully conscious of herself now, her person and her whereabouts. . . . She was Hannah Bascombe, daughter of and heiress to Iron Ike, richest woman in the world and keystone to industries by the hundreds and dollars by the million. She was sitting by herself atop a mountain in Syria, nursing a smooth, round glazed jar containing a bitter-sweet, aromatic, pungent-smelling substance that, when consumed, would provide her with the invincible weapon of time unlimited.

The contents of this jar represented the culmination of her desires. There was nothing any longer that could stand in the way of her achieving them. As always, she had won; this time against death itself.

And yet at this supreme moment of her life she was aware that she was no longer remembering clearly what those desires were, or what it was that had led her from the security of her mansion in San Francisco to this lonely and God-haunted spot, where she could no longer hide and stood, as it were, naked on the mountain side, beheld by the countless eyes of the universe.

Her thoughts wandered and refused to obey her will to keep them rigid and marshalled to her command. Instead they turned to that picture-book star of Bethlehem that she had seen reproduced in her childhood, with its four points of refraction like a diamond. This one in the west was like the pictures and could well be shining over Bethlehem.

She let her errant mind lead where it would now. The star conjured up Jesus again and led Him almost to her feet with His disciples, Peter, James and John; for this great basalt cone of Hermon tipped by eternal snow had looked down upon the scene of the transfiguration and had witnessed the clouds gather from which the followers had heard the thunder of the Voice:

'This is my beloved Son. Hear Him!'

'Hear Him!' the words seemed to echo in Hannah's ears and made her look about her. But there was nothing, no shadow or sound, or even breath of wind. She placed the blue-glazed pot on the rock close beside her.

Here, where they had been spoken, the words took on a new meaning; they became so simple and touching that they seemed about to press those unfamiliar catches at her throat that released the tears. God spoke to the hearts of these simple, faithful, believing men and asked of them only that they hear the words of His Son. And she thought that all that God seemed ever to have asked of the world was that it listen to the words of Jesus. . . . She knew that she herself had lived a lifetime with God in her mouth and never once had permitted Him into her heart.

She looked suddenly into that Hannah who had thought to capture the goods of the world and saw her for what she was, a sinful woman and a failure as a human being. She had sinned against God and man, against nature, against herself, even against her father whom she had once thought to love so greatly.

For the first time she saw herself no longer as his victim but knew that she had made him hers. He was a strong man whose one weakness was the love he bore his daughter and which surpassed the limits set by nature. She had supported not his strength but his weakness. She, who had been a woman and with whom the gift lay, had failed him in the immortality through succession that all men craved. Unloved, unwed, a dry, barren, self-elected spinster, she had chosen to deny life to his blood and had tried to grant perpetuity only to his money.

A wind stirred from Hermon's top, and Hannah shivered, for she was an old, frightened and miserable woman, alone with herself on a secret mountain top, holding by her side a cold, smooth, pottery jar that once she had been certain was her heart's desire.

She looked down at it, reposing there on the ancient rock, glistening in the nightlight, casting even a small moon-shadow, and tried to think why she had wanted it so much, what it really meant to her, and why she was sitting there beside it. She could not remember very well, though faint echoes seemed to reach her of standing before grinning men taking down her words and shouting her defiance of the government and their tax-collectors. But these surely were dreams of a past, too mean and wicked to entertain where the eyes of Him were so close that He could see into her soul.

Her mind fled from these memories; the life that she had led, the deals, the coups, the counting-house, the books and ledgers, the trades and purchases and ruthless acquisitions. She begged them to be dreams, this terrible devotion to a useless, tragic purpose that had set her at odds with the land of her birth and brought comfort and happiness to no one.

Let these be evil dreams swirling like the mists over the crumpled hills at Hermon's foot; reality must be what had happened to her since she had come to Palestine, the tears she had shed at Nazareth, the green and yellow field where David had once stood armoured in faith, the glade at Capernaum burning with the buried fire of the stones once touched by the feet of Jesus. Reality was the moment when she had stood in Jordan and prayed that her sins be washed away.

She looked again at the glazed jar at her side for which she had striven so mightily . . .

Ah yes. The stuff within was there to help her defy the Angel of Death and grant her the years for which she had been prepared to sell her soul. This was the last remnant of the ancient food that had sustained the patriarchs through generations. How long would she live then? A hundred years more? Two hundred? Knowing the secret, if one kept returning each century to refresh oneself at the source of this fruit of life that had once been God's gift to the mankind of His creation, need one ever die?

Under the starlight the pinched, acquisitive look returned to her face for a moment. Nothing was so important except that Hannah should not die.

Yet the very next moment the vast, frozen slopes, the clarity of the blazing heavens, the intense and solitary mountain from whose slopes His voice had sounded seemed to ring with the denial of this thought, for here on Hermon the truth flickered all about her like an aurora borealis.

Why was it important that Hannah live for ever? More and more the old dreams with their terrors seemed to fade. What had she, the Hannah who sat there contemplating this land so filled with beauty and the tenderest memories of man, to do with denying herself that eternity that Paul had written was the gift of God and the sign of God's mercy, the right to become one with the universe again and rejoin Him once more?

She remembered what Dr Levi had said to her once when she had asked him his beliefs with regard to life and death and God.

He had replied, 'I believe neither in life nor in death, only in transition in the journey that God bids us to take. As nothing comes between soul and body of child and father, so nothing separates man from God, his Father and fashioner. He is within us and all about us. When I am not what I am now, He will still be. I shall never be without Him. I shall never be lonely or afraid, for when the journey is at its end I shall find Him.'

She thought of Joe Sears and what he had promised her as the reward of life eternal, and she saw now, at her feet as it were, the possessions of the world that must fall into her hands. There she sat, a withered and arid queen atop a filth heap, sole owner and possessor of it all, down to the last stick and rag that man raised him as a roof and used to clothe his nakedness.

When had she last been happy? She could remember now. At Nazareth and Galilee and in the hills of Judea. Ben-Isaac was happiness, the expression in his eyes and the caress of his voice when he called her mother or the gentle Hebrew 'Imma'.

Memories of things that had brought to her swift pangs of joy came to her: the sight of a brown, sweated back in the hot sun, hewing a homeland from the desert; the green mist of young trees covering a mountainside denuded for long dry centuries of foliage; the curve of a Galilean hill; the deep blue of the Lake and the myriads of tiny coloured shells on the fringe.

And across those dark and frosty hills to the west, where now the great star gleamed for one last moment before it set, a Man had said, 'He that believeth on me hath everlasting life.'

She was swept back to that grove of ordered cypress with the single smooth pillar of the synagogue at Capernaum, where every leaf and stone and blade of grass, every hummock, twig and branch cried out that here it was indeed that Jesus once had stood and spoke those words which were to move the world:

'I am the bread of life; he that cometh to me shall never hunger; and he that believeth on me shall never thirst . . .'

There it was that the gift of eternity was made to man. 'Who so eateth my flesh, and drinketh my blood, hath eternal life; and I will raise him up at the last day.'

Hannah's thoughts turned once more to her father whom she had believed to love so greatly that she had dedicated her life to him and for his sake had been prepared to sacrifice even the peace and rest that comes with death. He seemed close to her there, and she felt that he must have known and had forgiven her for loving him sinfully and for being weak, human and corruptible.

Loneliness for him swept through her bleakly and an aching sadness filled her as she looked back to how they had loved one another and yet how blind and barren was that love.

But who was her father? What was he? In a sudden access of panic Hannah felt that she did not know, that she was as one suspended between the layers of the universe, abandoned and forever lost.

She cried aloud, 'Father . . . father!'

To whom had she called? Who was her father? Was it Iron Ike, who had petted and spoiled her all his life, now mouldering in his million-dollar mausoleum in San Francisco? Or Dr Levi, who had fought for her soul ever since they had come to Israel?

Or was it Him who dwelt behind the curving arch of stars that drew their bow of eternal mystery across the Syrian sky?

Her lips began to form words. 'Our Father which art in heaven . . . Hallowed be thy name . . .'

She could feel peace and understanding begin to flow into her, twin currents from sky and mountain. She continued, 'Thy Kingdom come. Thy will be done, as in heaven, so in earth', and spoke the words of the prayer Jesus had taught His disciples until it was finished.

The stars paled and it grew lighter. Behind her the tip of Hermon turned to rose. Then the first ray of the returning sun slipped past the peak and splintered against the glazed pot at her side, and Hannah Bascombe looked down at it with a little shudder.

For it all seemed so clear to her what a moment before had still appeared dark, fearful and confused. She was not certain what it contained, this stuff made by an artless people with their simple and ancient beliefs, or what its properties really were, should she partake of it. She knew only beyond peradventure of a doubt that eternity was not contained in a glazed earthenware pot, and that she, Hannah Bascombe, had nothing whatsoever to do with or no wish for it, or what it purported to offer, nor ever would again.

She arose, barely able to stand, chilled but at peace at last. She wrapped her cloak about her against the cold and commenced to retrace her steps back to the village.

But she halted after only a few paces and looked back to the jar reposing on the rock, now illuminated by the yellow of the fully risen sun. And she remembered that the men below believed in it wholly and that they had made a sacrifice to give it to her. Since she no longer had any use for it, it might be a kindness to return it to them. She hobbled back, picked it up, and, carrying it lightly but securely, took the path back to the village.

Chapter 30

'And I said, Should such a man as I flee? And
who is there, that being as I am, would go into
the temple to save his life?' — *Nehemiah* vi, 11

It was some eight hours after Joe Sears had been mysteriously
missing at the scheduled time of departure of the caravan for
Israel that Dr Levi went up to the quarters assigned to the women,
and to which they had returned upon the postponement of their
leaving, and called:

'Miss Adams . . .'

At once Clary appeared at the door. She asked anxiously, 'Is
there any news?'

Dr Levi replied, 'I cannot say as yet. You asked me to let you
know as soon as we had heard something. I have spoken with a
native boy who was sent by Barzillai. He was very frightened. He
had just come down from the hills. He said that there was a mad-
man or a demon up in one of the caves, that he had seen him and
heard him howling . . .'

Clary stared at him with a kind of bewildered incredulity. 'But
Joe was not mad. Surely you cannot believe . . .'

'It is the first report of any kind that we have had. I am going
to investigate.'

Clary asked, 'Let me come with you. Please do. I . . . I may be
able to help somehow . . .'

Dr Levi remarked, 'You are not afraid of demons, then?'

Clary replied, 'I am only afraid for Joe.'

'What is it you're afraid of?'

'I don't know. But I have been frightened ever since Miss Bascombe came back yesterday, exhausted and chilled, with the jar
that had been given her. She offered it to me. I refused.'

'Yes?' asked Dr Levi. 'Why?'

Clary looked bleak and did not reply. Dr Levi said, 'Never
mind. I believe I know. What did you do with it then?'

'I acted on Miss Bascombe's instructions. I called Joe Sears and asked him to return it to Barzillai.'

'And you were frightened then?'

'Yes. The expression on his face.'

'What was it like?'

'Evil!'

'Miss Bascombe . . .?'

'She is sleeping.'

Dr Levi nodded. 'It is probably just as well that our departure was postponed. She was in need of the rest. Very well. You may come with me. I believe you have the courage to face what may have to be faced. Bring an extra torch.'

While she went in to fetch it and don a warm garment Dr Levi reflected on the strange people that had been brought into his ken on the heels of the return of his nephew – Hannah, the woman obsessed; Sears, the charlatan, playing upon her obsession; and the girl who loved him and did not dare to acknowledge it to herself because of what she knew him to be.

They had been thrown sharply into relief against this new nation, which was going through one of its periodic and historic regenerations, during which the Children of Israel were making another of their touching attempts to walk upright in the face of the Lord.

Yes, Dr Levi thought, it was a tender moment in the life of this country reborn and which he both loved and pitied and understood. It would change again, it would err, stray and wander from the paths he found so beautiful and brave; but now for this brief moment it contained all that was great and lovable of Israel, and he was grateful that he who had travelled so widely, lived so diversely and seen so much had been given these moments of sharing the rebirth of his land, his people and all the goodness that had inspired them in the five-thousand-years struggle against themselves.

This Israel, he concluded, returning to what lay immediately ahead, could help anyone who had not crossed the borderline and was beyond help for ever. It was this that he had not wished to say to Clary. And yet if she loved this man, who was not evil but only foolish, misguided and weak, then she, too, must face what was to be. He pitied her for what she might find, but would not deny her the human right to grow through suffering.

She returned carrying an electric lantern and wrapped in a camel-hair coat. Dr Levi noted that the fear and anxiety had passed from her countenance. It had been replaced by a self-possession in which were mingled determination and the kind of calm that women can achieve when their minds are made up.

She slipped her arm into his. A small figure crept out of the shadows and they could see the whites of frightened eyes. It was the native boy. In his own language Dr Levi said to him, 'Come. You shall only point out the cave to me and then you may run as fast and as far as you like.' He held out his hand, which the child took eagerly, and thus the three proceeded to climb diagonally away from the village up the path that led to the dark mouths of the caves that honeycombed the cliffs above.

Sears' defection had first been noted the morning the caravan had been gathered at the outskirts of the village to begin the return journey to Israel. Farewells had been taken from their hosts and they were ready to begin their descent into the Hauran when Clary called attention to the fact that Sears was not there. No one could remember exactly when he had last been seen.

A quick search of their quarters and its vicinity failed to turn him up, nor did he answer to shouts and calls for him that went echoing up the gorge. When an hour's hunt by the Palmach men under Avery, Schlomo and Ben-Isaac failed to reveal so much as a clue to his whereabouts, Dr Levi had called off the departure.

As the hours had worn on and no trace of Sears could be found he began to think that perhaps real tragedy, which thus far they had escaped, had struck them. Dr Levi knew nothing of Sears' actual arrangement with Hannah Bascombe but was aware, from what Sears appeared to believe, and from his point of view, that everything depended upon Hannah consuming the substance presented to her by the council of Beit Jebel. From the very beginning he and Sears had been locked in a battle for the soul of Hannah Bascombe. Sears had lost, and it was for this reason that Dr Levi feared for him.

It was not divine justice or the visiting of God's punishment upon him with which he was concerned, for Dr Levi did not believe in a police deity. On the other hand, he was a Jew, a devout man, as well as a scientist and a humanitarian, and he knew the self-destroying qualities of evil, and that as man sins against whatever – God, nature, or his fellows – he has already sown the seeds of his own punishment, must impose his own sentence and serve it to the bitter end. He was aware of God in man; that the working of evil denied Him and banished His presence, creating an imbalance in the human being that sooner or later brought about his destruction, since, according to Dr Levi's philosophy, man could not live without God.

He had thought it quite likely that when Sears had heard that Hannah had rejected the fruit of the Tree of Life he had made an end to himself. When the boy had come with his report of the thing in the cave that howled he feared something even worse had befallen Sears.

It was late afternoon when they reached the narrow ledge that ran along the face of the escarpment. The boy, clinging nervously to Dr Levi's hand, led them past the five large caves which dominated the village, then climbed higher, to the one that Dr Levi had explored for prehistoric tools and remains early during their stay, and pointed to a smaller orifice, the opening so narrow that a man would have to bend double to enter it.

At first glance it did not look like the entrance to a cave at all, but when Dr Levi leaned down and flashed his light into it he could see that although the gradient descended steeply it then seemed to level off into a much larger enclosure.

Dr Levi asked the boy, 'Are you certain?'; and when he nodded, leaned down and shouted into the opening, 'Sears! Joe Sears!' Clary, too, dropped to her knees and added her voice to his.

They listened but could hear no reply. But the ears of the boy may have been more sensitive than theirs, for the look of terror returned to his face, and he squirmed away suddenly and fled down the narrow ledge in the direction whence they had come.

Clary asked, 'What is it? I heard nothing. Do you believe the boy saw Joe go in there?'

Dr Levi replied, 'It is the only thing we have to go on. I will look. Will you wait here?'

'Let me come with you.'

Dr Levi said, 'It takes a different kind of courage to explore a cave. Some people are unable to bear the narrow confines, the airlessness and the darkness.'

Clary said, briefly, 'I have no courage. I have only the will to go. If he is there he may need help.'

Dr Levi nodded. 'Do not use your flashlamp yet,' he said. 'There is no use expending the batteries of both at the same time if mine proves sufficient. Remain close to me. I will lead the way.'

But first he fished into his pocket and produced a ball of string and a small iron spike. He wedged the piece of steel into a crevice at the mouth of the cave and fastened the end of the string securely to it.

Clary said, 'You think of everything, don't you.'

He smiled. 'Obligatory equipment for spelunkers. Never go into a cave without laying a trail back to the entrance. That is just common sense.'

She said quickly, 'Poor Joe. If he came in here he would not have thought of that.'

'That is so.'

'Then let us hurry . . .'

'We must not hurry either.'

He squeezed into the narrow opening and Clary followed him. Then, unrolling the light twine behind him and carefully studying the terrain and what lay ahead with his electric torch, he set off down the narrow passage.

They moved cautiously for perhaps a hundred yards through a number of small chambers, really no more than a series of layers split in the rock when the mass had been shifted by earthquake or pressure. The air grew heavy and musty. Dr Levi was looking concerned. Several times he paused at side passages that branched off from the main tunnel before proceeding. Suddenly he held up his hand and stopped to listen.

A far-off, muffled sound travelled through the tunnel, but whether it came from human or animal throat could not be determined. Dr Levi said to Clary gravely, 'I think we are approaching the end of our search. Have courage.'

He proceeded again, the passage descending gradually and

then turning a corner abruptly, where it ended in a pocket, a small chamber like the lair of a beast of prey.

Joe Sears was there, picked out in the yellow beam from the torch in Dr Levi's hand. He was down on his hands and knees, his rump high, his head pressed close to the uneven rock floor of the cavern like a prize-fighter who has been smashed head first into the canvas and who has just begun the weary and painful attempt to arise.

His clothing was torn, his hands black with dried blood where they had been abrased on the sharp rock of the passages; he had a cut over one eye and the blood had streamed unheeded down the side of his face and neck, staining his collar. His lips were bruised and darkened. He was trying to push himself up with his left hand. The other was still gripped about a bottle. A broken electric torch lay at his feet.

Clary cried 'Joe!' and started forward, but the hand of Dr Levi restrained her.

Slowly Sears turned his head and saw them, but the eyes that glared out of the mask of the battered face were at first wholly glazed, blank and uncomprehending. Yet he was aware of their presence, for slowly he lifted his head from the floor, gained his knees and eventually lifted himself to his feet and stood spraddle-legged and swaying as he stared into the glare of the torch.

'Joe! You're hurt!' Clary moved into the circle of light. This time Dr Levi did not hold her back.

Sears recognized her. He shouted at her suddenly, his voice reverberating horribly in the confined chamber.

'Wha' the hell do you want? Followed me to get some of the stuff, eh? Well, there ain' 'ny more, Violet Eyes. I've had it all. Go back to your goddam so'jer boy.'

Clary turned pleading and horror-stricken eyes to Dr Levi. 'He's mad!' she whispered. 'He's lost his mind. What shall we do?'

But Dr Levi stepped close and for a moment let the beam of his light cut directly into the pupils of Sears' eyes. Then the scientist leaned his head forward and sniffed. He was filled with a sense of overwhelming relief. 'No,' he said loudly. 'He isn't mad. He's only drunk.'

Chapter 31

'This then is the message which we have heard
of him, and declare unto you, that God is light,
and in him there is no darkness at all' – *I John* i, 5

THE word reverberated hollowly from the dripping walls of the chamber. Sears' wavering gaze found Dr Levi now. He bawled at him, 'Tha's right, sourpuss, 'm drunk – plastered, blotto, stinking! An' wha's it to you, Levi? You and your goddam fruit of the Tree of Life! You wan' know where it is? 'S in me. I've had it. All of it. I can't die. Tha's why I'm drunk, and I'm gonna get drunker.'

Dr Levi said, 'Many a man would be happy if he were convinced he could not die.'

Sears broke into a dreadful laugh. 'You can talk, Levi. You're gettin' off at the nex' stop. I got to ride this planet for the nex' five hun'red years.'

Dr Levi asked, 'What has suddenly gone wrong with immortality?'

Sears turned his glaring reddened eyes on the old man and bawled at the top of his lungs, 'Me! Sears! You old fool. Sears, the big angle-guy and bull-thrower. I'm sick of the sight and sound of him. What do I do a hundred years from now?'

Dr Levi nodded and then said, 'One minute of genuine repentance on earth is worth more than . . .'

Sears' angry bellow interrupted him. 'Who the hell is repenting? I don't repent a goddam bit. I just think Sears stinks. When I take a drink I forget what I'm so scared about, and Violet Eyes and her boom-boom boy and the whole goddam mess. So here's to us.'

He worried the cork out of the bottle, gave them both a foolish smile and tilted the bottle to his lips. He held it there for a moment, but his throat did not move to swallow, for it was empty. It had evidently been so for some time, for his drunkenness was beginning to wear off.

Sears held the bottle before him a moment, staring at it, and said, 'Christ, what am I going to do now?' Then he hurled it against the opposite wall, shattering it. The effort pitched him forward on to his hands and knees again, and he remained there for a moment, shaking his head like an animal. Clary went down on her knees beside him, her eyes filled with tears, but she did not touch him. She did not know at the moment what to do or say.

Dr Levi pursued his soft-voiced, even inquiry. 'You consumed the fruit of the Tree of Life?' he asked.

Sears produced a horrid parody of the old man's way of speaking as he repeated, mimicking, 'You consumed the fruit of the Tree of Life? Sure I ate it. What the hell do you think? I'm a wise guy, ain't I? Nobody was going to make Sears the patsy on this deal.'

Dr Levi asked, 'In just what way, Joe?'

Sears glanced at him balefully. 'I'm out in the cold. Hannah no eat, Sears no get paid. Everybody's got something but me, ain't they? Violet Eyes here has her soldier boy if she can keep his mind off belting Arabs with his goddam hand-grenades, Hannah's got religion, Ben-Isaac's got a home, and you got your goddam turnips and beets. I was the sucker.'

Dr Levi said, 'Yes, Joe, you were the sucker.'

'Well, I ain't any more. I got the stuff in me to make me king of the world. I got the fruit of the Tree of Life burning in my blood. I'm the only one who's going to find out what happens tomorrow a hundred years from now.'

He blinked and shook his head, and when he spoke again his voice had fallen and was filled with a note of horror. 'Only now I've got to live with Joe Sears all alone into eternity and face the bastard morning, noon and night. And I'm scared. Oh Christ, I'm scared.' He put his hands before his face and commenced to tremble.

Clary put her arms about his shoulders and said, 'Joe. . . . Joe. . . . Poor, poor Joe . . .'

Sears shook her off. 'Okay! Look at me and laugh. Joe Sears

is scared stiff. It's a big joke. I gotta laugh myself. Let's all laugh!'
He cackled dreadfully, and then begged, 'For God's sake go away
and leave me alone. It's too late for anything.'

Clary touched the hand that he had bruised and cut when he
battered himself against the sharp rocks in what must have been
his wild panic flight into the darkness of his cave to escape from
his knowledge of himself, there to hide from all eyes like a
wounded animal. 'Joe! No one is laughing. Won't you try to
listen?' She turned in her need and anguish to Dr Levi. 'Can't
you help him? Don't you understand what has happened to
him? Is there nothing you can do?'

Dr Levi came over to where Sears was kneeling with Clary at
his side and looked down for a few moments at the pair, a half-
humorous, half-sympathetic expression on his face.

'Yes,' he replied. 'I think perhaps I can.'

He squatted down on his heels in the dirt on the floor of the
cave, his torch held before him so that the light did not shine
directly on the figure of the miserable man, and said to Sears,
speaking quietly but with the authority needed to penetrate the
panicked and befuddled brain:

'Come with me, Joe. . . . Let us begin at the beginning. The jar
of the substance called the fruit of the Tree of Life which Hannah
received from Barzillai that night and brought back with her
from Mount Hermon untouched – how did you get it?'

'Clary gave it to me to return to Barzillai with the message
that she no longer wanted it. That's how I knew I was cooked.'

'And you stole it?'

'I kept it. What difference did it make to them? They'd given
it to Hannah. They were through with it. Hannah didn't want
it. It was a loose ball. Was that stealing?'

Dr Levi reflected. He said, 'It is a fine point. Technically it
was not. You are right. Particularly since there was a third party
involved who likewise refused it.'

Sears took his hands from his face and stared at Dr Levi. His
eyes were more able to focus. He asked, 'Who was that?'

'Clary.'

Sears repeated 'Clary?' and brought his gaze to the girl kneeling at his side.

Dr Levi said, 'Oh yes. When Hannah returned that morning with her mind made up not to touch it, she offered it to Clary. She was tempted. What woman, believing she had the opportunity to defy the processes of ageing, would not have been? But she resisted the temptation.'

Sears shook his head again in another attempt to clear it. 'Clary had a crack at that stuff and passed it up?' he said, incredulously. 'Why?'

'Because,' replied Dr Levi, 'she could not bear to think of living on in a world which, when your life-span was ended, would no longer contain the man she loved.'

Sears twisted his head about and stared for a moment at Clary with a long and intense effort, then turned back to Dr Levi. 'Are you crazy?' he asked. 'She hates my guts.'

Clary did not speak. After a moment of silence Dr Levi addressed himself to Sears again. 'So it really was, as you say, a loose ball. And you then decided to have it yourself. Why?'

Sears replied, 'I told you.'

'Any other reason?'

'What was there left? I saw Clary's face when she thought Ben-Isaac had got it on the side of that ravine . . .'

Dr Levi said, 'What a strange thing for a disappointed lover – to commit longevity.'

Sears said harshly, 'Who are you trying to kid? Are you trying to make me look ridiculous?'

Dr Levi nodded solemnly. 'Oh yes. It is another thing that you must face. If you are to be saved, you must first be made to look ridiculous. We must all be made to look a little ridiculous before it is over. That is the salvation of everyone, that God is not at any time ridiculous . . .'

Sears, who had tried to follow, shook his head in an attempt to clear it. He said, 'I don't get it.'

'We shall come to that. How much of the substance did you eat?'

'All of it.'

'And what effect do you believe it will have on you?'

'The same as on the others – Barzillai, the priest, the old tanner – that I'll live to be three or four hundred years old . . .'

'And you still believe that?'

Sears' gaze could fix now. It fastened on Dr Levi and contained a quality of anguish, misery and desperation that tore at Clary's heart-strings.

'Yes,' he replied. 'Isn't it true?'

'No,' said Dr Levi.

In the thick silence of the gloomy cave all three could hear the ticking of Sears' wristwatch in the time it took Dr Levi's reply to penetrate. Then Sears cried, 'What?'

The old man said calmly, 'I said no, that it was not true.'

Clary was almost as shocked as Sears. She said, 'Dr Levi, are you joking?'

'Not now. Later we will joke about it.'

Sears looked incredulous. 'What do you mean, it isn't true?'

'I mean that you could have eaten twice the amount of that substance, ten times the amount, a hundred or a thousand times. You could consume the contents of a jar every day for a year. You could, if it were possible, live on nothing else, and in the end it would not add ten minutes, not so much as ten seconds, to your normal span of life.'

Relief came into Sears' eyes, but was immediately replaced by doubt.

'What are you trying to give me? You brought us here. You told Hannah you had discovered the fruit of the Tree of Life and led us here to get it for her.'

'It was what you wished to hear, perhaps, but not what I said. I offered only to lead Miss Bascombe to a village where lived some very old men and where there was the legend of the fruit of the Tree of Life surviving from Biblical times. But since there is no Tree of Life, and never was, how can there be a fruit thereof?'

'Then the whole thing's a phoney, a hoax?'

'Oh,' said Dr Levi, 'I don't doubt that *they* believe it. It is just that I don't. You see, Mr Sears, I do not happen to be superstitious.'

Sears cried, 'I wish to God I knew what was the truth, what you really do believe!'

'Ah,' replied Dr Levi, 'you have mentioned it. I believe in God.'

Sears stared at him, searching his features.

'It is really quite simple,' Dr Levi continued. 'You cannot believe in God and mumbo-jumbo too. There is not room for both. To be free of one, you must admit the other.'

Sears made a tremendous effort to understand. He repeated slowly, 'If I believed in God . . . then . . . then I would not need to believe in . . . this.'

'Is that not plain common sense?'

'How can I? What must I do . . . ?'

Dr Levi said, 'Try asking it of Him. It is not difficult.'

Sears suddenly bent and put his hands to his face again. 'O God, help me,' he groaned.

Dr Levi arose. 'Yes,' he said, 'God help you. He has never failed anyone. He will not fail you. Good night.'

He turned, looked back once more to smile cheerfully at them, and made his way out through the arch way of the inner cavern. Soon his footsteps died away and his bobbing torch was lost to sight.

After a little, Sears said, 'If it's the way I see it, I'm lost. If it's the way he says, I'm the damnedest fool that ever lived . . .'

Clary switched on her light. 'We all believed it – you, Hannah, myself. I suppose that's what Dr Levi meant by facing the ridiculous. We're all grown people. We should have known better. All except poor Hannah, who was obsessed. But when the test came she was able to reject what she thought she had most wanted.'

Sears said, 'What about Ben-Isaac?'

'What about him, Joe?'

'I thought you and he had made it up – that you were in love with him.'

She said, 'I'm here with you, am I not?'

Sears nodded as though he still did not realize what she was saying. He began to sway. He said, 'Oh God, I'm sick. Stand by me, Violet Eyes, if you're on the level. I don't know whether I'm coming or going. What was it the guy told me? Tell me, kid; I gotta hear it again.'

Clary repeated what Dr Levi had said.

Sears asked, 'How can I know that I believe in God?'

Clary looked at him, at loss for words for a moment. She sai
'I don't know.' And then she continued, 'Perhaps in the end v
all come to it, because, as Dr Levi says, God is never ridiculoi
and we so often are . . .'; and then she added with a kind of hel}
lessness, 'I don't know, Joe. But I believe what Dr Levi said. N
harm will come to you. . . . And you did ask God to help you.'

He swayed again and began to retch. 'I'm sick,' he repeate
'Sick, through and through . . .'

She put her arm about him and supported him and held h
clammy head. When it was over he staggered to his feet, gaspin
and bracing himself against the wall of the cave.

'How do we get out of here?' he asked. 'I didn't know whe
I was going when I came in. All I wanted was to crawl away ar
hide.'

Clary flashed her lantern and picked up the end of whi
twine at the entrance to the pocket. She said, 'Dr Levi left
something to guide us back to the light.'

Sears examined the twine thoughtfully and nodded. 'Okay
he said, 'let's go.' And then he added, 'You lead me, Clary . . .'

Chapter 32

'Abide with us: for it is toward evening, and the
day is far spent' – *Luke* xxiv, 29

HEY came down from the stony slopes and snow into the spring
the lowlands, and the little party marched through the green-
g of wild olive, pines and young ilex bursting into bloom, the
lden and scarlet rain of flowering broom, meadows aglow with
d poppies and purple thistles, river beds filled with pink and
ite oleanders.

Sometimes, when the terrain was rougher and the going diffi-
lt, Ben-Isaac would drop back from the patrols that still
arded the travellers, pick Hannah up in his arms and carry
r.

She would protest at first, but he would swear that she had no
ight, and she would lie with her head leaned against his
oulder, as they picked their way through some fragrant glen,
d dream that he was her son.

He helped to create the dream, for he petted her, spoiled her,
ked with her and behaved with the extravagant possessiveness
the boy grown into man who knows that he can twist the
other who loves him around his finger.

Always during these times when he carried her he would
eedle and beg her to remain in Israel.

'Stay with us for always, Imma,' he begged, 'and in the evening
en I am home from the fields I will come to you and take you
in my arms like this and sing to you of our beautiful land and
w dear you are to me, like this:

"For see, the winter has passed,
The rain is over and gone
The flowers appear in the land;
The time of singing is come . . ." '

Hannah smiled. 'You said that to me the first time you came

to see me in San Francisco. How long ago that seems ...'

'It is our greatest love-song. And I was in love with you from the moment I saw you.'

'How shameless you are. It seemed to me you had eyes for no one but Clary. Are you in love with her, Ben-Isaac?'

He laughed. 'Of course. But that is different. I shall marry Clary, settle down and till the soil like Uncle Nathaniel. Israel needs food to feed all those who will come. And you will see how I will take care of you if you would only stay with us.'

Hannah said, 'You would do nothing of the sort. You would be off fighting the Arabs somewhere, or drilling, or leading armies.'

'Why, if it *should* happen, little warrior mother, then I promise to take you with me and you shall ride in my jeep. I saw you that day we fought the bandits, and you weren't any more frightened than I was. Stay here, Imma. We need them like you in Israel.'

'Have you spoken to Clary yet, Ben-Isaac?'

'No, but I shall soon.'

'Do you think Clary is in love with you, Ben-Isaac? She older than you.'

He looked at her, disturbed for the first time. 'I will make her love me. And I was old while I was still a child, Imma. This land will woo her as well as I.'

Hannah said, 'Set me down, Ben-Isaac'; and when he did she walked alongside him for a moment in silence and then said, 'Women are strange creatures, and Clary is a strange girl. Clary has never loved anyone. She has only loved luxury, and I provide for that. Now I do not know any longer, but I would not want your heart to be broken.'

He refused to be discouraged. 'You shall dance at our wedding, Imma, if only you will remain here.'

Hannah smiled again. But in truth her heart was heavy at the thought of leaving.

Sears often marched with Dr Levi, for there was much on his mind. On the first of these occasions he had dropped into step alongside him and said, 'Thanks, Doc.'

Dr Levi replied, 'You are welcome.'

'I was pretty sick back there, you know.'

Dr Levi nodded gravely. 'Yes, that is true. You were.'

'It still isn't all — well, there are a lot of things that aren't answered yet.'

The old man nodded again. 'There may be some things, even, that will never be answered. In others I may be able to help.' He gave Sears his warm and encouraging smile that led the younger man to burst out:

'Those guys back there in the village who were three and four hundred years old . . .'

'Which ones?'

'Barzillai — Amalkeh.' He stopped, for when he thought of them and their agelessness all the old fears returned again. How could he be sure?

Dr Levi asked, 'Who said they were three and four hundred years old?'

'They did,' replied Sears, 'but . . .' He reflected and swore. 'Damn! Can it be that simple?'

'Perhaps . . .'

'But they were old. They looked old. . . . The tanner scraping his hides with a prehistoric flint . . .'

'Oh yes. Interesting, was it not? I said you would find that there. And did you see the women grinding corn as they did ten thousand years ago? Such sights stimulate the imagination powerfully . . .'

'How old actually were they, then?'

'Who can say? In that climate, and living under those conditions with none of the pressures of modern life, believing in the contents of their little magic pot, some of them might conceivably reach an extraordinary age. Several remembered such astonishing things, historically speaking.'

'Such as . . .'

'Soldiers,' replied Dr Levi. 'The soldiers of Napoleon, Soliman, and — Coeur de Lion! But, in a primitive community in which there is no printed word, who can say for certain what is actual memory and what the imprint of tribal, legend-into-memory stories and experiences handed down from father to son?'

Sears felt a return of the fear and desperation that had assailed

him in Beit Jebel. 'But if it isn't true that they live so long, what
the racket then?'

Dr Levi smiled. 'A very old one, I suspect,' he replied, 'an
Biblical in its implications. The Lord rewards His faithful. I
you were desirous of raising the standards of a community, how
better could you accomplish it than by letting it be known tha
the worthy in the eyes of God were to be elected to somethin
closely approaching life eternal. It keeps the electors in powe
and the uninitiated on their good behaviour.'

Sears reflected upon this. Then he cried, 'But they can't ge
away with it. Their fraud is bound to blow up in their faces. Whe
one of the elect turns up his toes the whole village must kno
the stuff has been a flop and the game is over.'

Dr Levi smiled again. 'Oh, I thought you would have notice
how simply and cleverly they got around that. No one kne
who received it and who not. The elders guarded the secret fo
the power it gave them. And the recipient, sworn to secrecy
would never tell.'

Sears said, 'I suppose if a man was given it and believed in i
hook, line and sinker, it might help to keep him alive longer.'

'It might.'

Sears fell silent a moment. Then, 'What if Hannah had take
it?'

'Ah,' said Dr Levi, 'but she didn't.'

'Look here. You were never fooled. You knew from the firs
that the stuff wasn't on the level, didn't you?'

Dr Levi turned his bland blue eyes on Sears. 'Oh no. I kne
nothing of the kind. . . . I do not know it now.'

Sears stared at him, the old horror returning. 'But back the
in the cave you told me . . .'

'That *I* did not believe in it because I am not superstitiou
You remember I told you that belief in God and superstitio
could not occupy the same space. Believe in God and you hav
nothing to fear.'

For all of his inner anguish, a stubborn expression came t
Sears' face. 'That leaves me no choice, then, but to believe i
God . . .'

'In the end man eventually comes to the realization that the is no other choice.' Dr Levi fell silent for a moment as he trudged alongside Sears. Then he gave him a glance of sympathy and said, 'But, if it will help you, I will remind you that I am a scientist.'

'How will that help me?'

'The pragmatic approach, of course, calls for experiment ...'

Sears stared at him. '*You* had some of the stuff ... ?'

Dr Levi looked almost guilty. He said, 'Ten years ago, when I first visited the village, I prevailed upon Barzillai to let me consume a portion – for test purposes, you understand ...'

'And ... ?'

Humour gleamed in the eyes of Dr Levi. 'I have aged perceptibly.'

Sears looked at the old man with something almost resembling affection. But then he said, 'You never believed in it. That still leaves it up to me.'

'Oh yes,' replied Dr Levi cheerfully. 'But I thought that a practical demonstration might comfort you ...'

It was Sears' turn to walk in silence for a time. Then he asked, 'Dr Levi, why did you take Hannah to Beit Jebel?'

'I told you.'

'What, to make good the things Ben-Isaac told her in San Francisco? I don't buy that. What was your real reason?'

Dr Levi regarded Sears earnestly. 'Do you, who went into the heart of Mount Hermon and emerged there from no longer the same man who entered, really not know?'

Sears did not reply. He thought that perhaps he did know, but he did not wish to think about it. He was not yet prepared to face it.

Ben-Isaac said, 'Clary, will you marry me and become a farmer's wife?'

'No, Ben-Isaac. But I am very proud that you have asked me.'

'Are you really, Clary? How quickly the "no" came to your lips. I am asking you because I love you.'

'Ben-Isaac, my dearest – isn't it better to be honest?'

'You have never really loved me, have you, Clary? Not even that night when I held you in my arms and felt your heartbeat.'

'I love you very dearly ...'

They were resting in the same rocky defile close to the border where they had encamped the first night, waiting for the moon to set before attempting the final recrossing of the border into Israel. Ed Avery and Schlomo were out with the Palmach men testing and patrolling the area, but Ben-Isaac had remained behind. He was without weapons. Clary had noticed that ever since the fight in the ravine and their arrival at Beit Jebel Ben-Isaac had gone unarmed. Clary sat on the same rock where Sears had talked to Ben-Isaac during the first night-watch, and the boy lay at her feet looking up at her. He said, 'I told Hannah that I was going to marry you. She said that you have never loved any one, that you loved only luxury. Is that true, Clary?'

'It was, Ben-Isaac.'

'But you have changed. Yes. You have. I have too. I don't want to kill any more. I want to make things grow.'

Clary had a memory and a flash of insight. 'Like the Russian with the little tree . . .'

'He was a better man than I. I killed an Arab with a shot in the stomach, but the Russian made something live for Israel. And Uncle Nathaniel took my sin upon himself.'

Clary said, 'You fought in self-defence, Ben-Isaac.'

He nodded. 'Yes, I know. But it does not make any difference. It is still a sin to kill. My uncle is right. We have talked together for many hours. I want to be like him, Clary . . .'

She said, 'You will be, Ben-Isaac. He is the finest man I have ever known. You are like him – brave, gallant, honest.'

He took her hand. 'Stay here with me, Clary. You don't know yet what love is. You will learn to love me as I love you, and to love Israel when you have worked for her, as Israel will love you in return. The land has lain dying, and together we will help to bring her to life again . . .'

'But Hannah. . . .' Clary started to say, when the boy interrupted her:

'Hannah will stay here,' he said intensely. 'You will see. Hannah will never leave Israel. She cannot.'

When she smiled at his conviction he moved to the rock beside her, looking like a young faun, ardent, beautiful, pressing his suit in the moonlight surrounded by the scent of night flowers.

'Clary,' he said, 'have courage. Listen to your heart . . .'

She gave a little cry. 'Ah, Ben-Isaac – my dear . . . I am.'

For the first time understanding came to Ben-Isaac. He did not relinquish her hand, but he sat silently beside her trying to master the sickening realization.

Finally he asked, 'Joe Sears?'

'Yes.'

The boy cried almost in anger, 'How can you? How can you love a fellow like that? You know what he is, what he is like!'

She did not reply, and a moment later he asked, 'Is he in love with you? But he must be.'

Clary shook her head. 'I don't know. I don't think he knows. Perhaps he is incapable of loving anyone – like I was. I must go back, Ben-Isaac.'

'Clary, why? I would make you forget Sears . . .'

She turned to him. 'There is more involved even than Joe, Ben-Isaac. It's too long a story, but I must return. I have a date with my self-respect. It is my home. I have left a life unlived there. I must make it up.'

'Alone?'

'Yes,' she replied, 'if necessary – quite alone.'

He showed then who he was and what he was: the sensitive, understanding human, the boy-grown-into-man. He said:

'There are deserts and wildernesses other than sands and mountains that must be made to bloom. Sometimes you find them inside of you. Good luck, Clary. God bless you.'

He leaned over and kissed her, and they clung to one another for a moment.

Sears came by. He said, 'The boys are back. It's all clear. We'll be starting off in ten minutes . . .'

Chapter 33

'Yet a little sleep, a little slumber, a little folding
of the hands to sleep' – *Proverbs* xxiv, 33

THEY crossed the border into Israel without difficulty and were
met by their jeeps just above Dan. That night they slept in their
trailers at Metullah. Mail from the States awaited them. By the
next day Hannah appeared again to be caught up in the intricacy
of her affairs.

It was the 9th of May. A boat leaving Haifa on the
14th. Their departure from Metullah was set for the following
day.

On the way back they passed once again the grove, the German
hospice and the little Church of the Loaves and Fishes at Ain
Tabigha on Lake Galilee.

Perhaps it was the persistent pleading of Ben-Isaac, or just the
sudden glimpse of the beautiful lake seen shining through the
stand of oak, willow, fir and plane trees, its surface and shores
so closely linked to Christ's ministry, that made Hannah suddenly elect to interrupt her homeward journey. She picked up
the car speaker and ordered the chauffeur to stop.

She remained silently looking out upon the scene that catches
the throat of every traveller no matter how often he comes to it.
For Hannah the association was even more poignant. It had been
in the vicinity of these very shores that the most beautiful voice
ever to resound on earth had spoken the words that at last had
reached through to her soul: 'He that believeth on me hath everlasting life . . .'

Sears, who was in charge of the arrangements for the return,
came forward, inquiring, 'Is anything wrong?'

Hannah became aware of his presence on the road outside the
car and said, 'No. It is just that I cannot bear to leave.'

Sears thought of his loading problems and Hannah's reputation for demanding efficient service. He said, 'I'm afraid we'd

better push on, Miss Bascombe, if you wish to catch that boat. We're just about going to make it now as it is.'

The old woman leaned out of the window of the car.

'Let me stay here one more day,' she said. For the first time in their relationship, Sears found himself touched by her.

He said 'Of course' and dropped back to give the orders.

Ben-Isaac gave a cry of triumph and quoted an old proverb: 'Remain in Israel a day; remain there for ever.' He leaned over and kissed her on the cheek.

Hannah fell back in her seat as though the effort had exhausted her, but she said, 'If I could, I would indeed stay here for ever.'

They made camp again by the edge of the lake with the permission of Father Hofstatter. And thereafter one stolen day followed upon the other.

It seemed as though Hannah could not bring herself to leave this spot where the winds of Time blew from Hermon to the lake of Galilee, raising the echoes of the long-gone centuries.

Here in Israel, between the two worlds of the ancients who searched for God, and the triumphant, unconquerable young who fought for independence, she had breathed the air of freedom once more and herself had experienced the liberation of her spirit from the dark chambers where it had been so long captive.

But it developed also, after a time, that she was so worn and tired that to go on was almost more than she was capable of undertaking. Nothing more was said about the boat.

She lay in a deck-chair by the lake, a light blanket over her legs, or remained in bed in the trailer, from the window of which she could look out upon the lake and the cliffs of Jordan opposite. Ben-Isaac read to her, or she talked softly and endlessly with Dr Levi. If at home the wheels of her enormous empire might slowly be grinding to a halt she did not seem to care.

It was evident to all that she had changed greatly, but to Sears most of all.

There were things about her appearance that puzzled him besides the dissipation of the fierce and challenging vitality that had always animated her. Things were different, as though a portrait of someone in accustomed pose and with which one was long familiar had suddenly moved upon the canvas and subtly altered its position.

Now that she huddled in a chair by the lakeside, he saw how really tiny she was, and how by posture, imperiousness and inner fire she had created the illusion of size and command. In relaxation she appeared to have shrunk; the delicate wrist-bones were even finer and more bird-like, the blue-veined temples more waxen and defined, the face beneath the piled-up hair smaller and pinched.

But one day it all became clear to him as though a veil had been lifted. Ben-Isaac was reading to her. When he paused to turn a page, Sears saw her glance at him without his being aware of it and smile secretly.

Always, up to that moment, Hannah's face had been a paradox, a countenance divided between the living and gelid. All of her intelligence, cunning, zest for living, and even humour, had been centred in the upper portion of her face about the fine, bony nose, the clever eyes with their folds of wisdom at the corners. All of her lost youth and wasted past were entombed in the frozen area of her harsh, uncompromising mouth and chin.

Now the upper and lower portions of her face had been brought into harmony; the warmth of Palestine had thawed the icy tundras of her nature. The thin lips, stiff from the wind perpetually blowing from a chilled heart, were warmed by a different current and at last were able to test the quality of a smile.

And there was another thing that Sears noted with something of a shock. Looking at her hands lying in her lap, he saw that they were no longer balled into tight, possessive fists, curved inwards at the wrists with convulsive grip symbolic of her clutch upon all she had and life itself. Now they lay naturally on the blue covering, open and relaxed, beautiful, well shaped and ivory white.

A soft greyness appeared to have come to her skin. All her vitality still centred in her eyes. But for the rest there was very little left of the Hannah Bascombe any of them had known. What was there was an old, old woman, very small, very tired, lying in the Galilean sun.

On the sixth day of their stay at Ain Tabigha Dr Levi came to

Hannah to speak to her about a matter that had been preying on his mind. It had to do with the fact that the time had come when he must return to Metullah and his work. Clary and Sears were there, but Ben-Isaac had gone north to look at a piece of property that was for sale, and he was not due back until the next day.

'It is a small thing, growing vegetables,' Dr Levi said, 'but they depend upon me.'

Sears saw how quickly tears sprang to Hannah's eyes, and how even more swiftly she suppressed them.

'I have been selfish, have I not?' she said. 'Yes, you are right. You must go. I have stopped the clock for all of you long enough, and for myself as well. They will be awaiting me at home.'

Dr Levi sat down by her side and leaned forward, an expression of affection and eagerness on his face that was almost boyish, as he said:

'Cannot you remain here with us? I know that Ben-Isaac, who loves you as a mother, has been trying to persuade you to stay. Let me add my entreaties to his. We need you. There is a place here and a sharing in what is happening for every human soul that will come to us. And perhaps you still need us. I ask you to stay.'

Sears thought what a strange ending it would be to the train of events he had started what seemed such a long time ago if the richest woman in the world were to give up everything to return to the atmosphere and emotions of the pioneer times of her father.

After a moment of silence Hannah asked, 'When will you go?'

Dr Levi replied, 'Tomorrow, when Ben-Isaac returns.'

Hannah nodded. 'I will let you know my decision later to-night, or in the morning. You have been so kind to me, now I would like to be alone to think about it.'

They went away and left her dozing and dreaming by the lake-side.

Chapter 34

'And if the blind lead the blind, both shall fall
into the ditch' – *Matthew* xv, 14

THAT afternoon Hannah retired early. Sears wandered over to the trailer and found Clary. He said casually, 'How about a turn on the lake to cool off? You look hot and tired. I've found a boat.'

They had not been alone together or spoken to one another much since the night in the cave. Yet each had known the time must come when speak they must.

Now that the moment was at hand Clary did not hesitate. 'Yes. I will come, Joe. Hannah won't need me. She is sleeping.'

They walked in silence along the north shore of the lake. There was no breath of wind and the heat had settled like a moist blanket on the valley. Clary was wearing a sleeveless, white linen frock that showed off the healthy tan and firm muscle tone that had come to her arms and shoulders. For coolness she had her brown hair piled Grecian style on top of her head, but the wide spacing of her eyes, her colouring and the perfect oval of her face gave her an Egyptian look. The perverse challenge that had so shocked and irritated Sears in the days back in San Francisco had vanished; the semi-sickly hot-house quality of her person had been supplanted by the health that comes with sunshine, outdoor life and a mind that has lost many of its fears.

A ten-minute walk brought them to a clump of reeds in which was drawn up a flat-bottomed boat with a pair of oars.

Clary asked, 'Whose is it?'

Sears replied lightly, 'Probably belongs to either Peter or John, or maybe James, the son of Zebedee.'

He helped her in, noting the warmth and firmness of the hand she gave him, and that as she sat on the rear seat she did not go through the old feminine routine of ostentatiously pulling her skirts down over her brown knees. She was as unself-conscious as a cat.

Sears pushed the boat out into the water across the shallows of millions of tiny, coloured Galilean shells, climbed in and, settling the oars in the rowlocks, began to row slowly away from the shore, and in silence.

It was less hot on the surface of the lake, and when they were out on its broad expanse they found a riffle of wind that swept down the valley from Hermon and carried a reminiscence of the cool that lay about its slopes. It was welcome, for the Galilean trough was like a furnace, even though the sun had edged to the hills and was about to sink below them.

The western sky was glazed with red, the last rays were shed at Naphtali's ragged crags; and when they faced opposite, a white moon had already climbed up over the Jordan bluff, hanging in a pearl sky. The cliffs of Jordan, rising steeply from the eastern shore behind Ein Gev, were purple, grey and terracotta.

They had been rowing in silence for perhaps a half-hour. Sears revolved the boat slowly. Clary cried, 'How beautiful! . . . What an unearthly beauty! . . .'

Sears cocked an eye at the moon and said, 'Corny, but effective. I didn't bring you out here to discuss the backdrop, Violet Eyes. I wanted to talk to you.'

Clary said evenly, 'That's why I came, Joe . . .'

He nodded. 'There are a couple of things we need to get straightened out. First of all I wanted to say thanks for what you did up on the hill there' – and he indicated Hermon with his head – 'when Sears went a little off his chump.'

Clary seemed about to speak, but he held up his hand, resting his elbows on the oars. 'Wait,' he said. 'Let me get this part off my chest. You're a good kid; you stood by me and helped me when I was in a bad spot. Why, I wouldn't know. But we were all sort of screwy and emotional and off our trolleys up there, and what I wanted to say was maybe that's just the kind of person you are and it didn't mean a damn thing. Or maybe you and the kid had a falling-out, or something – how would I know? But if you've still got a hankering for the boom-boom boy – why, I'm letting you off the hook.'

Clary considered before she replied, and then she asked merely, 'And what if I do not want off the hook?'

Sears said, 'I'm not a nice guy, Clary.'

'I'm not a nice girl, Joe.'

The man grinned suddenly. 'We're a pair of first-class twentieth-century stinkers, aren't we?' Then he added, 'Okay. I was just talking. Who do I think I'm kidding? We're in love with each other, aren't we?'

Clary agreed. 'I suppose so.' Now she was watching him somewhat warily.

Sears backed water gently for a moment and brooded over the thought before he asked half mockingly, 'Well, Violet Eyes, what do we do now?'

Clary thought, too, and then replied, 'I don't know, Joe. I wish I did.' There was no coquetry behind the statement. He could feel its sincerity.

Sears said, 'The first time I saw you behind that desk in San Fran and you took off your specs you knocked me for a loop. I thought you were the best-looking thing I'd ever seen. And I didn't like you for sour apples . . .'

Clary managed a faint smile. 'When did you change your mind, Joe?'

Sears said, 'I was coming to that. Remember the night we got to talking about what life meant to us and I told you about being the kind of guy who reads the buy-everything ads, get-a-house, get-a-shiny-car, get-a-wife, get-a-kid, get-the-works – '

Clary nodded. 'Yes. I do.'

'That night I'm lying in bed, thinking about nothing, when up pops the whole scene ready-made, just like the full-page layout. There I am driving up to the front door of the bungalow in the new super-dynapower Airflow Six. Across the well-water Shady-Green lawn comes the Little Woman to greet me, holding the eight-year-old Junior by the hand. She is wearing a blue frock and a red checkered apron over it. The kid yells out the apppropriate slogan about there's Dad with the new car and dinner is ready on the new atomic electric range. Only the Little Lady has your face, and the kid has both of ours, and I'm lying there for at least five minutes before I shake myself out of it, liking what I see fine.'

Clary did not reply to this. There had been something almost mischievous and boyish in Sears's expression during the telling of this. Now he broke out a new pack of cigarettes and extracted two, offering Clary one, and when he looked up from the operation a hardness and bleakness had come to his face again. He said:

'You're not a bungalow and checkered-apron girl, Clary.'

Clary drew on her cigarette so that the end glowed. Dark had fallen upon them swiftly, even though it was silvered by the climbing moon leaving the frowning line of Trans-Jordan and mounting into the sky.

'No,' she said. 'I am not.'

'Even if you were, you wouldn't like the way I went about getting 'em for you. I'm a twister and a corner-cutter, Clary. You nailed me the first minute I walked in on you. I want all the shiny things on the counter, but I won't go for the patsy routine to get 'em. I want 'em on my own terms.'

Clary said in a flat tone, 'That's what you discovered about me five minutes after you had begun to talk to me.'

He said, 'Yeah, I know, but you've changed.'

She shook her head. 'Not basically, Joe.' Then she said, 'I'm thinking of you on my terms.'

He said, 'It won't work, will it? What's changed, what's any different from what it was a couple of months ago except that we got each other under our skins? When we go home I've got eighteen hundred bucks saved up out of what Hannah's paid me and no job. You go back to your work with Hannah. If she's got rid of her obsession and quits fighting the tax-collectors, you'd even have it a little easier. You're running the Bascombe mansion and I'm in L.A. getting tossed out on my ear by producers or editors when I come around for a job. Where do we fit together?'

Clary replied, 'I don't know, Joe'; and then she added with a sudden firmness that surprised him, 'But somewhere I feel that we do.'

Sears said, 'I could understand your going for a guy like Ben-Isaac. There's a man. No kinks and all the guts in the world.'

Clary said, 'In some things you underestimate yourself, Joe;

and you don't know much about women. I told you once you have enough courage for me.'

Sears laughed a short laugh. 'And I still say that when the going got rough up there in Syria I dogged it and let the others do the fighting.'

Clary said, 'Yes? I don't remember that. All I know is that when the shooting began *your* only thought was for me, and for Hannah's safety. You risked your life for both of us.'

Sears said with sudden savageness, 'I didn't want my meal-ticket punched by an Arab bullet.'

'Was I your meal ticket too?'

Sears did not reply. Clary asked, 'What makes you so hard, Joe?'

Instead of replying he went back to his fears. 'What would our life be like together, the kind of people we are? A job, a grind, the drudgery of trying to make both ends meet on the one hand, or me living off the drippings from Hannah's fat on the other. Where do we find each other? Where would there be room for the warmth of what has happened to us somewhere along the line?'

When he paused Clary said, 'Go on. Talk, Joe.'

He said, 'We're haggling like a couple of employment-agency sharks. Neither of us wants to let go what we think we can get, or what we've got. What would it lead to? In the grind of doing the same thing over and over again, working that goddam tread-mill, we'd grope for one another in bed occasionally and maybe find one another, maybe not. It kills what you'd want to make of a woman. Soon there'd be nothing left, not even the remember-ing the days here and what they were like . . .'

Clary asked, 'Could one forget so quickly what one learned – and all the memories: the land, the feeling of the nearness of the sky, Ben-Isaac, and Dr Levi, and what he said about God . . . ?'

Sears jammed his oars into the water so that they came out of the locks and nearly pitched him backwards. He swore, mastered them and rowed hard and unevenly, though gradually his strokes became smoother and calmer, and in the end he rested again and let the boat glide soundlessly up the moon's silver path on the glassy surface of Lake Galilee.

He said, 'It's no use, Clary. I wear blinders. I'm afraid to look. I don't want to look. I'm afraid to admit that I want to believe and that I want help. I can't take it that Levi taught me a lesson and that I turned to him when I was in a jam. There's a hole in me as big as that mountain, and all my pride has drained out through it.'

'And yet, you know,' Clary said out of the darkness, 'that is the time when I seem most able to love you and when it seems as though there were nothing I would not do for you if you asked me.'

'Including marrying me?'

'Now, yes.'

'Now . . . ? Since when? What makes you decide?'

Clary replied, too quickly, 'Since the night in the caves on Hermon at Beit Jebel.'

He was wary at once. 'When I made a fool of myself? What has that got to do with it?'

Clary cried, 'No, no, Joe. Don't you understand? When you confessed to the kind of person you knew you were; when . . .'

He interrupted her harshly. 'Confess is a word I don't swallow, kid. I made an ass out of myself and I got scared. But one scare doesn't change a man. I'm no different than I was before. I'll always cut that corner . . .'

Clary said, 'But you are, Joe. You are different.'

He asked, 'Tell me something. If I had asked you to marry me before – that night, would you have?'

Every impulse in Clary urged her to tell him the lie he wanted to hear, but her own stubbornness would not countenance it, or her lips form it. She said, 'No.'

He was sure he had her now. 'Why not?'

Her own patience was being tried. She was beginning to feel lonely and embittered at what was happening to them. She replied, 'You make it very hard for me, Joe. I don't want to hurt you.'

Sears said, 'I've been hurt before. Believe me, its a novelty to have someone not want to do it to me.'

'A woman can be in love with certain things in a man and yet at the same time despise him and feel contempt for his weaknesses, and hate him for having them and making her despise him. She can love a man and see the abyss yawning before them. She can love that same man and be afraid, as of hell, because of what she believes him to be.'

Sears said flatly, 'Bunk. If a woman loves a man, she loves him, and there's an end to it. He can be the biggest scoundrel on two legs and . . .'

'Oh God!' Clary burst out. 'You like to wear your weaknesses like chains and rattle them. Cannot you leave me mine? I told you that I was not a nice girl. Yes, I would have gone to hell with you or for you, but I would not have married you, or brought your children into the world, or tried to make a life with you.'

It was strange the scorn she could put into her voice for one she so loved. 'There are no more caves for you to run into and hide yourself, Joe Sears. You've faced yourself once and you can never escape from yourself again. You've abased yourself like a man and a human being before your conscience and your God. You've prayed for help. Do you think you can take that prayer back?'

He fell silent upon this and did not speak for a long while. The luminous dial of his watch caught his eye and he glanced at it.

'Do you know what time it is?'

'No. Is it late?'

'A quarter to midnight.'

'We must go in.'

'We haven't solved anything.'

'That's right, we haven't solved anything.'

'Except that we're in love with each other and don't know what to do about it?'

Clary cried, 'Oh, Joe, I'm so miserable . . .'

He began to row in the direction of the dark clump of trees and the two trailers' blazing light on the shore that marked the location of Ain Tabigha.

But when he had grounded the boat and stood to help her ashore he felt the trembling of her hand and lifted her out then in his arms and kissed her again and again while she returned them, both swept away by the passion they had restrained so long until they were breathless and dizzy and near to being overcome by their desire for one another.

Yet, like all lovers caught up in the maelstrom of human urgency and close to helplessness, they paused to hold apart from one another for one last look, a kind of farewell to the people they were before their final union should change them for ever.

And in that moment they recaptured themselves.

Clary moved backwards, out of his embrace and away from him. 'No, no, Joe. Please!' And then she added with a kind of gasp, 'That we knew . . .'

He did not try to take her again. He said only, 'Yeah. That doesn't solve anything either.'

They walked slowly back to their camp, side by side, with their fingers intertwined, each lost in the thoughts, fears and self-accusations that still tormented them.

Chapter 35

'This is my rest forever: here will I dwell: for I
have desired it' — *Psalms* cxxxii, 14

WHEN Sears and Clary returned to the hospice there were
lights burning and signs of unusual activity for that time of
night, a sense of coming and going that lay about the building,
figures that passed before windows, and even as they approached
they were aware of a chanting that came from somewhere in the
house.

Neither spoke, but their fingers clasped more tightly, and while
they were not aware of it a kind of urgency came upon them
and they hurried their steps.

In the garden, not far from the chapel of the Loaves and
Fishes, its cupola bathed in the silver reflected from the now
high-riding moon, they encountered Dr Levi walking with
Father Hofstatter. The two men were conversing in low tones,
but they ceased and looked up as the two approached, and Sears
and Clary could see that their faces looked oddly strained.

Clary, the more sensitive and intuitive, stopped, her hands
catching at her breast. 'Dr Levi — Father Hofstatter,' she cried.
'What has happened? Is anything wrong?'

The two men exchanged a glance. Then Dr Levi said, 'My dear,
you must prepare yourself for a shock. We have some grave
and sad news to tell you . . .'

Sears stepped to Clary's side and put an arm about her waist.
He did not need to be told, nor did she. It seemed as though they
both knew at one and the same time, and yet they did those
outward gestures and said those things that one always
did.

Clary cried, 'Something has happened. Hannah is ill?'

Dr Levi said quietly, 'Hannah is gone . . .'

Sears felt the girl tremble and tightened the grip of his arm.
He said, 'Gone — where? What do you mean?'

Dr Levi said gently, 'I am sorry to have to tell you this, but Hannah died an hour ago.'

Clary put her hands to her face and murmured, 'Oh no, no. Not possible . . .'

Father Hofstatter stepped forward and placed a hand upon her arm. He said, 'She died peacefully in her sleep. Everything that could be done has been done. Dr Ascher is on his way out here from Tiberias, but he can do no more than verify. She was tired. She is at rest. Take comfort.' And after a moment he turned and went up towards the hospice.

Sears found his voice. He said to Dr Levi, 'What happened to her? Was she taken sick? I don't understand it.' He was deeply shocked and a sense of guilt pervaded him. His mind somehow short-circuited all that had happened and left him filled with a sense of failure. Had he not in some manner contracted to keep her alive for ever . . . ?

Dr Levi said, 'Let us sit down here and I will tell you . . .'

They were close to the angle of a low grey stone wall that contained the terrace looking towards the lake with its bright moon-path stretching boldly to the dark shoreline at their feet. They disposed themselves there, with Dr Levi facing them so that the moonlight fell athwart his expressive features. Sears took out a cigarette and gave one to Clary.

'Good for the nerves, kid,' he said as he lit it for her. By the flare of the match he saw that she had a grip on herself again. 'Okay, Doc . . .'

Dr Levi began. 'It was shortly after nine o'clock. I was walking alone in the garden smoking an after-dinner cigar when I heard Hannah call from her trailer, "Dr Levi, is that you?" I answered her. She then said, "I cannot sleep. Will you come to me, please?"

'I went inside and joined her. She was lying propped up in her bed, looking out over the lake. The moon was then yet so low that its light was shed upon her face, and I could see her expression. But the night was warm and fretful, and I thought this, perhaps, was why she could not sleep.'

Sears asked, 'What did she say?'

Dr Levi reflected a moment before replying. Then he said only, 'She needed comfort and reassurance. There were things that were troubling her as they trouble all of us when we grow old and know that we must face the inevitable . . .'

Clary asked softly, 'Were you able to help her?'

Dr Levi did not answer her question directly. Instead he said, 'We talked together for a long while. More than an hour perhaps. I could see then that she was very pale and tired; indeed, all of the colour seemed to have left her face, but its contours were soft, and her hands relaxed. I thought that she would be able to sleep now and suggested that I leave her to rest.

'But she asked me to remain, saying, "Stay here with me a little longer." I sat there silently at her bedside.

'After a while she spoke again, saying, "Please, Dr Levi, will you give me your hand?"

'I placed my hand in hers, and she clung to it tightly. I was reminded somehow of the way a child that cannot sleep clings to the hand of her father . . .'

Sears asked, 'Did she say anything before she died?'

Dr Levi replied, 'She spoke twice. Once, she gave a deep sigh and said, "It seems as though never before in all my life have I known such peace."

'A little later she opened her eyes and looked at me. She said, "I will stay here, Dr Levi." Then she closed them and seemed to relax and go to sleep. I waited another fifteen minutes or so for her sleep to become deep so I would not disturb her when I left . . .'

He paused for a moment before he concluded softly, with deep and paternal tenderness, 'But when I went to disengage my hand from hers I became alarmed.

'I looked at her more closely. Then I knew that nothing would ever disturb her again . . .'

They remained silent for a long time after he had finished. Clary was the first to speak. She said, 'May I go up to see her, Dr Levi?'

'Yes,' he replied. 'You may.'

Clary arose and walked with a firm step across the moon-bathed gardens towards the trailers, while the two men sat and watched her go. Sears asked of Dr Levi:

'Ought she?'

He replied, 'Yes. Let her go.'

A little later her figure reappeared, framed in the lighted doorway of the vehicle. Leaving Dr Levi seated on the wall, Sears sprang up and went towards Clary. She remained standing in the doorway waiting for him. When he reached her he was startled by the expression on her face.

He said to her, 'What is it Clary? Can't you cry?'

She looked at him as though she had not understood him. 'Cry?' she said. 'But she's so happy . . .'

Chapter 36

'Be thou my strong rock, for an house of defence
to save me' – *Psalms* xxxi, 2

AFTER the simple interment in the small cemetery behind the
Hospice of Ain Tabigha, Ben-Isaac remained with his uncle, but
Sears and Clary, by a kind of common understanding, wandered
off together without speaking, and almost by instinct their footsteps turned eastwards along the shore of the lake.

It had been on Clary's responsibility that Hannah had been
buried there in Galilee, for when it was suggested that arrangements be made for her to be taken back to San Francisco she had
cried to them from a full heart:

'Oh no. Let her rest here where she found the only peace and
happiness she ever knew. What has she who lies here to do any
longer with those things that are back there at home?'

Sears had said only, 'After all, her father is buried in the crypt
in San Francisco.'

Dr Levi had suggested softly, 'She is already with her
Father . . .'

Ben-Isaac said, 'She would not have left me'; and Clary, 'Does
one not respect the wishes of the dead . . . ?'

Sears had looked at her questioningly.

'Have you forgotten the last words she spoke?' In the ensu-
ing silence she repeated them: 'I will stay here, Dr Levi.'

The burial was a simple one, attended by those who had been
with her and had known her in Israel: Clary, Dr Levi, Sears,
Ben-Isaac, and the chauffeurs and staff who had driven and
looked after the expedition. Ed Avery and Schlomo, with a
half-dozen of the Palmach men, had come down from
Dan.

Father Hofstatter had read the burial service. Ben-Isaac had
recited the Twenty-third Psalm, 'The Lord is my shepherd; I
shall not want', that had brought comfort to Hannah in an hour

of need and Dr Levi spoke his farewell with the lines from the Kadish:

"Only the body has died and has been laid in the dust. The spirit lives eternally in the shelter of God's love and mercy. Whence shall come our help and comfort? Our help cometh from God. He will not forsake us nor leave us in our grief. Upon Him we cast our burden and He will grant us strength according to the days He has apportioned to us. All life comes from Him; all life to Him returneth; all souls are in His keeping."

And thereafter Hannah had been covered with the soil of Galilee . . .

Sears and Clary arrived at the clump of reeds, where the flat-bottomed boat still remained as they had left it. They did not go out in it but climbed in and sat down facing one another and remained there for a time without speaking, each given up to thoughts.

For Clary it was a kind of last leave-taking from the woman she had known and served so long and with whom her life had been bound up. Well, it was over and done with. The cord was cut. The dead had been mourned.

She said, 'Give me a cigarette, Joe.'

He lit one and handed it to her. 'Hard hit, kid?'

She replied, 'It's over now. One cannot remain too long sad over something that was filled with beauty.'

Sears nodded and lit a cigarette for himself, and with the gesture found the ease to speak the thoughts that had been his. He said, 'This makes it all a little tougher, doesn't it?'

'What, Joe?'

'What we couldn't seem to solve out there on the lake the other night.'

There was something in the way that Clary was looking at him, something reflective and knowledgeable about her expression, that he could not fathom.

She said, 'I suppose so. I hadn't thought about it until just now.'

He asked her bluntly, 'Do you love me?'

'Yes, Joe, I do.'

'Would you marry me?'

A half-smile came to the corners of her mouth. 'Are you proposing to me, Joe?'

He said, 'I'm asking.'

'Yes, Joe, I would.'

'Don't kid me, Violet Eyes. You're an heiress now.'

Clary asked, 'Are you afraid of marrying money, Joe?'

'No. I'm not. I could be very happy wedded to a lot of it. But you'd be a sucker to marry a failure like me now, even if you think you're in love with me. Sooner or later you'd regret it and throw me out. We'd both be better off, maybe, if you did it now before I acquire more expensive tastes than I already have.'

Clary's smile dried up. She reached into the pocket of her frock and produced a cablegram that had been sent on from Tiberias and handed it to Sears. She said:

'Maybe this will set your mind at rest. Braverman, who signed it, is the family lawyer . . .'

Sears glanced at it and stared. 'Oh no!' he said. 'Does that mean . . . ?'

Clary nodded. 'Hannah died intestate. I always knew it. She refused to draw up a will because it would have meant acknowledging that one day she would die.'

Sears said, 'The hell you say. But then you . . .'

The girl shook her head. She was singularly calm and unmoved. 'No. There is a closer relative, an aunt on her father's side. There is a grand-nephew of hers living. He will get what is left, but the bulk of the estate will go to the lawyers and the tax-collectors.' She suddenly remembered something and the smile illuminated her face again. 'Wasn't it wonderful, Joe, that she died not caring?'

Sears thought for a moment and then said, 'But what about you? What kind of a raw deal did she give you? Did she sucker you into devoting your life to her for nothing . . .?'

'No,' Clary said, 'she didn't. When I came to her she set up a lifetime trust fund for me, and I have the income from it.'

Sears did not say anything, and if he felt relieved he managed not to show it. He was watching Clary, for something about her eyes and the expression about her mouth was faintly amused and told him that she had not yet finished what she had to tell him . . .

He was right, for she continued after a moment, 'So you see, Joe, you will not have to worry about becoming a rich woman's plaything and being discarded like a broken toy. You are going to marry a poor girl after all.'

Sears was not yet ready to be amused. He said, 'I don't get it.'

'Oh,' Clary said with an astonishing lightness, 'Hannah took no chances of losing me. There were three swords suspended over my head. The trust became voided if she dismissed me – or if I left her . . .'

'And the third?'

'If I got married.'

Sears stared at her, unbelieving. 'Is that on the level?'

'Yes. Are you very disappointed, Joe?'

Sears said, 'God, but she was wicked. She was revenging herself upon you for her own self-imposed spinsterhood.'

Clary shook her head. 'No, she wasn't wicked. She was sick. And, besides, I acquiesced.'

'You were too young to know what you were doing.'

Clary said, 'I think that she would have changed it some day. I always felt that. If she had lived to return home I am sure she would have done so. In her own way she cared for me . . .'

'But now nothing can be done. Is that it? With marriage the trust fund ends automatically.'

'Yes, Joe. Knowing that, would you still want me to marry you?'

He did not reply, but again watched her warily.

Clary said, 'There is another way. Do you want me to live with you, Joe? It is the only way to get around the trust fund. If you want it that way, I will do it. But you must make the decision. Or I will marry you and lose the money, if that's what you wish.'

Sears glanced down at his soft, well-kept hands for a moment and did not look up when he started to speak.

'I care about money a great deal. I always did. It means a hell of a lot. When you've got it it keeps up the morale and makes you feel comfortable and decent. When you know where your next meal is coming from you can afford to think about the other guy a little. Only a fool kicks money in the teeth if he can have it.' He looked up at Clary. 'I take it that what you are offering me is the girl and the money too. Wouldn't I be the biggest sucker in the world to let that go by?'

Opposite him, on the other side of the small boat, Clary folded her hands and met his challenging gaze. 'Yes,' she said evenly. 'You would.'

'And wouldn't you?' he added. 'We're both products of our times; we're both not fools. As between struggling against poverty with a twister of doubtful earning ability and having your cake as well as eating it, the logical choice is pretty clear. You must have thought of that.'

'I have, Joe. It was I who made the suggestion. But it is you who in the end must make the decision. I will do whatever you say. Which is it to be? Or do you wish to consider it?'

Sears was already doing so.

And he was thinking odd thoughts for a Joe Sears. It was almost like the time he had the bungalow vision with Clary in the checkered apron, only now it was himself he saw in the role of so many of his fellow-citizens who toiled at some routine job from morning until night to win a living for their families and themselves, giving their lives, their juices and their energies in some drab and habitual performance that could be exchanged for dollars which in turn could be taken to the store and traded for food and clothing, and he was amazed at its sudden and inexplicable attraction for him. It even took on a faintly heroic quality, and he had a weird picture of reversal in which it seemed that perhaps the simple patsies, the members of the herd, the suckers, the faceless men who poured out of stores and offices and factories at quitting time were the wise and the worth-while.

And he thought, *'Maybe it's time I tried life from the sucker angle, just for the novelty of it.'*

But he knew he wasn't fooling himself. He had been deeply stirred by what had happened to him in the village of Beit Jebel and the cave of Hermon, and the direction in which his thoughts took him now was that – he might as well admit it – you could beat any game, but you couldn't beat yourself. He had learned the terror that accompanies looking into one's soul.

He said to himself that he did not want to be a crook or even the kind of person who would balance like a tight-rope walker on the line bordering between honesty and dishonesty and kid himself that he was treading on solid ground. But he knew that he would be tempted to go on trying it all his life because he was Joe Sears. Yet now he found that he felt a sudden feeling of strength and support. From now on he would have to face not only himself, that Sears with whom he could not bear to live so much as a hundred years, but her as well.

For a moment he rejected the idea and fought against it. He even in his mind accused Clary and thought to himself that she was weaker than he when the chips were down. It had been her idea how to get around Hannah's trust-fund set-up by coming to live with him instead of marrying. What kind of ethics was that?

Yes, Clary was weak. He had known it from the first. But her weakness made her human. It brought her down from that pedestal where too many women were elevated back home, to where they became no longer warm, approachable or needful of their men. And he knew at that moment that her very weakness gave him strength, just as his must to her. When they returned home they would both once more be like swimmers struggling in a wild and dangerous sea that always threatened to become too much for them. But they could support one another.

And finally he had one more queer thought as he considered all that had happened and what his decision was to be, and this was that there was a kind of divine and dramatic neatness and logic to the outcome of the affair that maybe a guy ought not to tamper with too much.

It was almost as though Hannah had planned it that way. He had worked a game on her for his own ends and made her his victim. Well, it had all turned out differently from what anybody had thought. She had escaped him, herself, and everybody else and apparently died happy, and none of those who had looked to living on her money would have a cent of it; not even Clary, who had been ready to sell her youth and her birthright for it. As for himself, he was right back from where he had started, except that he was no longer alone.

He looked up at the girl opposite him and saw not the exquisite eyes, ripe lips, oval face or perfect features, but a warm and somewhat miserable, puzzled and needful human who was prepared to give him whatever he wanted that lay within her power to give.

Sears suddenly smiled a wry smile, and, bunching up the five fingers of his right hand, he reached over and knuckled Clary gently under the side of the chin. He said, 'Aren't you the brazen hussy? Isn't it enough having one bastard in the family without having a lot of little ones running around besides? We get married.'

Clary took his fist and held it to her brow for a moment with her two hands and then put it against her cheek. A moment later he felt her tears run over it.

Sears asked, 'Did I say the wrong thing?'

Clary shook her head and held his fist the tighter, clinging to it.

'It's just relief, Joe. Don't you see that it solves everything between us. . . . If you can be strong where I am weak, I need never be afraid again – of anything . . .'

A moment later she asked, 'Are you sure that you will be happy, Joe, married to me, starting again from the very beginning?'

He eyed her with a new gravity and tenderness. 'No,' he replied. 'I'm not at all sure. But that's the way I happen to want it right now. It's true enough that only a sucker won't take a handicap when it is offered to him, but it's also a fact that everybody admires the scratch man . . .'

He took one of her hands, balled it into a fist, covered it with his own that was free and held it close to his cheek, and there they sat a few moments longer gazing into one another's faces, luxuriating in the doing of it and the looking into eyes that were no longer clouded or fearful. Then, gently and quizzically, Sears leaned over and twice rubbed his nose against hers before he kissed her.

Chapter 37

'Why leap ye, ye high hills? This is the hill which
God desireth to dwell in; yea, the Lord will dwell
in it forever' – *Psalms* lxviii, 16

AT the Megiddo Hotel, in Haifa, Ben-Isaac found Clary at her
packing. He asked, 'May I come in?'

'Yes, Ben-Isaac, do.'

He was still dressed in the shorts and half-sleeved khaki
jacket he had worn on the trip, but he looked thinner and older.
The passing of Hannah had affected him deeply.

He sat down on a trunk and watched Clary for a moment.
'That is a melancholy sight,' he said. 'There is nothing so sad as
to see someone you care for packing to go away. Will you come
back, Clary?'

'I don't know, Ben-Isaac. Perhaps some day.'

'Is it true that you are going to marry Joe?'

'Yes.'

'Do you think you will be happy with him?'

'I don't know, Ben-Isaac. What matters is that we need one
another and could not bear to think of living apart. That in
itself is happiness.'

'Yes. You are right. I envy him.'

'And you, Ben-Isaac?'

He looked at her gravely before replying. 'My uncle has bought
me the farm I looked at not far from Dan. It is near the Ayeleth
Hashahar Kibbutz, where Ed Avery and Schlomo live. I will raise
wheat and corn. I will think of you a great deal. And I will love
you always . . .'

She was watching him, too, now, curious as to what was to
come.

He continued, 'One day this love will be shifted from one
part of my heart to another. I will meet and love a girl of my own
people. She will come to me and we will work together to build

233

this nation and make it strong, and our children will join us in this work. . . .' He stopped. Clary thought, *'So must the ancient prophets have looked when the future was revealed to them. How very wise, how very old he is . . . and how very generous. He is freeing me . . .'*

His face changed, the lines smoothed for a moment, his smile was almost mischievous. 'I suppose you'll never forgive me for that. I meant it as a wedding gift . . .'

They leaned forward by mutual impulse and kissed one another with tenderness.

Sears had a last talk with Dr Levi in the bar of the Megiddo Hotel, where the two went for a final drink together before leaving for the pier.

Dr Levi ordered his dry Martini and savoured it, studying its colour in the light before he tasted it.

'Probably the last one I shall have for a long time,' he said, then toasted Sears and drank half of it down.

Sears asked, 'What will you do now? Where will you go?'

'Back to Metullah and my vegetables.'

Sears studied him with a smile that was almost affectionate. 'Then it is really true,' he said.

'What is true?'

'That in Israel Dr Nathaniel Levi is only a grower of beans and carrots, sprouts and radishes.'

The old man raised his glass. 'May Dr Nathaniel Levi never be more in Israel than a grower of cabbages and beets, peas and spinach.'

'All right,' said Sears, 'I'll drink to that. I suppose you are right. When people are hungry they need bread.'

Dr Levi asked, 'And what will you do now?'

'Go back to the U.S. Find a job. Work at it . . .'

Dr Levi said, 'I wish we could persuade you and Clary to remain here with us. We need you. We need every man. You see, I do not hesitate to proselyte for Israel shamelessly. And yet we have something to offer too. Who knows when once again upon this earth there will be given to man the opportunity to share the sweet and agonizing birth-pains of a nation.'

Joe nodded and ordered another round, and sat steeped in thought until it came. Then he said:

'Yes. I know what you mean. It's a temptation for any man. It fills you up and for a little while makes you think you are more than just a piece of dirt. But it isn't for us any more. It's for kids like Ben-Isaac . . .'

'Or kids like me,' Dr Levi said gravely.

Sears laughed. 'Or kids like you. But then you have tasted of the fruit of the Tree of Life and are older than Methuselah and wiser than Moses. You can afford to start all over again. But not us. We're going home. We're a different breed. We're trapped by what we've built for ourselves. We don't fit anywhere else any more. Many of us think our civilization stinks, but it's the only one we have, and most of us have learned how to live with it. And, besides, in a way we love it. Clary and I are Americans after all. You can't kiss that off. We want our children to be born there. It's our homeland. You can try to be tough and say that that doesn't mean anything, but it does. You're an American, and that makes you a certain kind of guy; maybe not the best in the world, but that's how you are and where you belong.'

Dr Levi nodded and said, 'Come back to visit us some time. We shall think of you often.'

'If we can, we will.'

Dr Levi lifted his glass again. 'Shalom!' he said.

Sears met the toast. 'Shalom! And thanks again, Doc.' They drank.

The tedium and disillusionment of departure weighed heavily upon Sears and Clary.

The sun was tropic hot and beat down upon their heads with furnace heat and glare as they stood at the rail of the *Esdraelon*, looking down upon the confusion of the long dock at Haifa and the boy and the old gentleman who stood there shouting up those futile inanities and last-minute repetitions that are called forth by sailings when all farewells have been made and last things said, and still the vessel obstinately remains moored to the dock.

Yet neither Sears nor Clary could tear themselves away from the rail, nor could the pair below achieve the gesture of turning away and walking out of the lives of the two above them with whom their destinies had been so closely enmeshed.

Sears looked down and wondered what had become of the mystery that had clothed Dr Levi and his nephew. He saw now only a stoutish old gentleman, wearing a black hat and carrying a cane, who soon would go back to a small village in the north, to hoe his rows and pour water from a can on to his onions and beets with perhaps that same tender gesture he had seen in all Israel when water was poured out over something living. He would be content to do this, and perhaps sometimes go to the top of a hill to fancy that he talked with God, until the end of his days.

There did not even seem to be any of the glamour, dignity and young, god-like quality about the bronzed face and figure of Ben-Isaac, staring up at them and waving his hand from time to time. There were so many more like him all about, in the throng crowding the dock area for farewells, it seemed; tall men and boys, bronzed as he, self-possessed and hard, hauling on lines, or whacking a cant hook into a bale or crate with the gusto and vehemence of knifing an enemy.

He, too, would now settle down to his land and his building, marry and rear children in the endless, tedious process of days that set in when adventure and those rare happenings that lift the favoured few out of the ruck for a little are over.

Well, he, Joe Sears, and the girl there at his side who was to become his wife had had it too, their moment of madness and inspiration. And now they were on their way back to take up the struggle against the deadly, sapping drug of living for the sake of surviving, and what would ever be left of those high moments that had come to them?

He stole a glance at Clary, standing next to him, smiling down at the two men below, but he could not guess what she was thinking, or whether she was smiling with her heart as well as her eyes. Yet he felt she must think and feel as he. How could you escape it? He felt angry suddenly at the loss of his illusions. He wished he were a giant axe to cleave the hawsers that bound them still to the dregs of their adventure. Where and how could he lift up the life that he was to begin with Clary?

The *Esdraelon* hooted three times. The flurry of waving and calling broke out once more from the pier below.

'Shalom!' called Dr Levi.

'Write to me!' cried Ben-Isaac.

But this time the lines were slacked away and slipped into the water; the ship shuddered to the beat of her engines. Water appeared between her flank and the dock.

They stood there waving endlessly as slowly the figures on the pier diminished.

The ship moved forward, then backed and turned, and pointed for the opening in the mole, the golden beach that curved to Acre, and then the calm and sunbathed sea. And still the two remained at the rail and did not speak. But Sears saw Clary's eyes cling to Carmel's headland as they turned, and linger on the green valley that was plunged like a sword through the hills, pointed at Jezreel and the ancient Tell of Beth Shean.

And Sears, too, found himself turning to look back upon the land and the sky, the valleys and the hills with a curious ache in his throat and longing in his heart. And even as he looked he knew that the spell of Palestine was once again upon him.

He gazed upon the coast and the heights behind it rising in the heat-haze to the blue. There, far off to the right, were the frowning ramparts of Judea, athwart which lay Jerusalem; lost in the valleys were the sites of the ancient heroes, Samson and Saul and David, who had fought and sinned and repented, strayed and fallen, and in the end had always returned to God.

And Sears thought, as he looked out upon this land, that there slumbered the beginnings of man's conscience; that there, and there alone, it seemed as though man could find himself again and hold fast to what he had found.

His lips silently formed the words 'Naphtali' and 'Galilee' as he looked upon the dark hills and peaks in the distance and thought of Hannah, purged of all the darkness that had imprisoned her for so long, sleeping in the cool of the grove at Ain Tabigha; and when he thought of her he found, to his astonishment, that he could see only her hands that for so long had been knotted into tight fists of possession, and now they were open and relaxed, as he had seen them in her lap on the shores of

Galilee. And thinking of them brought to him, too, a feeling of peace.

He found, too, as he gazed out upon the endless mystery of the hills, that he could picture Ben-Isaac once more, and Dr Levi, as they had been with all the glamour, force and drama with which they had been invested. There, north behind the ramparts of Naphtali, hidden behind the lines of hills, was Hermon where the boy had climbed the savage ravine, laughing and careless in the face of death, and proved himself more battle-god than man. He thought once more of the silent watch when he spoke with Ben-Isaac of his uncle who went up on a mountain-top to talk with God, and the picture was no longer either strange or eccentric.

Hermon was there, hidden away, but in his mind he could see the long snow slopes, the triple peaks, and feel the magic and solitary grandeur that hung about this mountain that had looked down upon the birth of man's discovery and belief in God.

It was God's mountain. Scripture and tradition had said that God and His Son had conversed there. He, Joe Sears, had fled, howling like an animal, into a dark cave cut into the bowels of that mass. There he had found the person who was himself. He wished he were not leaving. He wished he could see Hermon once more. There, on the mountain, they had all somehow come closer to God, if such there was, than they would ever come again.

He saw Clary's unwavering, thoughtful gaze as she, too, looked back upon all that was left of Israel, now sinking into the sparkling sea.

He turned to her and said, 'It's something to hang on to, isn't it?'

He had his reward in the tears that sprang to her eyes at last and the trembling of her lips, and the way that she took his arm in hers and clung to it with a kind of loving desperation, as though that were also something to hang on to and which, like the memories of Israel, would be her support in the difficult days to come.

MORE ABOUT PENGUINS

Penguinews, which appears every month, contains details of all the new books issued by Penguins as they are published. From time to time it is supplemented by *Penguins in Print* – a complete list of all our available titles. (There are well over three thousand of these.)

A specimen copy of *Penguinews* will be sent to you free on request, and you can become a subscriber for the price of the postage – 4s for a year's issues (including the complete lists). Just write to Dept EP, Penguin Books Ltd, Harmondsworth, Middlesex, enclosing a cheque or postal order, and your name will be added to the mailing list.

Note: *Penguinews* and *Penguins in Print* are not available in the U.S.A. or Canada

THE ADVENTURES OF
HIRAM HOLLIDAY

Paul Gallico

Familiar to millions from the famous TV series, newspaper copy-clerk Hiram Holliday is the last of the
big romantics. He comes to cynical, world-weary old
England on the eve of war in 1939 and straight-way
rescues a princess from a dragon in the middle of
Green Park. There follow hair-raising adventures all
over the Continent, including a spell as a clown in a
Montmartre circus, a spine-chilling escape from exe-
cution in a Nazi prison, and a tragi-comic duel fought
with ancient Roman swords beside the Appian Way.
Hiram even wins his princess in the end!

Also available
CONFESSIONS OF A STORY-TELLER
FLOWERS FOR MRS HARRIS
JENNIE
LOVE OF SEVEN DOLLS
LUDMILA AND THE LONELY
MRS HARRIS GOES TO NEW YORK
THE SNOW GOOSE AND THE SMALL MIRACLE
THOMASINA
TRIAL BY TERROR

Not for sale in the U.S.A. or Canada